SO1OMON

J. D. Whyman

To Katie,

For five years of unwavering support, endless encouragement, and the countless times you pretended to care about my writer's block. You're the real author here—I just put the words on the page.

P.S. I promise the next book will take less time. (Maybe.)

Chapter 1

Damn, morning TV is terrible.

Even though hundreds of channels were open to him, nothing good was on. Nothing worth half-watching while wolfing down his soggy, off-brand cornflakes.

David flicked the channel up button on the remote, and a fake smiling blonde woman appeared on the screen waving her arms around like an inflatable tube man. You know, those crazy air dancers they had outside car showrooms in the 80s? She looked like one of those.

The young couple she was flailing at looked mystified and nervous. It was some holiday home abroad show. David's mum loved garbage TV like that for some reason. The woman was now trying to justify why she'd picked a house for them that was double their budget.

Silly cow.

David hit the remote again, his fake-flakes now resembling a gross yellow mush. He dipped the spoon and brought it to his mouth, globs of congealed flakes dribbling over the side and down his hoodie. Next on the screen was one of those family issue shows, those where the cocky host parades up and down the stage, gaslighting his guests.

The audience whooping and cheering every time a guest raised their voice or when a fight might break out. At that point, the psychologist waltzes on with a clipboard and makes someone cry. Classic trash TV. He left it on this one; it was just about entertaining enough for a hasty breakfast before getting the bus to college.

Right now, the host, an ostentatious simpleton with a likely permanent smirk, was berating a slim woman in her mid-twenties. The woman was wearing a dress only just covering a tattoo that likely crept all the way up her thigh. The screen's resolution was terrible, but it looked like one of those rose tattoos with Mum or Dad across in illegible script and drawn by someone who'd failed high school art class.

The woman was now in the host's face, unleashing a rapid torrent of expletives.

The bleeping guy is working some serious overtime here…

Two robust, bald security people circled the scene like vultures hunting for job validation. They wore *'two-sizes-too-small'* black t-shirts with *'SECURITY'* in giant white letters across the chest.

In case they forget what they're here for…

After a couple more minutes of the woman swearing at the host, with him occasionally looking to the audience as if to say, *'Would you get a load of this psycho?'* she took a swing at him, narrowly missing his nose.

"Unlucky," David said to himself.

"What did you say?" his mother said, walking into the kitchen; her hair was in a towel standing a good foot higher than the top of her head. She was wearing a bathrobe and carrying a mug. Her fuzzy light pink *'Prosecco princess'* slippers scuffed across the linoleum floor irritatingly.

"Nothing," David replied.

"You're going to be late," she said. *"Stop watching that rubbish and get a move on."*

"Such a hypocrite," David muttered under his breath.

Pretending not to have heard this, his mother turned back to the toaster. *Teenagers…*

Glancing back at the TV and taking another spoonful of milky yellow mush, the vultures put the woman in an arm lock and dragged her off stage. It hardly took the two of them, but it was important for them to prove their usefulness.

A single high-heeled shoe lay behind. The host walked over to it and kicked it off-screen. The audience laughed. He then raised his open arms to the audience.

"He thinks he's Christ the Redeemer," David said.

It cut to an ad break, another fake smiley woman laughing at how amazing her new washing-up liquid was, grinning maniacally while washing up a plate. She then picked up a lemon and sniffed it as she closed her eyes. David hit the power button. That was enough.

He chucked the rest of his breakfast in the bin and put the bowl on the side. His mother was leaning against the counter, waiting for the toaster to ping, her head buried in yesterday's issue of OK Magazine.

"*See ya,*" David said in her general direction.

"*What? Yeah, bye,*" she replied, not looking away from the images of glossy Z-listers. David grabbed his beaten-up backpack hanging on the back of the chair, threw it over his shoulder and walked out of the kitchen.

Chapter 2

Five years had gone by, and high school was finally over. College was now on the horizon, only a few weeks away, and David couldn't wait. This would be it. New mysteries, a way to reinvent himself. A fresh start. Five years of hell was over. Though he was excited, the anxiety, the paranoia, the past trauma - they were embedded in his mind all the time. Whenever he felt excited, optimistic, or even happy, they always whispered to him, reminding him of his past and what could still happen. That maybe it was him, not the place.

Just the idea of doing another two years at that school, doing his A-levels, sent a massive shiver down his spine. He doubted the school would even let him return. *Just as well...* But now he was free. He had managed to avoid any good friendships while there, but maybe this is where that could all change.

This was a fresh start, an opportunity to shed the skin of his former self, to shed his vulnerability, to grow. He would be a stranger – a blank canvas ready for the brushstrokes of a new life.

As he entered college, David managed to seamlessly blend into student life. His once-disparaged long hair was actually now a popular style choice. It showed him to be an individual and confident, and it wasn't long before other long-haired students started talking to him. After all, David had grown his hair out because of his love of rock and metal. This was apparently a common musical interest at college, and walking through the hallways, the thud of heavy metal emanated from phones, headphones, and tiny, terrible, tinny speakers wherever he went.

4

David felt as though he genuinely belonged here, not just his hair, but his clothes, which had always been an afterthought, were right on trend here. On one particular day, he counted 14 people wearing Metallica T-shirts. 14! Including himself. You found it almost impossible to contain his happiness at this observation. It wasn't long before he had a small group of friends, one in particular. Morgan had been, if possible, even more of a devout Metalhead than David and even played the guitar, much to David's envy.

The first few months of college were a revelation. They washed away all of the self-doubt, depression, anxiety, and paranoia that had haunted him for so long. The energy of college transformed David's outlook on life. It infused his weary spirit with a renewed sense of purpose.

David devoted himself fervently to physics, maths, and computers. After all, they had been his steadfast companions throughout those lonely high school nights. Ever since first immersing himself in those archaic 1980s video games all those years ago, he sought refuge in their pixelated landscapes, finding comfort from the gloomy nights that had always plagued him.

To David, high school had been like the relentless battle of Space Invaders. He was the frail 8-bit spaceship, tirelessly fighting against the relentless waves of bullies, each advancing step chomping away his diminishing self-esteem. However, the countless hours spent gaming had honed his skills to a razor's edge, allowing him to conquer almost any game he encountered before stepping foot into college. And it was this extraordinary gaming skill that he and Morgan both shared. Morgan's past had been similar to his. Endless nights of gaming into the small hours to escape the depression brought on by school life, and David was thankful for finally finding someone he could confide in. It also helped that Morgan was the best gaming opponent he had ever had.

But as he conquered every game he came across, David was hungry for new challenges. He wanted to cross the boundaries of the gaming world, to breathe new life into those vintage games that he loved so much but were no longer a challenge. And so, he began looking online, in special forums about hacking games and seeing all the possibilities that lay at his fingertips.

David fully immersed himself in these forums, which were a vibrant community of like-minded people who were also chasing challenges. It was another place where he found a sense of belonging. He made friends here, a different social circle. It was within this online environment that an audacious idea began to sprout. Why confine this rapidly expanding, though primitive, coding knowledge just to vintage video games? What if he could use these new skills to manipulate other things, like the software in college, for example?

So many possibilities were unfurling before him. So many challenges. But despite this infinite potential, questions lingered in his mind. Where should he begin? How far is too far? What path should he take? David was standing at a crossroads, a young, intelligent man with a newfound confidence ready to embark on a journey that would redefine his understanding of technology and himself.

Chapter 3

2011, Castle Hedington - Age 18

David had planned what he would do, and one evening, he was fortunate to have the house to himself. His mother was out with friends for the night, which meant she'd probably be home past one in the morning. Likely stumbling and making a racket downstairs on her return, so it was on these nights David prepared for an equally late night. Perfect opportunity to take on a lengthy gaming session with Morgan, or something perhaps a little more life-altering.

Opening the lid of his laptop, casting his pallid face in the glow of the white-blue light, David crunched his neck and pulled his chair nearer the desk. Clicking open his private browser, he navigated to the bookmarked forum devoted to amateur hackers he had chosen to join tonight.

Of course, these weren't the bad kind of hackers you hear about on the news. The state-sponsored ones who bring down government infrastructure or steal millions of email addresses to sell on. No, these were the nice kinds, the ones who find the weaknesses in software and tell the companies so they can fix it—usually called *'white-hat hackers'*. They did it for the challenge and the community. And, of course, sometimes the financial gain from the companies as a thank you. This reason probably ranked a little higher on the list of justifications, but that was just life. Computers cost money.

David opened the forum and scrolled to the *'join'* button. Members' names and avatars appeared before him, running down the right side of the screen in little windows—their status showing either offline red, away yellow, or ready to go green.

David created his new online identity and account. He'd given the avatar name some thought throughout the day and had settled on *Sadbutfalse*, a play on Metallica's *Sad but True*. He thought it was hysterical but presumed it actually wasn't. But that didn't matter; it was his new identity now. After setting up his account, he logged in, and the refreshed home screen bared all.

As David's eyes scanned the screen, he felt lost in the information flow. Each topic heading lured him in—little gateways to new knowledge and potential friends. Starting from the top, David read through every topic posted in the last month, navigating to ones discussing games in particular. He absorbed everything; he downloaded every toolkit, every code segment, and everything he thought he might find helpful.

Days melted into nights as David delved deeper into the forum's depths. He started immersing himself in discussions about cutting-edge encryption and finding software vulnerabilities. The forum became a place for his dormant potential to grow and evolve into what it could be. He even made friends. Probably not what you would call *real* friends, but they were interesting to speak to and gave David confidence. They all had strange usernames, things like *Gh0st4* and *Lastcall* - or Marcus as he preferred to be called. The people David met on this forum seemed incredible, they were teachers, mentors. And now friends. As he continued his cyber-education, the world continued to open up to him. His imagination ran wild with all the ideas, possibilities, that lay ahead.

During one such profound moment, David's resolve solidified as he stumbled upon an interview featuring a prodigious computer geek who had hacked his school network, uncovering flaws in its security and leading to a booming career in consulting. This computer prodigy now resided in Mayfair, his account overflowing and his recognition global. David yearned to emulate this path, and for all he knew, it was entirely possible.

And so, one night, David perched at his desk adorned with an array of energy drinks, crips, and chocolate bars. He positioned his laptop closer, queuing up Metallica's latest album on his trusty iPod, drowning out the mundane world outside. The echoing thud of his mother's footsteps abruptly dissipated as she left the house for another night out, slamming the door behind her a little too enthusiastically.

As David cracked his knuckles in anticipation, he opened his browser and navigated to the college proxy network. He began isolating its impregnable IT systems, swapping between windows of code and virtual machine viewers.

Hours bled into each other as he delved deeper into the source code. His fingers performed a choreographed ballet on the keyboard as he started adding his lines of code, swapping out snippets and replacing new ones. The hacker forum became his new home, where he diligently scoured for existing code that could expedite his progress. After a gruelling battle of trial and error, he finally breached the college's systems. The file system map materialised on his screen, revealing a vast expanse of organised folders brimming with information.

David stood before a virtual treasure trove of sensitive information. As he gazed at the human resources files, confidential payslips, and even medical records belonging to the on-site nurse, he felt an inexplicable pull towards them. They were like forbidden fruit, tempting him with the promise of power. But David knew giving in to such temptation would be a grave mistake. Instead, he remained guided by his unwavering moral compass, leading him towards righteousness, the white-hat code, as it were.

He consciously resisted the temptation of quick money and determined to stay away from the allure of illicit gain. He set his sights on a brighter future built on integrity and honour, like the prodigy guy who now ran his own consulting firm.

I'm gonna be just like that, this is how he got his big break. I can do that too, why couldn't I? I have the same skills, well kinda, I'm getting there. Hell, I just managed to break into my college system after only a few hours! I mean come on...

Amidst the labyrinth of data, David's focus homed in on the student grade directory. A list of approximately 400 folders sprawled before him, labelled with the student's surname, first name, and date of birth.

David scrolled until he found the folder bearing his name, his pulse quickening with exhilaration and uncertainty. Eagerly, he clicked open the portal to his academic past, only to discover another list of subfolders, each labelled with the name of a study subject and its corresponding code. The folders housed all the coursework, exam scripts, spreadsheets with grades, everything that would dictate his academic fate.

David marvelled at the revelation that he had writing permissions - the ability to actually go into the files and change whatever he wanted.

His existing grades were already pretty decent. Mostly good with a smattering of distinctions. They were just fine and didn't need any alteration. The fleeting temptation to toy with his records, though, did flit across his mind and was swiftly dismissed. His aspirations reached higher, aiming for a nobler cause after all.

His gaze shifted to Morgan's file, a spark of intrigue kindling in David's eyes. While not mirroring his decent achievements, Morgan's grades held respectability. The urge to gift his friend an academic boost tugged at him. But this was not the mission. He was there to prove to the college that he could find a way in, and he had. He wanted to let them know how he did it and get the credit he was after.

Drawing upon his newfound knowledge, David composed a brief script containing logic and proper syntax designed to infiltrate each student's grade folder with his manifesto. Would his real intentions be deciphered—that he was there to help—or would he be condemned as a digital trespasser?

A single line materialised on the screen in stark black letters:

'User ID login vulnerability exposed, accessed via SQL injection: 105 OR 1=1, D. Mills.'

These words harboured a potentially disruptive potency, a simple signpost aiming to highlight the college system's vulnerabilities, positioning David as the omen of a necessary change. His finger hovered over the Y-key, caught between anonymity and revelation. Doubt crept in.

What if they don't get what I'm trying to do? What if the IT guys think I'm attacking the system? What if they expel me? Or worse? No, this is the right thing to do. I'm helping them, they'll see that. It's the right thing to do. But do I just do this anonymously? Should I put my name on it? If I don't, I won't get the credit. No house in Mayfair, no worldwide fame. I have to do it.

With a breath, he pressed down, surrendering to fate. Whatever it had in store.

Leaning back in his chair, David relished a fleeting moment of reprieve. His heart raced. He watched the little pixelated envelopes fanning out and inserting themselves into every student's folder.

David foresaw the chaos—a tremor shattering IT administrators' unawareness, shockwaves rippling through the system. The realisation was that the system was easily breached, and David was the one to thank for bringing it to their attention.

Amid the excitement and a little anxiety, David realised that he had initiated an irreversible change, altering his fate forever. His life's trajectory had shifted, pointing straight up. The door to opportunity was wide open, welcoming his imminent arrival. Unable to contain his excitement, he sent a message to Morgan outlining all that he'd accomplished.

Chapter 4

A stern looking police officer had picked David up one morning from his house. Ringing the doorbell just before David was due to leave for college. His mother had answered the door, princess prosecco slippers and hair in a towel tower without a second thought to who would be calling round this early. She'd opened the door, and instinctively taken a small step back as in disbelief. The officer had introduced himself and asked to see David. Answering his mother's shouting, David had peered around the kitchen door, backpack on his shoulder, and just stood still. Still as the stillest thing you've ever seen. Utterly grounded to the spot, petrified even. The officer had walked towards him, but David just stood. Eyes wide in confusion.

The police interview room was a strange space. It was brightly lit, the overhead fluorescent tubes buzzing slightly and too bright to stare at directly. Four worn-out chairs huddled around a scarred metal table, etched with countless dents and marks of desperation and aggression.

Once likely a pristine sterile white, the walls bore the scars of time and turmoil. Cracks snaked across the faded paint in the corners. The room exhaled an air of neglect, the stale scent of aged misery clinging to its every crevice.

David's mother occupied a chair beside her son. Her posture was rigid. Her outward appearance of stoicism was a thin veil, failing miserably to mask the discontent that simmered beneath. Every furrow on her brow seemed to scream disappointment and unresolved frustration. Her gaze lingered on David.

"David, do you realise what a mess you've made?" Her voice, tinged with boredom, cut through the heavy silence.

"I was just trying to prove a point," David said, frustration tingeing his tone.

"Proving a point?" She scoffed. *"You jeopardised everything."*

DI Harrison observed the exchange, a very slight hint of sympathy flickering in his eyes. He cleared his throat.

"Your son seems to have a knack for technology."

"Too much of a knack, if you ask me," she retorted, her impatience now evident.

"Mrs. Mills, we're just trying to understand David's actions," the inspector said in a gentle tone.

Her response was a weary sigh.

"It's always something with him. Trouble, trouble, and more trouble."

David faced the looming consequences and the loss of all of his equipment. But what clawed at his soul was the void left by the absence of his mother's admiration. His intentions were genuinely noble, but they had cast a dark cloud, smothering the pride he had hoped to elicit.

Christ, why can't she just be even slightly proud? It was a hell of an achievement, and yeah, it didn't quite pan out as I expected. But come on, just be a little impressed, even the cop seems to be. A bit anyway.

As DI Harrison studied the scene, his gaze flickered over the room's dismal image. The atmosphere was heavy, and the weight of impending consequences on the two people before him was palpable. Yet, despite this, a glimmer of empathy stirred within him. It was not merely a small case of cyber vandalism before him but a snapshot of a fractured family.

David had always been a lonely figure, lost in the addictive glow of his laptop screen. His mother had long known his penchant for isolation and his unwavering love of technology. However, DI Harrison's comments about David's arrest for cyber-vandalism and his menacing threats against the college meant to nurture his future changed everything. His mother's indifference was striking. She didn't even spare him a glance as the charge was read out, her eyes devoid of disappointment or fury.

Why is she being so silent? Am I really being charged with this? I can't believe it, no this isn't happening. I didn't do anything wrong! I was trying to help them, the stupid bastards. How can they be this dumb? And why is mum not saying anything? Does she really not care? Well, screw her then, whatever.

He had always held onto a foolish hope of gaining admiration from his mother. However, she could not understand the complexity of the charges against him for breaching the college's security systems. To David, gaining access to confidential student files was an intellectual challenge rather than an intention to commit any wrongdoing. He saw himself as a white-hat hacker, motivated by nobler motives than personal gain or cyber-terrorism. He aimed to expose vulnerabilities in the system, which genuinely malicious people could exploit. Despite attempting to explain his intentions to his mother, he was met with indifference or dismissive nods.

Yet, everything had changed this time. David had veered dangerously close to the precipice, planting what he thought were harmless notes within the virtual confines of his classmates' files. He insinuated that he could access their grades, medical records, addresses, and phone numbers. It was a daring gambit. A desperate cry for recognition he couldn't allow to fade into obscurity. When he revealed this reasoning to DI Harrison, a glimmer of understanding spread across his face, an ember of comprehension that sparked an idea.

And still, his mother remained aloof, her demeanour hovering on the precipice of boredom. She had been suddenly pulled from her mundane daily routines, leaving her boring office job to face this annoying trial. She frequently glanced at her wristwatch. Her restless eyes revealed an impatience to escape.

Her impatience was palpable as she let out a frustrated sigh.

"Are you going to charge him or what?" she demanded, her tone laced with irritation. David was taken aback by his mother's apparent lack of concern for his fate. It almost felt like she didn't care whether he ended up in jail. Detective Harrison, too, was surprised by her indifference. He cleared his throat loudly, breaking the tense silence that had settled over the room.

Ultimately, the evidence against David was substantial. While David had accessed the unauthorised parts of the college's servers, he hadn't stolen any confidential information. His honesty and unguarded vulnerability in DI Harrison's presence partially swayed the tide of his fate.

Instead of a sentence befitting a wayward youth, a decision was made for David for an alternative path. The inspector mentioned a small local cybersecurity company that had received a sizeable government grant. The company aimed to cultivate the raw talents of young, diverse computer prodigies like David and shape them into responsible IT professionals. By doing so, they hoped to protect society while earning a decent, honest living.

However, complete absolution would remain out of reach for David. The charge would forever smear his criminal record, branding him with the stain of his actions. Moreover, he would also be expelled from college, the very place he was trying to help. The police also confiscated his laptop, which really annoyed David. They took everything he loved, except for his game consoles, which they didn't consider dangerous.

The other world, the friends he'd made on the forums, were gone now. His mother had told police that she would never buy him a computer again. His access to the digital world was severed, and now he stood at a new junction in his life. One he most definitely had not wanted. He would soon embark on a two-year forced career in IT as per DI Harrison's wish, and who knows, maybe it wouldn't be so bad. Hell, even a few years later, he might be able to return to his intended life.

Chapter 5

Life had dealt David a challenging hand from the start. A hand so cruel and unyielding it could have broken the spirit of a lesser soul. And it almost had many times. While lots of people would remember their childhoods as a mix of ordinary moments; a blend of joy and sadness, for David, school experiences acted as a defining element in those memories. They forever stained his memory with the dark hues of torment and anguish. The corridors of high school were transformed into a twisted labyrinth where his vulnerability was mercilessly preyed upon.

David's torment began in 1998 when he was five, an age where the world still held a hint of magic and wonder. But for him, the magic was replaced with a bitter dose of reality as he was thrust into the unfamiliar territory of a new home and school—the aftermath of his parents' painful divorce. The stark reality of their separation became a target for the other kids, their surprising cruelty latching onto the vulnerability of his parents' situation. They revelled in their power over him. Like sadistic puppeteers. Mockery, torment, and beatings became their weapons of choice. Day after day, David found himself caught in the crosshairs of their cruelty, enduring a relentless onslaught, leaving him battered and broken mentally and physically.

The physical abuse ceased when David's mother stepped in after teachers refused. Threats to pull him from *that wretched school* briefly halted the onslaught forcing teachers to intervene, yet the scars etched into his impressionable mind remained unhealed, poisoning his thoughts and self-confidence. Resentment toward his parents brewed within him, their separation the catalyst to everything he went through and the vulnerability he felt. It erupted in outbursts here and there, defiance, and a constant shroud of negativity tainting his home life, eventually leading him to become more and more isolated.

At age seven, David moved a junior school down the road, the hope that a fresh start would hinder any further psychological damage. As David reached junior school, hoping for a respite from the trials of his earlier years, fate revealed its cruel hand once again. This time however, it was a gang of four girls a couple years older.

Their stocky, towering figures stood completely out of place with the rest of the class and were generally avoided. They descended upon David with such malice that David couldn't understand. No reasoning whatsoever, just springing from hidden corners in classrooms and hallways, their nails sharp and poorly painted, scratching at his arms, leaving crimson trails of pain in their aftermath. Kicks to his shins and yanks at his mid-length, curly brown hair became their usual routine. But it was in the classroom that their true sadism revealed itself.

"Come on, David, let's play a game!" The ringleader's voice echoed as the girls circled him in the classroom, their compasses wielded like weapons. They suddenly lunged at him, leaving puncture marks etched on his arms and hands. Walking through the hallways, David always kept his hands in his pockets, hiding the compass marks. He pulled his jumper down over them, desperate not to give more fuel to the other boys in the class. He couldn't let them see.

The stigma attached to reporting the girls made it impossible to ask for help. The mere thought of the boys in his class finding out he was being bullied by girls was unbearable. And so, the cycle of abuse persisted.

But as David moved on to high school at eleven, he discovered the nature of his torment was a chameleon. Ever-changing, adapting to his newfound vulnerabilities. Psychological warfare became the weapon of choice now, a weapon deadlier than any fist or nail or compass. By now, everyone had identified him as the shy, introverted kid with his hands in his pockets, trying not to be noticed by anyone. This, instead, had the opposite effect. It acted as a siren's call, as it were, serving as an invitation for his classmates to subject him to unrelenting psychological torture. At the age of sixteen, David found himself burdened with a textbook case of social anxiety disorder.

"Anthro...anthropophobia, I think. That's what they call it. The wuss is terrified of people or something," a voice had murmured, and laughter echoed through the corridor.

The consuming dread of people, a condition given the grandiose name of anthropophobia, wrapped its hands around his fragile psyche, squeezing tighter with every passing day. Word of David's affliction spread like wildfire through the school, reaching not only his class but even the other years. It became a twisted game to them, a sick fascination to exploit his anxiety for their sadistic pleasure. Every joke and every humiliation became a piece of his identity. The HDP, the Humiliate David Project - people even had homemade badges - was an insidious creation borne out of their sadism and became a living nightmare.

Chapter 6

In David Mills's appearance, you'd find a man cloaked in the subtleties of a chameleon, his face blending seamlessly with his surroundings. His slender frame gave the air of an inherent vulnerability like a mere breeze could snap him in two. Yet, beneath this timidity lay a yearning, an insatiable hunger to belong, to be embraced by a world that often felt so far away.

David's lifelong quest for acceptance was a constant struggle. His looks, a blend of a high fashion model with his sharp cheekbones and narrow chin, intrigued and unsettled those around him.

Unfortunately, his personality contained quirks his mother deemed abnormal and repelled those she considered *"normal"*, whatever that was. His narrow, pale features and sunken eyes gave him an almost vampiric appearance, and despite his best efforts to fit in, he never really succeeded. The more he tried to be someone he wasn't, the more he felt like an outsider. David remained hopeful that someday he would find his place in the world, but had generally accepted that his struggle would continue until then.

David was pretty intelligent, certainly above average anyway, and was therefore a decent target. When he started high school in 2005, the popular kids took great delight in exploiting this, subjecting him to merciless harassment. They found ample material in his love for chess, using the chess club newsletter as ammunition for their constant bullying. High school became a five-year nightmare for David - a relentless onslaught of confidence-destroying negativity, ultimately leaving him isolated and devoid of even the most basic interpersonal skills. Yet, within the confines of his incredible imagination, he discovered a refuge offering some relief from the crushing weight of his everyday problems.

Video games became David's first lifeline. Countless nights were spent huddled in his tiny bedroom, the computer screen's glow illuminating his pale face as he clutched the game controller in his cramping hands. Each button press, each small victory, served as an escape, letting him rise above the misery of his reality.

But David's interests extended beyond video games. He was also passionate about computers, spending hours on them. Tinkering with the hardware and software led him to explore the internet and everything it was capable of. Every line of code and every system tweak opened new possibilities.

David was fascinated by space, too. The cosmos. The night sky, full of mysteries, captivated him. David would venture outside on those freezing nights when the world was still, and the chill nipped at his skin. His eyes locked on the twinkling lights above. He would stand in awe, thinking about the formation of stars and planets and their movements through the skies. Back in 2003, on his tenth birthday, he'd gotten a telescope that forever changed his perspective. It was not a flimsy, run-of-the-mill department store one, good only for spying on neighbours, but a powerful one allowing him to glimpse the actual planets, albeit limited to the larger ones.

On that memorable August night in 2003, David stood shivering in the icy darkness of his garden, his breath visible in the frigid air as he delicately adjusted the telescope's focus. And there it was—Saturn, its luminescent sphere adorned with a ring of ethereal beauty, suspended in the vast, inky blackness. It shimmered in the eyepiece as though caught in the tight grip of an invisible cosmic hand, and David's breath caught in his throat. From that moment, he knew he was meant to study the stars.

For David, these weren't just hobbies. They were vital. They connected him to a world he could shape and mould, where he could be the hero of his own story. As he immersed himself in video games, computers, and astronomy, hope sparked. Maybe, just maybe, he could find a better future among the pixels and stars.

2015, Castle Hedingham, Essex

Now at twenty-two, having left college a few years earlier, David had focused his life on work - granted this hadn't been optional, and further study through part-time courses on the side.

David was good at science and maths but struggled with other subjects. This made it hard to pursue astronomy. However, he didn't give up. He put aside his love for the stars and worked hard to improve. Eventually, his hard work paid off, and he secured a place at Queen Mary University in London, his first-choice institution. The prospect of immersing himself fully in the study of astronomy thrilled David to no end.

He had entered the living room that evening, having just received his acceptance letter earlier in the day, ready to bring up a subject he sensed would meet with a peculiar reception from his mother. She sat engrossed in her knitting.

"I've made a decision. I'm going to university," David announced, gauging her reaction.

His mother paused her knitting, looking up with mild interest. *"University? What for?"*

David hesitated, anticipating her response. *"Astrophysics."*

She glanced over the lump of wool in her lap, *"University seems a bit late now, doesn't it? I mean, you're getting on a bit. Besides, I figured after all that hoo-ha at college would be an issue."*

David ignored the latter part of her comment.

Actually, that hoo-ha, as she put it, probably made my prospects even better. It made for a hell of a personal statement.

"Yeah, it might be late," David replied. *"But I want to give it a shot."* Her tepid response, though expected, stung more than he cared to admit.

"I'm going to be a bit older than most students, but I think it's the right move," David added, seeking some form of acknowledgement.

His mother smiled faintly. *"Well, dear, it's your life. If it's what you think is best. Good to have a plan and all that."*

Though her response lacked enthusiasm, there was an unmistakable sense of relief in the air, a subtle acknowledgement that David's departure was welcomed. His decision to go to university seemed met with more peace than excitement.

David set off on his undergraduate journey, diving deep into the wonders of astrophysics. He enjoyed every moment spent unravelling the mysteries of the universe—learning about the creation of stars and planets, the movements of celestial bodies, and the tantalising riddles posed by black holes. Graduating was a milestone, but for David, it was just the start.

His thirst for knowledge and unyielding curiosity drove him to pursue a PhD in cosmology after his three-year undergrad course was done, but this time with computer science, committing himself to another four years of intense study. The previous three years had been academically fulfilling, expanding his intellectual horizons. However, his social life was practically empty. There were no romantic interests or invites to parties - just solitude in his small student room. It became his refuge, with bare walls and a board filled with schedules, deadlines, and doodles of black holes.

Chapter 7

2021, Queen Mary University - Age 28

Today held an unusual vibe. For years, David had agreed to venture to the University Student Union on this exact day. Morgan had made David agree to the plan, and now it was the day David lacked enthusiasm. He was nervous—more than nervous—flat-out panicking. His final PhD viva, his academic journey's rigorous examination, loomed just hours away.

Seven years of university, all for this day…

Hunched over his desk in the cramped dorm room, David felt engulfed by disarray. The room mirrored his chaotic state. Papers and textbooks lay scattered, neglect curling their edges, covering the worn wood of his desk. It looked like a storm had ransacked the space, leaving chaos in its wake. Colourful post-it notes, once orderly on the shelves, now floated aimlessly, their reminders useless against his impending judgment.

He anxiously re-read his thesis for the tenth time that week. His eyes traced the meticulously arranged lines and diagrams that spanned its 100 pages. A collection of electrical schematics and astronomical equations adorned the pages. They formed an intricate web of knowledge that, to the uninitiated eye, would appear as an esoteric lexicon of absolute gibberish. David checked online again for any contradicting papers. He knew it was his typical anxiety acting up, yet the gnawing doubt persisted, threatening to undermine the confidence he had so painstakingly built over the last few years.

I mean there won't be anything, Christ I only checked this morning. There won't be anything, just relax. Relax! You've got this. Four years of breathing this stuff and its done. Well almost done. One more challenge, it won't be a challenge though. They'll love it. Probably. They've read it already. But I've got this. Morgan's done it, I'm sure. I'm sure he's passed his. God, I hope we both pass, that would be so cool. Come on pull yourself together David.

Nervousness consumed him. It twisted his gut into knots and sent jolts of apprehension through his veins, but there was no turning back now. He needed to appear confident and prepared for any challenge the panel would throw at him. But for now, he needed a distraction. He had done everything he could and needed to take his mind off the thesis. He clicked open the folder labelled *'blog'* on his desktop, a digital space where his thoughts could roam free.

Writing about space and computer science theories on this online platform provided a brief respite from his rigorous studies, a momentary escape from the suffocating weight of academia. Deep down, he knew these thoughts might be seen as mad ramblings, the products of an overactive imagination. Yet, it offered a sense of solace. Dreaming up new ideas about the universe, wormholes, and time travel had been sparked by books like Carl Sagan's *Contact*. Though it seemed crazy, David hoped that some sliver of truth might be found in those far-reaching theories someday.

An hour had passed, and David leaned back in his chair, the old joints creaking in exhaustion. He stretched his arms and felt his joints crackle, then cradled his head with clammy hands, tracing the furrows of anxiety etched into his temples. He felt a mix of fatigue and exhilaration as he reviewed the two pages of text he had written—a blend of scientific eccentricity, lunacy, and a sprinkling of genius. With a decisive click, he hit the *"publish now"* button and let out a long sigh.

Glancing at his Casio wristwatch, he realised the time to leave had come. There was no point in delaying any further. David reached for his bag, its worn fabric frayed at the edges, placed on the messy bed that seemed to mirror his equally messy and chaotic mind. But before he could grasp the bag's handle, a buzz erupted from his pocket, jolting him from his thoughts. He retrieved his phone with its worn, cracked screen. It was a text from Morgan. He'd decided to study just physics, computers weren't really his thing. That was more David's arena. Morgan had even deferred starting university until David had finished his court-appointed IT job and could get in. Morgan was probably coming to the end of his viva.

"Passed it mate! You can officially call me Doctor, and see that you do! See you after. Good luck!" The text, a simple yet genuine message, felt oddly

foreign even now. David smiled, thankful for Morgan's friendship over all these years—a blend of intellect and approachability that occasionally sparked a hint of envy. But such emotions were fleeting. Rereading the message, David sensed the weight of the pressure to succeed now, not just for himself but also for Morgan.

Relief washed over him next. He wouldn't need to console Morgan. Sympathy wasn't his strong suit, yet he couldn't bear witnessing Morgan's disappointment. With a final check of his messy room, making sure he hadn't forgotten anything crucial, David stepped into the dimly lit hallway.

Chapter 8

Nerves returned once he was outside. They wracked David's body like a swarm of hornets. His PhD viva loomed ahead, an ordeal as formidable as it was crucial. Four years of dedicated pursuit weighed on him like a leaden cloak, suffocating his every breath. Despite his knowledge and preparation, the gnawing unease in his gut refused to subside.

David trudged toward the computer science building, his stomach in knots, his heart racing. Sweat dripped down his forehead, his once-neat hair now a twisted mess. Each step felt like a Herculean effort as if he were wading through quicksand.

Inhale, one, two, three, four, hold, one, two, three, four, exhale, one, two, three, four. Stop panicking damn it, it's fine. Just focus on the sounds, the sky. Whatever. Just chill out.

Finally, he arrived at the courtyard, his nerves at a fever pitch. As he walked up the stairs to the building, his brain buzzed with a thousand thoughts and fears. He felt like a lamb walking into the lion's den, waiting for the predators to pounce. The air was thick with tension, every sound amplified to a deafening roar. David knew what lay ahead was a test of his mettle. He took a deep breath and stepped through the doorway, ready to face the biggest challenges of his life.

Arriving a generous twenty minutes early, David sought refuge against the cool, white-washed hallway's textured surface. Its roughness offered a comforting contrast to the anxiety raging within him, a grounding sensation that quieted his racing thoughts. As he closed his eyes, the familiar texture stirred something deeper—an echo of another time when discomfort had led to change.

He was nineteen then, feeling equally trapped in his own skin, the weight of isolation pressing down. The frustration had built until it could no longer be ignored, igniting within him a sudden need for movement, for independence. It was this restlessness that drove him to ask his mother to teach him to drive—a big step in reclaiming control over his life.

Ok, seat belt in, hands - what did she say? Ten and two that's it. God stop trembling, relax. Why is my stomach rumbling? Oh, I don't like that, breathe... Ok next ignition on, ok, and handbrake down. Gear in one. Now gently press, shit, stalled. Ok ignition on, press down and away we go...

Hyperventilating and teetering on the precipice of vomiting, he mustered the resolve to press forward. With each cautious turn and gentle acceleration, he began to conquer the paralysing fear that had kept him captive for far too long. And when the engine was finally silenced, an unfamiliar sense of pride washed over him—triumph. It was a feeling he was desperate to feel again.

David glanced at his watch with a slight smile tugging at his lips. The seconds ticked away like a metronome, each passing moment bringing him closer to the test that awaited him. To his astonishment, just moments before he was about to enter the room, he got a text from his mother, wishing him luck. For a fleeting moment, cynicism threatened to dismiss the message as intended for someone else. Still, David set aside his scepticism, if only for this moment, allowing a flicker of hope to ignite.

Christ she actually remembered?

David's trembling subsided as he crossed the threshold into the room, yet perspiration dampened his brow, tracing paths down his temple. His grip on his thesis tightened, his knuckles turning white as he clung to the manifestation of his academic journey. The next few hours were gruelling, though the bombardment of questions and incredible concentration did wonders for his nerves, which dissipated within moments.

Time seemed to stretch, a chewing gum-like distortion, as minutes turned to hours, each passing moment bringing him closer to the precipice. David's stomach grumbled loudly, breaking the deafening silence in the room as the panel conferred.

God, I hope they didn't hear that. Why did I skip breakfast? Oh yeah, I know why. Nerves. I reckon they haven't looked up at me once in five minutes. What are they whispering?

His anxiety grew as the silence lingered until finally, the life-altering words he'd been waiting for were spoken:

"Congratulations, Dr. Mills."

A surge of relief washed over him like cool water on a sweltering day. It was a moment he would never forget. It was as if a massive burden had been lifted, the weight of uncertainty thrown aside. David's legs threatened to buckle beneath him. His body swayed with the ebb and flow of emotions coursing through him.

With unsteady steps, he approached the three men, their expressions a mix of sternness and approval. He extended his trembling hand, the sheen of sweat glistening on his palm, and with each firm handshake, he showed his thanks. As he left the room, a renewed sense of purpose surged within him, his steps infused with a buoyancy he had longed for, his path illuminated by the radiance of a hard-fought victory.

The journey back to his halls of residence unfolded before him, the familiar surroundings aglow with a golden hue of accomplishment. Each step reverberated with quiet pride, the jitters subsiding as his palms began to dry beneath the crisp January sun. His once-tangled curls danced playfully in the gentle breeze as if celebrating his triumph. Yet, the evening still lay ahead, an uncharted territory he hadn't traversed in what felt like forever.

Morgan had insisted they venture to the student union, an agreement made years ago, a promise to embrace the celebration that awaited them. The whole venue buzzed with rugby World Cup excitement the last time David joined Morgan at the union. Its magnetic pull capturing the attention of sports enthusiasts, free snack lovers and budding alcoholics alike.

Sports held little interest for David. But Morgan, with his relentless pep and uncontainable enthusiasm, had convinced him that diving into the sports scene would magically make them social butterflies. An opportunity to escape the clutches of solitude, or so Morgan proclaimed with a fervour akin to a preacher in a fish market.

David had an epiphany after an excruciatingly awkward twenty minutes spent near the bar, nursing a Diet Coke as if it held the secrets of the universe. With a determined stride, he ventured forth, weaving through the crowd like a studious Moses, his eyes scanning for a familiar face. It was like hunting for a needle in a haystack, except the haystack was a bunch of chatty, cheering, drunk sports fans.

Five minutes of wandering aimlessly later, David threw in the towel, gulped down the Diet Coke, and made a swift exit, feeling more foolish than ever. Tonight, however, would be different. Probably.

Chapter 9

As he reached the Union piazza where he was to meet Morgan, David's heart pounded as he approached the familiar scene of his past embarrassment. The air seemed charged with anticipation, as if the very universe held its breath, waiting to witness his return.

Would anyone remember me? Probably not, I didn't exactly make much of an impact last time, did I? The awkward, shy nerd who always appears to be playing peek-a-boo from the sidelines?

David's nerves tap-danced down his spine, setting off an anxiety firework display in his mind. He prayed to any celestial being listening that his past antics hadn't become the stuff of local legend. But alas, uncertainty clung to him like a stage actor to a spotlight, refusing to exit stage left.

Clad in worn-out denim jeans and a Metallica shirt that had seen better days, David attempted a confidence-summoning ceremony. He could practically hear the fabric chanting mantras of empowerment, trying to give him an aura makeover. However, fate was cruel—cue Morgan's appearance.

Morgan, the epitome of suaveness, strutted in like a fashion messiah. His shirt was so white it could blind oncoming traffic, and those black jeans? They hugged him tighter than a kid clinging to a cookie jar. To top it off, Morgan was wearing a dark blue velvet blazer as well. The guy was a walking charm offensive, making David's outfit look about as exciting as yesterday's leftover chilli.

David might as well have worn a sign saying, *"Please ignore me while I try to blend into the wallpaper."*

"I thought this was supposed to be casual," David said, his voice tinged with a hint of self-consciousness, gesturing to his faded grey T-shirt.

29

"It is, mate," Morgan replied, a grin playing on his lips, his eyes dancing with mischief. *"Just wanted to look good for the girls."*

David glanced down at his T-shirt, its worn fabric suddenly imbued with a sense of inadequacy. His mind raced, contemplating the idea of girls being interested in him, of his newfound academic stature as a potential attraction. It seemed unlikely, considering his past experiences and the countless rejections that stung like bees on his fragile ego. But a secret optimism flickered deep within him, a flicker of hope.

"So, you gonna get wasted tonight?" Morgan asked, his words catching David off guard.

David blinked, mentally doing a cartwheel to keep up with the sudden detour in conversation. Alcohol wasn't his favourite indulgence, his delicate relationship with his mind and intellect making him wary of anything that might impair his mental abilities. But tonight was a special occasion, a night of celebration and liberation.

"Probably not wasted, but yeah, I'll have a drink. Couldn't hurt, right?" David responded, his voice laced with cautious excitement. Morgan, the cheerleader of reckless merrymaking, whooped and clapped his hand on David's back with a painful thud. *"What could go wrong?"*

Morgan and David found themselves standing in a line, a bunch of eager students stretching about fifty feet from the entrance of the union. Dazzling white and blue spotlights cast a blinding light, illuminating the crowd who were literally buzzing with anticipation. The sound of techno music seeped into their ears, a relentless pulse drowning out their conversation. David felt a hint of disdain for the pounding beats reverberating from the small smoking terrace above. Its thumping rhythm assaulted his senses. It was pretty annoying actually.

On the other hand, Morgan fidgeted excitedly. Enthralled by the electrifying atmosphere and pulsating music coursing through his veins. David forced a weak smile, nodding along with all the fervour of a bobblehead.

A group of women stood directly behind them. Their laughter wasn't in any way infectious. It was more like high-pitched guffawing. Their giggles sounded like a choir of frogs experimenting with stand-up comedy, punctuated by sips from a concealed bottle. Amidst them stood a towering, slender figure draped in black from head to toe, black lipstick serving as a portal to the abyss of her presumably enigmatic soul. David's curiosity pricked at the sight. He had never seen someone like her, her unconventional looks defying the norms he had grown accustomed to. There was an odd attraction to her, something that beckoned him. As she lit a cigarette, a plume of acrid smoke enveloped David, a suffocating cloud invading his lungs, forcing a cough as involuntary as a hiccup.

Part reflex, part protest against the foul odour lingering in the air. He took a small step forward, seeking respite from the smoke that wanted to poison him from within. Morgan, observing the girls' antics with an amused twinkle in his eye, rolled his eyes and let out a dismissive chuckle. In response, the girls croaked and giggled even louder, their annoying laughter mingling with the beat of the annoying music.

After an excruciating and seemingly eternal fifteen-minute purgatory, they finally got inside. David had almost forgotten what the place looked like, the memories of previous nights consumed by the relentless march of time and general repression. The foyer sprawled out before them, immense and overwhelming. Past the ticket stand, a central area served as a meeting place for students, a cloakroom already smothered in students holding out jackets and bags, a pizza stand that smelled absolutely incredible. To the left, a large archway beckoned, leading to the alternative music room with the promise of familiarity and a sense of belonging. David's eyes lit up as he recognised the familiar beat of *Master of Puppets* by Metallica, its heavy guitar riffs reverberating through the entrance hall. It was one of his favourite songs, a companion that had accompanied him through the darkest nights of solitude and the brightest moments of inspiration. It was probably his favourite song. He knew deep within his soul that that was where he belonged. All the other social misfits would be there too. After all, he was wearing a Metallica T-shirt, for God's sake!

"Morgan, let's go in there! It's Metallica!" David exclaimed, his voice brimming with anticipation.

Morgan cast a sardonic glance at the alternative music room, his eyes glinting with mischief, and mockingly shook his head.

"Ah, but dear David, it appears to be a gathering bereft of the fairer sex. A congregation of sausages, if you will."

Why the hell is he talking like that? Idiot, too excited to speak normally. Christ I wanna go in there.

David's frustration smouldered, a simmering resentment lighting up his gaze.

"So what? The music is so much better!"

Morgan laughed, his smile mischievous, his gaze never leaving David's face.

"We'll check it out later. Behold, Room One beckons." He gestured to a more expansive archway, double the girth of its predecessor.

We better go in there later, not listening to this rubbish all night.

As they walked through, David couldn't help but be impressed by the grandiosity of Room One. It was colossal. Filled with a sea of bodies swaying and thrashing to the loudest and most discordant music he had ever heard.

This music is crap...

Strobe lights flashed in sync with the beat, casting a kaleidoscope of colours, painting the room in an otherworldly glow like a mad painter's masterpiece come to life. Encircling the fervent mob stood tiers of railings, each layer packed with hundreds of students tapping their feet and swigging from plastic pint glasses splashing beer over each other without a care in the world. Morgan wisely chose a spot at one of the railings away from the chaotic centre, a vantage point offering a better view and a semblance of respite from the sensory bombardment.

"Better view, mate," he said, his voice barely audible amidst the deafening music, his words punctuated by the pounding bass reverberating through their bones.

Chapter 10

The nightclub throbbed with a bass so insistent it asserted dominance over the dark room. David found himself awkwardly wedged between Morgan and a pair of women, the rhythmic assault enveloping them all at the railing's edge. The sultry atmosphere was punctuated by flashes of green and red spotlights.

One of the women, occupying David's immediate attention, appeared just as uncomfortable and out of place as he did. She stood about his height with a slim, elegant figure accentuated by curly shoulder-length brown hair. Now and then, the spotlights revealed subtle streaks of dark blonde interwoven in her hair, creating a mesmerising play of colours David couldn't help but notice. To him, she was the epitome of textbook attractiveness.

Her face was soft and gentle. Her nose had character. From this angle, he could see that she had plump lips and a long neck disappearing into a white backlit blouse. Surprisingly, the buttons were done up a little higher than he'd expected to see in this place, giving her a fairly conservative look.

David's gaze dared to drift lower, and he saw that she wore a blue, or bluish, mid-length leather skirt. The booming bass and ear-splitting decibels were a thin veil for his surreptitious glances, though he couldn't shake the feeling that he was acting like a voyeur.

Jesus David, stop staring at her. You're gonna creep her out. She is pretty hot though...

Clutching a coke, she peered into the liquid depths, seeking wisdom from the fizz. It was either a silent protest against the uproar of the club, or perhaps just a moment of existential contemplation.

Morgan, ever perceptive, noticed David's fixated gaze and delivered a soft jab to his ribs, causing a brief surge of pain to snap David out of his reverie.

"*You planning on serenading her with silence or actually saying something?*" Morgan shouted over the loud thud of the music, his words struggling to be heard amidst the sonic assault.

"*I don't know, should I?*" David shouted back, his voice barely audible amidst the pulsating beats that throbbed through the air like a living entity.

"*Just say something, for God's sake!*" Morgan urged him, trying to offer support amid the chaos.

In that charged moment, a titbit from an obscure forum on social horrors flitted across David's mind like a ghost with an advice pamphlet:

What was it again, yeah it was something like its challenging but the fewer fucks you give, the happier you'll be, you have nothing to lose when meeting people. Yeah, that was it, or something like that. Just don't care what people think. It's challenging. Yeah, it bloody well is challenging. But I get it. Ok ok...

Repeating the sentence like a mantra, David took a deep breath and summoned the courage to tap the girl on the shoulder. Startled, she jumped and spun around. David froze, his throat drier than a comedian's wit in a funeral home. Summoning the courage of a timid lion, he managed to squeeze out a solitary, tremulous word.

"*Hey.*"

The girl's eyes bore into his, and an awkward silence hung in the air.

Is she gonna say anything? Did she even hear me or is she trying to psyche me out? If she is it's working.

Finally, she responded, her tone more of a statement than a genuine question, yet her voice held a certain softness, a slightly high pitch that charmed him. There was an undertone of certainty as if she knew her worth, and that first word transfixed David.

"Hi," she replied.

"*I'm David,*" he blurted out, unsure whether he'd bellowed his introduction or whispered it, considering the bass throbbing as if it had a personal vendetta against his eardrums.

Did I just shout my name in her face? Oh god. How loud was I just then? Stop overthinking it, David.

His inner voice jabbed at him, his insecurity sneakily tiptoeing in.

"Clara," she declared matter-of-factly, her eyes never leaving his.

The strobe lights continued their intermittent dance, making it difficult to discern whether she had blinked since their interaction began. Ultimately inconsequential, David scolded himself for hyper-analysing the situation as usual.

"Did you wanna go outside? Hear each other better?" he asked, his words drowned out by the relentless bass. He repeated the mantra under his breath, reminding himself that he had nothing to lose. It made sense, but the niggling worry still gnawed at him from the depths of his mind. The ugly, hateful nervousness stirred within him, blending with the pounding bass—a wretched tango of absolute misery.

As Clara's response emerged from the muffled chaos of the nightclub, it was as though her words had fought their way through a sonic battleground.

"Sure, yeah," she replied, her voice almost drowned out by the relentless noise. David strained to hear, but it seemed, to his astonishment, that she agreed to spend time with him and appeared genuinely enthusiastic about the prospect. A glimmer of delight danced in her eyes, concealed beneath the low-lit ambience. Casting a quick sideways glance at Morgan, David was met with a broad, knowing grin that said, *"You've got this."*

Emboldened, he followed Clara. His heart thumped in his chest as they moved from the epicentre of the auditory hell into the foyer. The noise subsided, replaced by the lingering scent of cigarette smoke wafting in from the entrance.

Suppressing a cough, David stood face-to-face with Clara, who had spun around to meet him in a small clearing within the smoking crowd outside the entrance. Her eyes remained locked onto his as if trying to work him out.

Over the next twenty minutes, they engaged in a spirited conversation, exchanging details about their fields of study. Clara was in the final stages of her Masters in journalism. A subject David had only a surface-level understanding of, primarily through glances at news articles on his phone before growing bored and moving on to Buzzfeed listicles. Looking at a list of the top 10 stupidest cats was ultimately more life-affirming than the current world news. Clara, however, looked unperturbed by his admission, her eyes alight with passion as she tried to convey the beauty of local printed journalism. David feigned moderate interest but enjoyed the enthusiasm in her voice.

To his slight disappointment, Clara didn't share his enthusiasm for physics or computers, but they discovered a shared love for heavy rock music, especially Metallica. Her eyes sparkled as she excitedly pointed at his Metallica shirt, revealing that she had seen them a few years ago at a festival. This new information made her even more attractive, adding to her already considerable charm. Those twenty minutes felt like a dream, a fantasy David had only dared to imagine on his happier days.

And then, Clara asked for his number in a twist that exceeded his wildest expectations. A surge of excitement coursed through him, electrifying his every nerve. With eagerness, David readily supplied his number, watching with anticipation as Clara tapped it in. He felt his phone vibrate in his pocket but refrained from taking it out.

I'm not showing her this second-hand thing, it's cracked and old and broken. Stupid mugger... Hers is nice and new and shiny and expensive, she'll think I'm a loser.

"Yep, got it! Thanks!" he replied, eager to dismiss any concerns about his less-than-stellar device.

Despite twenty minutes of engaging chat, he couldn't shake the lingering sense of shame that clung to his phone.

"I think I should get back to my friend," Clara said. *"I'll text you later?"*

"Yeah, awesome!" David responded, unable to hide his excitement. *"Look forward to it!"*

Clara's face then blossomed with an effervescent smile, illuminating the space between them as she leaned in toward David. Her arms extended, embracing him in a soft, tender kiss on the cheek. The warmth of her touch seeped into his skin, igniting a flicker of joy that swelled into a full-blown bonfire within his chest.

With a small wave, Clara pirouetted and began to make her way toward the entrance to the Union. David couldn't keep his eyes off her. With a smile stretching from ear to ear, he stood there, trying to wrap his head around the surreal moment.

As Clara melted back into the crowd heading inside, David watched her with a sense of longing, the pounding bass now felt less overpowering.

Chapter 11

As Clara vanished into the crowd of the foyer, evaporating like mist before sunrise, David's elation turned into urgency. He reached for his phone, fingers trembling with anticipation, eager to capture this fleeting connection. His thumb raced across the screen, adding Clara's name and the eleven digits of her number to his contacts list.

But as his eyes darted to the corner of his phone's screen, his heart sank like a stone. The battery level glared back at him with a menacing 1%. Panic surged through his veins, threatening to consume him. The chance of missing a message from Clara later, the lifeline connecting them, loomed. He couldn't bear the thought of losing her amidst the chaotic crowd.

Christ, I'd never find her in here. There must be a few thousand people! 1%? Seriously? Bloody ancient stupid phone, if I still had my phone, I'd have like loads of battery left. I can't wait til when I get home to talk to her, what if she thinks I'm ghosting here? Oh god. I gotta find her and tell her...

David took a deep breath, fortifying himself for the quest ahead. Clara was the Holy Grail, and he had to find her. Nothing about this appeared desperate or in the least bit creepy to David either. If anything, he saw tracking Clara down to be quite romantic. Walking into the foyer, he set his sights on the entrance to Room One, where they had met and where he had ditched Morgan, preying that she had returned there with her friend.

Please be there, please be there, please please please...

The chaotic hall enveloped him, but his focus remained singular. His eyes scoured the crowd, scanning for any glimpse of Clara. But the fates were clearly conspiring against him, as if mocking his desperate longing. Clara was nowhere to be seen, swallowed up by the vast wave of drunk students.

But amid the dashed hopes, a familiar face emerged from the swirling chaos. It was Morgan, surrounded by a group of guys David had never seen before. Their laughter just about punctuated the deafening heavy air. David made his way over to them, and at that moment, David realised that despite the initial letdown, tonight had been a wild ride so far and who knows what more would happen?

Chapter 12

"Mate!" Morgan shouted, beckoning him over to the group. David gave a thumbs-up and made his way over. Morgan couldn't wait to hear all about David's adventure. *"So, spill it! What took you forever?"* he said, his eyes shining with either curiosity or drunkenness. David delved into the tales of Clara, her love for Metallica taking the spotlight. Morgan glazed over at this point, but he didn't interrupt, recognising David's dire need to tell someone about the most interesting thing that had ever happened to him.

Morgan's attention rekindled when David reached the part about the kiss. He clapped him hard on the shoulder and gave him a small side-to-side hug, trying not to make it too awkward.

"That's amazing!" he exclaimed, a grin painting his face.

But a furrow on David's brow caught Morgan's eye.

"What's wrong?" he asked. David hesitated for a moment before replying.

"Phone's dead, and I can't find her," he said.

Morgan's expression dimmed momentarily.

"Ah, right," he said, a tinge of indifference clouding his response. *"No worries, though. Drop her a message later if she's not here. And while we're at it, let me introduce you to the flock!"* With that, he swivelled, showcasing David like a prize on *'The Price is Right.'*

"Hey! This is David he just pulled!" Morgan shouted, his voice cutting through the air with excitement and an exaggerated sense of triumph. The sudden spotlight caused David to blush, and he felt the weight of the group's gaze on him. He didn't recognise any of them, realising they weren't his fellow computer science or astronomy nerds.

As David scanned the assembled group, he couldn't help but size up their appearances. The man on the left was draped in a black suit.

And I thought Morgan was overdressed, Jesus. Guy looks like he's hitting up a funeral after.

The next figure, in a black hoodie covered in silver stars which appeared just about on the right side of tacky, seemed more backstage than cerebral.

No. Flipping. Way…

The third man was wearing jeans and a Metallica shirt.

Amid the shouting-conversation over the music, the Metallica man hand-gestured to David with the devil horns. His enthusiasm led to a dramatic swing of his plastic pint glass, inadvertently baptising a towering figure in a white T-shirt with a surprise beer shower; the giant looked as thrilled as a cat in a bath. Metallica-man ignored him.

The man next to him looked like a poorly assembled fashion experiment - green suit jacket meeting blue jeans - and bore an uncanny resemblance to Morgan, their jackets practically twinning. Maybe this was Morgan's way of meeting the group.

The ensemble collectively reached out to David, offering a medley of greetings. Hands jutted for handshakes, fists bumped in amiable gestures, and one overly zealous member even requested a high-five.

"Shots all around!" Morgan's enthusiasm was infectious, yet David hesitated.

"Shots? I'm more of a sip-it-slowly kind of guy, so no thanks," David said, pulling Morgan to one side out of earshot of the group.

"Why not?" Morgan countered, his tone tinged with annoyance.

"I don't really drink, not shots anyway," David said, the reality being that he didn't drink at all.

"Come on, we're celebrating here! A toast to you!" Morgan insisted.

"Okay, fine. Just one then," David finally relented.

"Agreed, mate," Morgan said, a triumphant grin stretching across his face.

Morgan led David back to the group before running off to the bar, leaving David behind to fend for himself.

What do I have to lose?

The group had surprised him, their warm reception had no mocking undertones. Instead, they embraced him, genuinely celebrating his small achievement with Clara, a sensation as unexpected as seeing a unicorn in a traffic jam. It was a novel and refreshing experience—a sense of belonging he hadn't felt in a long time. Or ever for that matter.

When Morgan returned, carrying a tray filled with eleven shots - one had tipped over - David crossed his fingers behind his back,

Please don't be tequila, or sambuca, or anything gross...

His prayer went unanswered. The initial shot was like a volcanic eruption in his throat, threatening to turn his insides out. Waves of nausea threatened to overpower him, but he fought against the urge to lurch forward, desperate to maintain his composure.

Noticing David's distress, Morgan patted his back reassuringly.

"Hang tight, mate. It'll pass, and then it'll feel amazing."

David managed a feeble smile, attempting to steady himself. Gradually, the nausea dissipated, replaced by a fuzzy warmth. Encouraged by this newfound sensation, David begrudgingly accepted another shot, his caution loosening.

As the group held out their second shots, a collective cheer erupted, and they threw back the fiery liquid in unison. Disgusted groans and involuntary shudders followed, creating a chorus of discomfort. Over an hour, the group guzzled at least five shots each, chased by several pints of cheap lager. David's head spun slightly, but overall, he felt surprisingly good—better than he had in a long time.

But amidst the fun, David's mind wandered back to Clara.

Clara!

He had almost forgotten about her in the whirlwind of drinking and talking. Anxious to check his phone, he reached for it, only to be disappointed. His smile vanished as he realised the battery was still dead.

Well yeah, what did you expect? It was on 1% hours ago, and she's probably gone home now. You missed her. She probably messaged you loads and thought you were ignoring her... which you kinda were...

The phone was dead. Dead as a doornail.

Chapter 13

Amidst the alcohol-induced fog, David's voice staggered through the air, laden with weariness and the remnants of the night's burden.

"Morgan," he mumbled, his words a struggle against the weight of exhaustion. *"Gotta go... dead phone... Need... crash. Clara."*

Morgan, himself somewhat under the influence, nodded in agreement and slurred,

"Yeah, may! Grey seein ya, ore-wa-sum nigh!"

With a wave that seemed more an act of determination than a gesture, David said goodbye to the group.

"Good t' meet y'all," David managed, his speech laden with tiredness and a muddled tongue. *"See ya."*

They responded with feeble waves, a few extending hands for a shake or attempting that awkward guy-to-guy side hug. Feeling as precarious as a Bambi on an ice rink, David pondered his balance. His head spun with a turbulent mix of alcohol and fatigue.

He stared down at the lifeless screen of his phone, a void of anticipation for a possible message from Clara. The walk back to the halls felt like an eternity, passing rows of university buildings, lecture halls, and student accommodations. The cold air bit at his skin, exacerbating the dizziness that threatened to take over. Time seemed to stretch, and the minutes dragged like burdensome weights as he strode up the steep road towards the mature student accommodation street. When he had first started here all those years ago, he was in awe of the kids who ran and cycled up these ridiculous inclines with ease. He remembered dragging a wheeled suitcase up this street and it nearly killed him. It was nearly 2 am when David finally stumbled into his room, only just on the precipice of coherence and consciousness.

With an ungraceful collapse, he flung himself onto the bed. He pulled the battered phone from his pocket and fumbled with the charging cable poking out of the wall, failing dismally to insert it into the port. David lay down trying to keep his eyes open, waiting for the telltale signs of life from the phone. After a few agonising minutes, the screen blinked on, casting a white glow across the ceiling. *Ding!* The sound jolted David awake from his drowsy stupor, his bleary eyes fixated on the bright screen. A text from Clara, sent a thirty minutes ago, materialised before him.

'Hey David, was great to meet you! Might be weird, but wanna come over? Got wine here, and my housemate's out.'

That single line acted as a bolt of electricity, instantly snapping David out of his intoxicated haze. The message left him breathless. *Ding!* Another message arrived, his heart pounding like a frantic drum.

'Hey, you still up?'

Fumbling with the tiny keypad, David eagerly typed out a response, his excitement noticeable in every keystroke.

'Hey! Yea, lov too! Where should I head?'

Send. *Ding!* Another message popped up within seconds, Clara's address marked with a lone *'X'* at the end.

Holy shit, is this real? Is this actually happening? Not sure about the wine, but she clearly likes me if she's inviting me over, right? No way is this just a friends thing...

Adrenaline surged as he leapt from the bed, shedding his lager-soaked clothes for a fresh, non-alcohol T-shirt. He gargled some mouthwash, his reflection in the bathroom mirror revealing a transformation. The anxious wreck that had entered the club had been replaced by a confident, handsome figure, albeit with slightly sunken eyes. A smile, radiant and unrestrained, adorned his lips.

Though a gentle spin persisted in his head, it resembled the playful swirl of a theme park ride, a sensation he could endure. David wasted no time. He scrolled through his contacts, searching for a local cab company.

"Sorry, all booked up," the operator's weary voice echoed through the phone. *"Nothing for at least two hours I reckon."*

David's heart sank, a weight of disappointment dragging him down.

Was I slurring too much? No way are they all booked up... everyone lives on campus! Well, except Clara clearly…Maybe I am slurring a bit, don't wanna risk me being in the car…

Clara's house was just three miles away, he knew the general area and how to get there. It was a distance he could easily cover in his car. His keys lay on the desk, mocking him. The worn key to his fifteen-year-old Ford Fiesta jutted out from the cluster, its metal reflecting the ceiling light into David's eyes.

No… I can't. Although, three miles isn't that far. I mean the streets would be empty now. Three miles would take like, what five minutes? That's nothing… No one would be around, plus I'm fine! It'll be fine.

A long yawn escaped his lips, and he stretched upward releasing a loud crack from his elbows. Determination mingled with apprehension as he grabbed his phone and keys. With a slight stumble, he left the room, stepping into the night.

Chapter 14

The coldness of the air wrapped around David, piercing his body with an unexpected jolt. Just moments earlier, he had been covered in the comfort of his soft bed in his warm bedroom; his mind lost in a haze of swirling thoughts. A mix of exhilaration and nervousness coursed through his veins, a potent cocktail of anticipation.

Could this actually be the night? The night I lose my virginity? Christ, I know that's a big jump from kiss on the cheek, but who knows? Right? She clearly likes me. I like her. A lot. She's perfect! God, will it happen though? Am I ready? I reckon I am...I think.

Yet, as David fumbled with the keys at the door lock, struggling to unlock his car, he attributed his clumsiness to a combination of nerves and a dodgy key.

Why can't I have flipping central locking on this thing!

The blackness of the night enveloped him, with only a single street light behind the small car park wall casting a feeble glow. The soft illumination made getting into the car challenging, forcing David into a clumsy tumble as he landed in the driver's seat. The subsequent struggle to pull the seatbelt across felt like an eternity until, with a loud click, it found its intended target.

Gotcha...

Twisting the key in the ignition, the engine roared to life, and David squinted his eyes, attempting to coax the blurry world into focus.

Wow that fog must have rolled in fast... maybe if I turn on the heater that'll help. Yeah, that makes sense...

Reaching for his phone, he opened the last message from Clara, struggling to type a reply with dexterity eluding him.

'Om ny way be ther soom x', he tapped out, oblivious to the

unforgivable spelling mistakes that adorned his message. He realised the egregious errors after reading it back after pressing send.

"Now is not the time for good spelling," he said aloud.

With a clumsy manoeuvre, David managed to coerce the car into gear, the clutch grinding in agony as first gear remained elusive. The car was far from being a good and reliable, it was practically ancient, and its gears proved tricky even at the best of times. Gingerly exiting the parking space, he drove up University Drive with exaggerated caution. Without indicating, he careened onto Hartford Street, blessed by its lengthy, completely straight road. Shandy Park loomed to his right, a group of students were sat in a circle on the grass clearly drunk but having a good time. But annoyance crept in as the road before him remained practically empty, save for a few vacant taxis.

Yeah so, they're clearly not all booked up are they… liars.

The illuminated storefront of a pharmacy materialised, marking the spot where he needed to turn.

Ah, I know this place. Left, I think. No wait right. Nah it is left. Definitely left.

With a hazardous, last-second decision, David's old Ford swung violently to the right, crossing into the opposing lane, narrowly missing a central reservation. A surge of adrenaline unsettling his senses, but he clung to the focus on his desire, the yearning for that elusive pleasure. His foot pressed down on the accelerator, the initial trepidation fading into the background.

However, the fog outside the windshield persisted, obscuring his view.

Heater's broken, I guess. Everything in this stupid thing is broken.

The thought nagged at him, reminding him of the faulty passenger window that refused to budge as well. The dimly lit road ahead appeared hazy.

Shit, maybe it's me. Probably so tired I can't see right. Or maybe the booze? Nah, I'm just tired that's all. I can still drive tired. But it is pretty foggy out there though.

Yet, despite the outside haze, a church materialised in his sightline, its grey stone bathed in a soft green glow coming from little spotlights placed within its various archways and empty windows.

Ah wow, look at that. Reminds me of that place, ah what's it called. Barcelona. Sagrada…something. Familia! That's it! Clearly not drunk if I can remember that! It's just missing the watery stonework, the epic spires and all that. God that place was awesome, like seeing Saturn when I was younger.

Same feeling. Out of this world. Actually yeah, just like seeing Saturn through the scope… Coming up from the metro and it's just like bam! There it is… so cool…

As shadows from swaying leaves danced across the spotlights, casting fluttering patterns like a hypnotic pendulum, David's gaze lingered on the sea of weathered headstones in the graveyard in front of the church. The forgotten occupants of those graves seemed to hold his attention for a moment longer than they should have. And in that transcendent moment, that pivotal juncture, something inexplicable happened.

Chapter 15

The silence of the night shattered in an instant. A deafening clash ripped through the air, assaulting David's senses and sending him into a blind panic. All David could manage was a sharp punctuating yell. Metal screeched, and his car lurched, he hit his head against the roof and at the same time he was yanked violently forward. His mind was fuzzy, impossible to focus on anything now. One split second distraction, and now this. But what was *this?*

What the..., ah ow... David rubbed the top of his head, then moved his hand down the back of his neck. *I... what?*

It had felt like he'd hit a speed bump way too fast. But he hadn't been going fast. Had he? The sickening ache spread across his neck and down his back.

Eyes widened with shock, David peered beyond the steering wheel, his hands were trembling with the adrenaline coursing through him. The previous *'fog'* as David had assumed, had now dissipated. It had lifted, revealing a confusing sight that defied all logic. David had expected to see nothing, perhaps a large speed bump a few yards in front of him, confirming that's indeed what he had hit. But no, instead it was a mass of mangled metal. Even in the darkness David could tell what it was, and his heart sank like a stone. It was a bike. Crumpled like paper, but definitely a bike.

Shit, oh no. Oh no... what? But... I saw nothing, there was nothing there. I would have seen... No. No this isn't happening. I... ow my neck, my head...

Its fractured frame exposed slivers of glistening aluminium amid scraped-off green. The rear wheel was nowhere to be seen, likely swallowed whole by the car's underbelly. The front wheel resembled a crumpled taco shell, the tyre clinging tenaciously to life. Spokes protruded like fingers from a battered hand pointing accusatorially to the sky. A lone reflector, carelessly thrown aside, cast a blood red hue beneath the glow of the streetlight on the pavement.

The vibrant colours of the bike's paint were now a canvas of total ruin. A mosaic of scratches and abrasions interlaced with patches of metallic green—the exact colour of David's car. Handlebars jutted out at unnatural angles. Disconnected brake cables lay to the side, ripped off clearly with massive force.

Oh God…

David surveyed the wreckage, imagining the power it had needed to become the tangled mess of scrap metal it now resembled.

How fast was I going? The speedometer was fogged up. Wait… was it fogged up? Like outside was fogged up? No, I bet it wasn't, I was fogged up. Couldn't see right. Maybe someone just ditched their bike in the road as a joke? Yeah, that must be it. A joke. Crappy joke, nearly killed me. Gonna cost a fortune to fix this. But still a joke. I'm ok. Hahaha cruel joke.

About fifteen feet or so ahead, just on the pavement where the streetlight stood, he noticed a crumpled heap of black fabric lying motionless in front of a desolate street bin.

What? Oh no. Oh God no. It's a bin bag, it must be. Or some student throwing clothes out. Yeah, that must be it. Wait. Is it though? What's that on the floor near it? Pool of… It's shining. Oh no. Blood. It's blood! Shit…

Uncertainty enveloped him in a stranglehold, his heart racing. Time halted, trapped within a whirlpool of guilt and dread. Clad in a black hoodie and denim, the figure rested, silent and seemingly devoid of life.

David's heart plummeted. A surge of guilt flooded David's veins, searing his conscience with a remorseful heat.

I… I hit him. I killed him. Threw him all that way… Me… I was drunk, probably still am, it's my fault. All my fault! I'm an idiot and now this guy is dead. Because of me. I did this. Me… I mean he was wearing black on a bike at night, so maybe it was kinda his… no. It was me! David it was you. You did this. Why did I have to drink? Thinking with my dick got someone killed. It's as simple as that. Wait… what now? What do I do? If I stay, I'll be arrested, sent to prison for ever. That's it. Dreams gone. No more life. Everything I went through for nothing. Best day of my life. Over. But… What if I run? I leave this guy behind and pretend it didn't happen, then I'll be ok. Right? But if I run, I'll have to live with this forever. Like forever ever, can I? Ah my head still hurts. But what do I do?

As David grappled with the agonising decision before him, his fingers clutched the steering wheel, their pallor an eerie white. Logic had abandoned him in this moment. He was used to meticulous deliberation, calculating every choice. But not now. It didn't work, his mind was too fuzzy, and time was rapidly running out.

A jolting clarity dawned - remaining at the scene would seal his fate, his life forever ruined. To run, to vanish into the shadows, was to wager with his conscience, plagued forever by guilt.

The car, still idling with a nervous tremor, served as a grim reminder of the precarious situation he was in. The usual clockwork-like engine ticking was stuttering, its rhythmic cadence being disrupted by intermittent silence. Tick... tick... silence... tick... splutter. Yet, somehow, the engine persevered. David lifted his hand to the top of his head, gingerly massaging the dull ache. No blood trickled down his fingertips though it felt like there really should be.

Ok. Need to decide. Now.

David clenched the wheel, his quivering foot tentatively pressing the accelerator. The small car crept ahead, skirting the remnants of the bike, each metallic fracture a punch to his gut. And then, as he drew level with the motionless body, an irresistible compulsion seized him —a desperate need to see. To see what he had done.

A quick look revealed a medley of partial truths—a young man, life snuffed out in an instant, lying motionless. The silver stars on his hoodie sparked a flashback.

Wait. Stars? That guy tonight had stars on a black hoodie. Weird look. But... how many more of those could there be? Wait, did that guy have stars? Wasn't it moons? Or something else, can't remember, ages ago - was dark too, couldn't see well. Alcohol. Ah head hurts, neck, everything. Stop shaking foot! What was his name? Oh, it won't be him. He's still out! I left early. Right?

His pounding headache mercilessly amplified his torment, each throb heavy with uncertainty. The name had slipped away, but the resemblance lingered. One of the man's arms was stretched out in a desperate plea for help. That tore at David. The other, hidden from his view, clung at an unseen wound. A wave of revulsion surged through David, threatening to consume him entirely.

The streetlight was shining judgemental glows on the battered car bonnet. David knew hesitation was no longer an option.

Ok I need to go, somewhere safe. But ok, first, the car. The car, what do I need to do to the car? Ditch it, right? Yeah, ditch it, but then they'll know it's mine wherever I leave it. Mark. Identifiers that sorta thing. What did they say in all those crime dramas, yeah that's it, a number on the car on the door sill thing. Whatever it is. Ok, there's one more, right? See this is why they burn cars in all those movies. Wait should I burn the car? No that's stupid, it's too busy round here someone would see me. No, I need to leave it somewhere normal and just take the numbers off. The windscreen! That's where the other one is, I'm sure of it. What do I need? Screwdriver, yes, a screwdriver, in the boot, I think. Toolbox. Need to be quick though, yes very quick.

With a quivering breath, he pressed down on the accelerator, the engine roaring to life with newfound urgency. The car lurched into motion and the sight of death slowly disappeared back into the darkness.

Chapter 16

As he urged the tired engine of his weathered Fiesta forward, its aged components hummed in begrudging unison. His gaze swept the dim expanse, finally alighting upon the entryway to a small industrial estate. Nearby, tall trees stood, their branches swaying with an ominous cadence in the night breeze.

Luck favoured David momentarily - no barrier or signs of a security office at the entrance to the industrial estate. He guided the car towards the single lane entrance, the change from silent tarmac to the crunch of gravel beneath the tyres making his skin prickle.

The narrow road before him looked almost like a forgotten backwoods trail flanked by trees.

Thank God it's dark, darkness is my friend, can't see much ahead, but it's definitely an industrial estate. Or something. Is it? If it's private land they'll have cameras right? Cameras. No, that's not good. So dark though. Thank you. Where is this road going?

Anxious to find a hiding spot, he turned off the headlights, plunging himself into the next stage of complete darkness, with only the cloud-obscured moon providing a smattering of fragmented light to lead the way. David navigated the path cautiously, his heart drumming in his chest loudly.

Maybe this is the place? Keep going, just a bit further, yes, a bit further. Round the next corner and pull up on the side somewhere, who knows what there is around here but clearly isn't much. Yes here. This is the place, I can do what I need to do in peace...

Yet, as the trail rounded the next corner, his aspirations were cruelly dashed by a large fluorescent yellow sign that materialised, *'Under constant CCTV surveillance, 24 hours a day.'*

"Damn it."

Well, there goes that plan, definitely be spotted here now, they've probably seen me already, probably sending a security guard to come check on the weirdo without headlights on. Need to turn back, running out of options I don't know what to do, what do I do? Oh God, okay just turn back and keep moving don't get flustered just breathe 1, 2, 3, 4 move go now, move.

Swinging the car around, David's brow furrowed with sweat as panic threatened to entirely consume him. He accelerated back down the path only turning his headlights on again when he neared the main road.

David was scared now, he needed to find somewhere to hide the car and fast, people would see the smashed up car at any moment as he drove past houses with their obscured windows on each side. Anyone could see him and report it. He continued, seeking refuge in a residential area off the main road. Glancing to the side, he saw a little tree-lined side-street and turned. The narrow path stretched ahead, lined by less than a dozen houses on just one side staring out onto the street, and what appeared to be a patch of unused land on the other. There was no flicker of light or sign of any activity whatsoever.

Ok this looks hopeful...

As he neared the end of the road, a grey bollard blocked the entrance to another pathway. Black wrought iron fences bordered this route, leading somewhere David guessed was the main road running parallel to the one he was just on. Ahead, and to his right the churchyard glowed in harsh floodlights that made him shiver.

Is that the same church that made me lose my concentration?

He parked the car at the foot of the grey bollard, turned off the engine, and felt grateful for the absence of streetlights. He slumped back in his seat, taking a deep, measured breath and counting to four to calm his racing thoughts. Although the breathing exercises were usually somewhat effective, they couldn't silence the whirlwind of emotions within him now. David closed his eyes.

Ok what do I need? Mum always said prepare for the worst, God she got that one right - she did give me that toolbox for the car though, that's still in the boot. Glad I didn't chuck it out now, monstrous thing, everything but the kitchen sink... Still, that should have what I need. Cheers mum.

Opening his eyes, he opened the car door as gently as possible. David stepped out into the frigid night air. The chill sliced through him, shaking him to his core, but it relieved him as the coursing adrenaline dissipated.

He inhaled slowly, savouring the crispness of the air, and stretched his arms wide, releasing a loud crack echoing down the deserted street. Panic gripped him as his eyes darted between the rows of darkened windows, searching for any signs of movement. Finding none, he closed his eyes, desperate for calm.

However, all that greeted him in the darkness behind his eyelids was the image of a partially obscured face, shrouded in a hood, lying motionless beside a nearby bin. Arms outstretched as if reaching for life itself while having it cruelly snatched away.

By me...

Slowly, David opened his eyes, expecting the nightmare to dissolve like a wisp of smoke. Yet, the image clung stubbornly to his vision, etching itself into his memory, refusing to be forgotten. He thought about inspecting the bonnet for damage out of a morbid curiosity. Still, the grotesque mental image of crumpled metal, blood, and a mosaic of blue and green paint deterred him.

The horror of such a sight would surely be too much. Possibly causing him to faint, throw up, or succumb to the suffocating weight of guilt and terror. David realised that regardless of the outcome, he needed to remove the license plate. He had to ensure this car couldn't be traced back to him.

With trembling legs, David took slow, uncertain steps toward the front of the car. As he rounded the front of the car, his gaze fixated on the bonnet. The reality wasn't as awful as his imagination had invented. A crater, roughly three inches wide, marred the left side just above the cracked headlight. The surface bore a constellation of small dents looking almost like spots on a leopard's fur. Faint grey scratches adorned a few of these dents, revealing the steel beneath the paint. It was clear—the bike had collided with the bumper, somersaulted onto the bonnet, and then skidded off missing the windscreen, the back wheel meeting its fate under the car's wheels.

Relieved his presence would be less conspicuous without extra attention-grabbing details, David chose not to linger, aware time was of the essence.

He moved to the car's rear and released the boot latch with a resounding clack. The sound reverberated in the silence, louder than he had remembered. His head swivelled from side to side, paranoia igniting once more.

He scanned the surroundings, but no curtains rustled, or flickering lights revealed prying eyes. For now, he was safe. David rummaged through the darkened boot, his hands searching for the large grey plastic box. He found it and placed it on the pavement, squinting to make out its contents.

Glancing at the license plate, relief washed over him that it was just a simple Phillips head one. He spotted the screwdriver he needed among the mass of tools. With the screwdriver in hand, he delicately and silently removed the first bolt securing the license plate. It relinquished its grip in a few seconds and fell to the pavement with a hushed ping.

David proceeded to the second bolt, his movements slow and cautious. As the final bolt gave way, the license plate swung downward, emitting a high-pitched screech that made David curse under his breath. He glanced over his shoulder and saw a light illuminate a ground-floor window, a mere twenty feet away.

Christ! No, you didn't see me, you didn't hear anything, nothing, go back to bed, I'm not here, need to hurry up…

Scrambling on all fours, David made his way to the driver's side of the car, so it blocked the view of the window. After a painstaking few seconds, he bobbed his head around to check the coast was clear. The light had vanished, and the curtains remained still.

Hastily, he removed the license plate and tucked it into his coat and moved to the front of the car. Doing the same again, he unscrewed the plate which was broken in two and clutched the fragments in his hands staring at them as though they now reflected his fractured identity. Broken, and never to be whole again.

Okay, next. Serial number, VIN or whatever, need to scratch that off, but where is it? Ah Google. Google knows everything, phone… please have some battery still, phone, Clara! Oh God I forgot about Clara!

Retrieving his phone from his pocket, he saw three unopened messages from her staring back at him asking where he was, if he was alright and the last stating she was done waiting and was going to sleep. David swiftly tapped out a brief message ignoring the red battery indicator, his fingers trembling with cold as they typed.

"Car didn't start. Sorry. Another time. Night. X."

He didn't concern himself with appearing rude or abrupt. At this moment, there were more pressing matters at hand. He knew he had to prioritise dealing with the consequences of his stupidity. Clara would understand, or so he hoped.

With only a sliver of battery life remaining on his phone, David opened the browser and hurriedly searched for the location of the VIN.

He found what he needed in just a couple of clicks, praying that his trusty screwdriver would be sufficient for the task.

David started hacking and grinding away at the VINs etched onto his windscreen, careful not to crack it, *not that it mattered now,* and below the front driver-side door. Each scrape of metal against metal punctuated the stillness of the night, causing him to catch his breath in quick, frightened gasps.

Ten agonising minutes later, his arm aching from the exertion, David took a moment to massage the soreness away. He then removed any other identifiable items he could find, collecting a few receipts, the MOT documents, and a smattering of opened mail, stashing them in his inside pocket alongside the remnants of the license plates.

Clutching an old rag from the toolbox tightly in his hand and wiping the beads of sweat from his forehead, David turned his attention to the task of wiping away any traces of blood from the car's exterior.

As he pressed the rag against the thin steel of the bonnet, it crumpled slightly under the force, making a sharp scraping sound. David fixated on every dent, assuming the blood would be visible in those depressions. But to his surprise, there was none. *Perhaps all the blood had stained the pavement?*

A sickening mix of relief and self-loathing washed over him. He had hoped to avoid being linked to the victim, yet he couldn't deny the wicked satisfaction he felt. Pushing those thoughts aside, David dragged the old cloth across the entire front of the car, manoeuvring between the metal slats of the grille and broken headlight.

With a tired sigh, David stood back and squinted in the darkness at the car's pitiful state. It had never been a well-behaved vehicle, but now, it resembled a deceased beloved family pet, lifeless on the side of the road, crushed beyond recognition.

Stuffing the rag back into his pocket, David turned toward the tree-lined pathway alongside the church and graveyard. Casting one last glance at the sad car, he took a hesitant step forward.

Chapter 17

God its cold, windy too, icy wind is like needles slicing into my skin, so dark, but it'll be light soon, where does this path lead? I think I know, it's by the church, the graveyard too - horrible irony, I hate it, the darkness doesn't feel natural, like its choking me somehow - twisting and curling around me, tight on my chest, I deserve this, my poor car though, I hope I never see it again, but I miss it, that old car was a part of me I guess. But not now, now it's part of a past, a horrible past, one I can't stop thinking about - but I must, just keep walking David, keep going, don't hesitate, forward, so tired though, exhausted and sober, yes sober now, very sober, the cold keeping me awake, but not for long.

The crackling and rustling of a nearby bush, whether caused by a startled bird taking flight or a scuttling rat seeking refuge, echoed through the alleyway. David's wide eyes darted erratically, his fear palpable, searching for the source of the sound but finding only darkness and flickering movements dancing along the periphery of his vision.

The ancient oak trees loomed over the path, their gnarled branches groaning and swaying ominously in the freezing breeze. Like skeletal fingers, jagged leaves drummed an eerie rhythm against the iron fences, intensifying the sense of impending danger.

The fractured shards of license plates, concealed in his hand beneath his coat were a burden, their sharp edges carving into his flesh.

His attempts to tread the narrow path with some stealth proved futile. The loose stones beneath his feet seemed to conspire against him, clattering with each step. The toecap of his shoe occasionally scuffed against the unforgiving ground, launching a solitary rock into the iron fence with a resounding twang that echoed like metallic laughter.

David's head spun on a perpetual swivel, his neck throbbing with an unrelenting ache. Yet, he paid no attention to the pain, his senses consumed by the primal instinct to scan the surroundings for any sign of danger.

The end of the alleyway beckoned like a light at the end of the tunnel, a dim yellow streetlight promising respite from the all-consuming darkness. He acknowledged this was a morbid thought, but in that bleak moment, it served as a bittersweet reminder that his life was forever altered.

As he neared the threshold of the streetlight's feeble glow, David cast a last glance over his shoulder, the relics of his shattered car staring at his from the dark, its lone headlight gave a small wink of reflected light. A final goodbye.

David's gaze darted left and right, scouring the deserted street for any flicker of life. The raucous noise of late-night partying had dissipated, leaving just eerie silence. The taxis, once speeding through the dark streets, had now retreated into the city's core. And, to David's immense relief, the piercing wail of sirens had yet to shatter the tranquillity. For now, anyway.

Although he knew their inevitable arrival was looming, it had been some time since the accident - although David had no idea how long, time was behaving differently now. Had it been an hour? Two? It felt like forever ago since his life had irrevocably changed. Still the sirens were kept at bay, though a single perceptive soul stumbling upon the scene - perhaps a weary worker from their night shift could bring the sirens to life. David's stomach churned at the thought.

David pressed forward, the first beams of dawn painting the sky. The air was dense with morning dampness and faint traces of exhaust fumes that made David's throat itch slightly.

As the minutes drew on, the darkness grudgingly gave way to persistent rays of light, relinquishing its grip on the world. David thought about the arduous journey home. His restless David thought about the difficult journey home. His exhausted mind acted like a relentless puppet master, continuing to shape his perceptions, conjuring bizarre shapes and illusions that teased the edges of his vision.

Classic paranoia, David. Just breathe. What's that near that gravestone? It can't be a person, no it's not, it's just my mind playing tricks - why does my own brain have to be so cruel? Kick me when I'm down, it's not fair. But that really does look like a person over there, but it has like a shimmer around it, a ghost, no don't be stupid, the ghost of the man I killed? No, stop it, David, breathe! Nothing there, look forward, tunnel vision, keep walking.

Each step heightened David's dread. The unavoidable encounter with the accident scene drew nearer, dragging him toward its grim embrace. There was no escape, no detour that could spare him from the harrowing reality awaiting him.

As his steps quickened along the worn pavement, a chilling hush wrapped the world in eerie suspense. The leaves stopped rustling, and the trees stopped creaking in the wind like God had just hit the mute button. It felt as though the very air held its breath, coiled with anticipation. Then, like a nightmare summoned from his mind, the sound he dreaded to hear clawed its way into existence, piercing the serene morning.

That wail, a blend of agony and urgency, shattered the peace, ripping through the fabric of dawn itself. Its crescendo surged, rattling the waking world and assaulting David's frayed nerves. Lights blinked on in the windows above the quiet shops, curtains flung wide, faces appeared, and David suddenly felt very visible.

Straining his eyes towards the main road ahead, David felt as though his heart might leap from his chest; the beats felt deafening to him - ricocheting against his ribs and threatening to break them. Ahead, figures in high-vis jackets clustered near the bins amidst the pulsing lights and chaotic swarm of police cars.

With a jarring finality, an ambulance screeched to a halt next to the police cars, doors slamming shut as two paramedics leapt out and ran towards the group of police officers kneeling by the bins. One police officer was pacing back and forth across the road, arms folded, and glancing left and right as though searching for a suspect. The paramedics were now kneeling beside the motionless figure, faces etched with concentration yet apparent futility. Two other police officers were busily unpacking a small blue tent from a duffel bag to shield the scene from onlookers.

Why did that alleyway have to come out here? Shock, it must be shock, I don't know where I am, disorientated, took the only road, alley, I don't know... but why here? Making me face it all again? So cruel, but no, this is the way, only way, to home, to escape...

As David walked down the main road, the grotesque theatre of life teetering on the edge of death unfolding before his terror-stricken gaze. He neared the boundary marked by blue and white tape fluttering across the road's width.

The officer patrolling the pavement glanced in David's direction and made a beeline for him with fast, deliberate strides.

Chapter 18

"W...what happened?" David stammered, his gaze fixed on the ground, avoiding the piercing eyes of the young officer, a man who couldn't have been older than thirty.

The officer stood uncomfortably close, a proximity that made David swear he could hear the rhythmic thumping of the man's heart. Or perhaps it was his own heart engaged in a fierce solo tango, a dance that had consumed him all day.

"Accident," the officer replied, his face a mask of sternness, devoid of emotion. His voice carried an air of seriousness that sent shivers down David's spine, a glimmer of suspicion lurking within. Paranoia, perhaps, as his mind played cruel tricks, determined to betray him.

He knows. Somehow, he knows, knows what I did - it was an accident! It was my fault, of course, don't give anything away, he's already suspicious, why else would I be here - they always return to the scene of the crime - every cop show, he knows.

"How long have you been out here?" the officer pressed further, his eyes cold and calculating, grey like a storm on the horizon and David was a small fragile boat sailing heedlessly towards it.

David's thoughts raced, frantically seeking a plausible response, but the words choked in his throat.

He knows...

"N... not long, sir," David stumbled over his words, his voice faltering.

Why did I call him Sir? That just makes me look weird, or more guilty, he'll remember me now, he can't be much older than me.

The officer remained silent, his gaze unrelenting, and David felt the weight of his presence bearing down upon him. It was as if the world had fallen into a muted stillness, with only the officer's existence and penetrating stare filling the void.

At that moment, the officer's interrogating gaze seemed to burrow straight into David's mind, as though searching his innermost thoughts for a confession. His eyes never left David's; not a single word was spoken. David was terrified. The officer had used this highly unnerving interrogation method to great success, frequently able to coerce a confession from the most stoic of suspects. It was a gift or a curse, as his fiancée often referred to it.

David's nerves betrayed him, his body trembling slightly. After a few more seconds of searching David's eyes, the officer relented and sighed, evidently reaching a conclusion. Perhaps this ragged, weary-looking young man was simply cold, tired, and a bit intoxicated. It was best to let him sleep it off.

"Hmm, all right. Make your way through there," the officer gestured toward the other side of the road, his voice tinged with barely contained tension. *"Get home, mate."*

David nodded, his movements slow and cautious, as he walked toward the lamppost, sliding through the narrow gap between the front of a mobile phone repair shop and the post. The sharp metallic scent of blood wafted through the air, mingling with the acrid smell of burnt rubber.

His gaze briefly met the paramedic, kneeling beside a figure lying motionless on the ground, shaking his head in a grim acknowledgement. It was clear that nothing could be done to save the man. The weight of guilt pressed upon David's conscience was a heavy burden. He knew, without a doubt, that he had taken a life.

If I'd called them when it happened, he may have been saved. I chose for him to die.

The license plates tucked within his inside pocket jingled mockingly; their weight intensified, and his pace quickened.

With each step, he could feel the scene behind him haunting his thoughts, sickening him to the core. The flashing blue lights in his periphery dimmed and then extinguished as he turned a corner.

He rubbed his neck and tugged at his shirt collar, fingers seeking solace in familiar gestures yet finding none. An itch on the back of his hand throbbed.

All in my mind, nothing there, guilt, paranoia, shame, evil, regret, disgrace, nothingness.

David scratched at his hand, the itch not subsiding.

David's footsteps quickened, pounding against the pavement like a guilty conscience desperate to escape. Shadows cast by the flickering streetlights stretched and twisted across the pavement, seemingly reaching out for him, clawing at the fringes of his sanity.

The world around him seemed to warp and distort as if reality was crumbling beneath the weight of his guilt. The night had become a playground for his guilt, a stage upon which his deepest fears danced in macabre celebration.

David's breath came in ragged gasps, his heart pounding in his ears, the pulse of his remorse reverberating through every fibre of his being. He stumbled, his foot catching on a crack in the sidewalk, sending him sprawling to the ground.

His palms scraped against the rough surface. Tears welled in his eyes, blurring the world around him as he lay there, broken and defeated, the weight of his actions crushing him like a vice. Tears not just of pain but of pure sorrow - they came in thick, heavy beads, rolling down his face, mixing with the blood on his hands and dampening the pavement. With significant effort, he clambered to his feet, wiped the tears away with a bloody palm and shuffled forward, eyes set on the distance.

Chapter 19

Navigating to his front door unfolded as if the universe itself conspired against each step of David's journey. His hand fumbled in his pocket, contending with the jumble of keys while his other hand gripped onto the license plates concealed beneath his jacket.

Once he had made his way down the hall to his room and fumbling again to open the door, David sidled over to the desk, its surface marred by the remnants of water rings and a thin layer of dust. The keys made a resounding clack as they landed on its worn and faded wood, their metallic echo permeating the quiet room. Dropping the license plates on the floor and flexing his cramped hand, David retrieved his phone from his pocket, casting a gloomy gaze on its lifeless screen.

Weary eyes then shifted to the charger plugged into the wall next to the bed, a slender lifeline snaking downward.

Like my own golden thread hanging taught in the hands of the Fates just ready to be severed...

David plugged his phone into the charger, anticipating a few agonising minutes before it would come back to life.

With a weighty sigh, he collapsed onto the bed, his body sinking into the mattress with an air of surrender. Stomach against the sheets, head cradled in his hands, he readied himself, mentally gearing up for the impending onslaught of exhaustion. When would the crash come? And once it did, what fragments of himself would remain discernible?

Fear and weariness bore down on him, smothering his thoughts like sharks encircling their prey, lurking and ominous beneath the surface.

He was navigating upstream in a turbulent sea, grappling with unseen currents that threatened to drag him beneath the waves at any moment.

Now, the feeling of plunging into the abyss took over completely, his awareness sinking into the depths of darkness. The hazy fog surrounding him was shattered by the faint hum from his phone, a subtle vibration nudging it just a hair's breadth across the bed. David's tired eyes glimpsed the brilliant white light emanating from the screen.

Rolling onto his side, he picked up the phone with clammy fingers, still slightly trembling. Launching the Facebook app, he steered toward the local Spotted group - a digital mosaic filled with news on current events, odd advertisements, and the often offensive comments sparking heated arguments between people with nothing better to do.

David's eyes were fixed on the screen, scrolling from one post to another with a sense of urgency. He scrolled through each entry with meticulous attention, carefully examining the details of every post made in the last two hours.

As he scrolled through the posts, his anxiety rising and falling over and over again, he finally arrived at the end of the page. A cautious but overwhelming sense of relief washed over him as he saw that there was nothing on the screen indicating a death or the discovery of his car. The tension in his body began to dissipate as he exhaled a deep breath, grateful his worst fears had not materialised.

Placing the phone under his pillow, David felt a glimmer of hope. Another exhausted sigh escaped his lips as he rolled onto this front again where sleep embraced him immediately - a surprisingly soothing escape from the events of that night. In his dreams, there were no intrusive thoughts - only a profound, weighty, and beautifully tranquil escape, as if his exhausted body had finally found refuge in the blissful oblivion of sleep.

Chapter 20

David's eyelids fluttered open, and he was met with a harsh, blinding light that flooded the room. The main room light persisted in its brilliance, its high-wattage bulb blending with the relentless sunlight streaming through the windows.

The amalgamation of brightness made it almost torturous for him to fully open his eyes as if each attempt sent sharp needles piercing into his retinas. Slowly, his pupils acclimated, allowing him to take in his surroundings.

A lingering sense of restfulness cradled David, but beneath the surface, weariness clung to him. Aches and strains throbbed within his body, refusing to release their grip. His arms extended overhead with a lethargic motion, a satisfying crescendo of cracks and pops resonating from the joints.

Hunger gnawed at his stomach, its persistent growls like those of a starving predator. His throat resembled an arid landscape, each swallow akin to traversing gritty sand dunes and shards of broken glass. Though the discomfort clawed at his insides, he momentarily dismissed it, mustering the will to swing his legs out of bed and rise to his feet.

His head was swimming in a turbulent sea of confusion and dizziness. Each attempt to stand proved an arduous struggle. His legs, burdened by an inexplicable heaviness, trembled under the strain. Reaching out, he groped for his phone, his fingers fumbling clumsily as he sought to unlock it.

Several messages littered the screen, of which most were from Morgan. *"Good night, mate! It was awesome!"* and *"Did you score with that girl in the end?"* Yet, amidst the anticipated messages, one stood out—

an unexpected text from Clara. A momentary pause hung in the air as David hesitated.

I bet she's angry with me, she won't want to talk to me ever again I bet, don't blame her, why would she ever want to be with me now anyway?

He clicked open the message. The words, *"Hope you got the car sorted, maybe see you another time,"* sprawled across the screen. *"No x, this time,"* David said to himself. This left a hollow unease in the pit of his stomach.

Not a big deal, it's not the most important thing in the world right now, is it? There are more pressing things to deal with, like my own life - my freedom, need to check... although, police aren't here, are they? So, they obviously don't know about me, yet. Still...

David delved into Facebook again, scanning each new post from last night with trepidation followed by relief. A surge of reassurance washed over him as he scrolled through each one.

Chapter 21

Holding the phone above his head, the screen bathed David's face in a sickly glow, casting an otherworldly pallor upon his features as he immersed himself in the Facebook group dedicated to Queen Mary students. His fingers danced along the screen, scrolling the labyrinth of posts spanning the last twelve hours. Mundane reminders of student nights out, lost pets, and items for sale blurred into a monotony that threatened to lull him into complacency. But then, amidst the banality, he stumbled upon a post that sent a shiver down his spine.

"Anyone know what happened last night near the church? Police and ambulances everywhere."

His eyes widened, pupils dilating as an all-too-familiar dread seized his sluggish brain. With hesitant anticipation, he delved into the comments:

"Yeah, heard about it earlier. Some student got killed. No idea who did it or who the victim was," read one comment.

"Hope they catch the bastard. Can't believe it," added another.

The rest echoed similar sentiments until David's gaze landed on a particular remark that caused his heart to plummet.

"It was Alex McCormick, riding his bike, apparently. He was at the SU last night, and someone got him on his way home..."

The name leapt off the screen: Alex McCormick. It was the same guy David had spent the previous evening with, the one he had hit.

A torrent of sorrow crashed over him, a tidal wave threatening to drown him in guilt. Alex had been a nice guy, funny too, he'd even bought the last round of drinks to celebrate David's viva success. Tears welled up in David's eyes as the unfairness bore down upon him.

It isn't fair. I didn't mean to do it. He shouldn't have been wearing all black... no, that's not fair I would have seen him if I'd been sober, it isn't fair...

Reluctantly, he scrolled through the remaining comments, encountering a flurry of rest-in-peace messages, angry accusations directed - at him - as he reminded himself, and a heart-wrenching comment from Morgan. Those few words struck David with the most force.

"Will miss you, Alex. Had a great time with you and look forward to seeing you later. Sleep well, mate."

The weight of grief pressed heavily on him, threatening to crush his already burdened soul. For a fleeting moment, he considered responding, offering his condolences, but the thought twisted his stomach, filling him with nauseating revulsion. He shut off the screen.

Paranoia slithered through David's mind, a serpent tightening its coils as he pondered the ominous prospect of the police uncovering his involvement. Each moment passed like the slow tick of a time bomb, and the mere thought of a knock on his door while he showered sent panic coursing through his veins. The freedom he once took for granted now dangled precariously, teetering on the precipice of irrevocable loss.

Temptation clawed at him, urging him to search for prison terms related to hit-and-run offences, but a glimmer of reason held him back. What if the police got his phone? He had seen enough crime shows - the mind-numbing entertainment that served as background noise during his assignment writing sessions. The guilty, dishevelled suspect would be brought in for questioning, vehemently professing their innocence, only to have their internet search history laid bare by a smug detective.

"You searched yesterday for how to remove large amounts of blood from a carpet," they would say with a hint of sadistic satisfaction - game over mate.

After a tense shower that he felt was necessary, David emerged into the shared kitchen. Though his mind was preoccupied with dark thoughts, hunger tugged at him. His stomach rumbled insistently, reminding him that nourishment was essential despite his reduced appetite. The aftermath of the previous night's festivities sprawled across the table—an array of empty beer bottles and scattered tortilla chip crumbs.

Amidst the disarray, David sat as a silent witness to both internal and external chaos. His imminent departure from the postgraduate halls loomed, a customary exit for recent graduates. However, his moral compass spun wildly, magnifying his self-doubt. Remaining meant inevitable encounters with Morgan, steering conversations toward the tragic demise of their newfound friend, Alex McCormick, or worse, prying into David's connection with Clara and David having to make up an excuse why he chickened out of going to see her.

In Morgan's eyes, David had chatted up some girl named Clara, likely snogged her, and then spent the rest of the night pining after her like an overeager, unrequited puppy. Poor David. He deserved a victory, a genuine triumph, but deep down, he knew he was destined for a solitary existence, fated to wither alone.

Shaking his head to dispel the self-pity, David pushed aside the emotional undertow threatening to consume him. He reasoned that these moments of weakness were just projections of his poor self-esteem onto others. Morgan's delight about Clara, once captivating, now felt burdensome. David, wanting to avoid scrutiny, did not want her investigative instincts activated, particularly given her aspirations in journalism.

David could no longer delay the inevitable; a barrage of congratulatory texts awaited him. Messages from distant relatives and grandparents, including a typical one from his mother: *"Congrats, David. Saw the Uni's Facebook post. Very proud. Time to get a job, eh?"* Though layered with genuine pride and tinged with exasperation, the text underlined a complex relationship. She didn't honestly care about David's pursuits; instead, she revelled in his success despite his tumultuous upbringing—a fact that he had yet to forgive her for.

After finishing a meagre breakfast, David resumed his phone perusal, seeking any updates. Alas, the silence was deafening—no news, no updates. Nada. The fragile lifeline of silence momentarily granted him a reprieve.

Powering down his phone, a decisive resolution crystallised within David. Escaping the deplorable confines of his current living situation became imperative. The shared apartment had become an unbearable and dismal place to live. Add to that the way he felt now, it would be doing him more harm than good to stay.

Rice cookers languished, with dark, greenish moulds invading the stale rice. Glasses dotted every available surface, sticky remnants of liquor clinging to them, and a mountain of unwashed pots and pans stood as a Jenga of culinary chaos. He had no desire to linger any longer than necessary.

Chapter 22

As David walked back to his room through the dim, windowless corridor, the ambient light cast a gentle glow that clung to the walls like a ghostly shroud. The corridor, flanked by aged doors, appeared to be in a constant twilight, caught between complete darkness and the bright clarity of day.

The walls were textured with layers of faded paint and subtle imperfections, absorbing the dim light and creating an intricate interplay of shadows and highlights. The worn surfaces bore witness to the passage of countless students who had lived in those rooms, their footsteps echoing through the years, leaving behind a palpable history etched into the very surface of the hall.

As David continued his journey down the hallway, offensive bumper stickers served as graffiti on patches of crumbling plaster. Messages like *"Knock if you're horny"* clashed with the otherwise diverse and individualistic expressions that adorned the hallway, like advertisements for student Bible reading sessions.

The air carried the faint scent of aged pizza and the lingering aroma of chicken instant noodles. The occasional sound of muted laughter and the muffled strains of music added a layer of vibrancy to the otherwise subdued atmosphere.

The small light fixture above his head flickered momentarily. Then, with a surge of power, it flashed, dimmed and blinked out entirely, plunging the hallway into complete darkness, save for thin slivers of light seeping from under the doors that lined the corridor.

As he walked down the corridor, a palpable tension filled the air, clinging to the walls like an unseen mist. His gaze darted left and right, catching glimpses of shadowy corners and worn doorways.

A disquieting flutter surged through David. It was not just a mental discomfort but a palpable feeling, like a brisk rush of cool air had engulfed him, heightening his sensitivity. The air around him appeared electrically charged, triggering a wave of shivers across his skin.

His dry palms turned clammy. The cool film of sweat formed a subtle sheen. He found himself nervously rubbing his fingers together, a long-forgotten twitch revived from the depths of memory.

A breath caught in his throat, anxiety and the instinctual fight-or-flight response taking hold as cortisol and stress hormones flooded his system.

What's happening? Why am I feeling like this, what is it about the light going out that's making me feel this way?

Closing his eyes, he lowered his arms and took a deep breath, desperately seeking refuge from the unsettling atmosphere of the hallway. Holding his breath momentarily before exhaling, David tried to regain control over the unsettling flutter that persisted within him. His heart rate, however, only slightly eased, and a persistent unease lingered. The light overhead sprang into life again but flickered erratically.

It struck him with sudden clarity—the trigger wasn't merely a product of the present gloom. No, it was a memory. One that hadn't just faded into the recesses of his mind but had been forcibly repressed.

A chilling echo rippled through David's mind, taking him back to the stark, concrete confines of Victoria Tube Station from a year ago. The disturbing threads of memory wove through the shadowy hallway, revealing the remembrance with a strange familiarity.

The flickering overhead light, reminiscent of the fluorescent tubes in the underground station, inadvertently revealed a past encounter. He recalled that evening at Victoria Tube Station when the flickering lights illuminated the concrete tunnels beneath the lively London streets. This memory, previously hidden in the shadows of repression, now unfolded with haunting clarity before him.

As David paced on the platform, the long yellow-white tube lights flickered overhead with a noticeable hum. Their uneven flickering echoed loudly in the otherwise quiet emptiness. He had thought he was alone, with just minutes to go before the next train arrived.

The platform exuded an icy coldness that could be tasted, a metallic tang lingering in the air. It felt peculiar, a departure from the countless times he had taken the tube since moving to London, finding solace in the bone-shattering jostling of the train rides, even finding them hypnotic at times.

From the corner of his eye, David was startled by the sight of a towering, pitch-black figure—the sole presence in this desolate London void. A silhouette, cloaked in darkness from head to toe, appeared silently, with only the bright white swoosh logos on black trainers cutting through the heavy gloom. A grotesque hood, tight and misshapen, concealed the wearer's face.

With predatory swiftness, the figure propelled itself toward David, a relentless force of malevolence eclipsing the vacant space between them. Panic clawed at David's insides, rendering rational thought an impotent casualty in the face of immediate peril. The figure closed the distance with alarming speed, reducing the gap to a mere ten feet.

Had terror not shackled him, David might have contemplated running, but the reality of imminent danger obliterated any kind of coherent thought. Now hauntingly close, the abyssal presence offered no reprieve as David cast a frantic glance over his shoulder, yearning for the salvation of a police officer or anyone at all. Fortune, however, betrayed him—there was no one.

Observant cameras perched high on their mechanical brackets captured the grim theatre unfolding below. Their unblinking eyes recorded every twitch of terror, each beat of David's frantic heart, but their mechanical gaze betrayed no sign of intervention. Panic's icy fingers tightened their grip on David's throat, amplifying the palpable fear that trembled through David's quivering hands.

A wave of dread coursed through David, intensifying the rapid beat of his heart. The hooded figure loomed over him, casting a stifling shadow that made David feel insignificant in the vastness of its presence. Its stocky frame, hiding unseen strength beneath the large black padded coat, stood as a powerful symbol of intimidation. David caught a fleeting glimpse of the hidden face.

Dark skin, obscured by the shadow of the hood, and dim eyes, their whites standing against the darkness, punctuated the face. The lower half was covered in stubble, and as the flickering overhead lights played across his skin, it revealed scattered small scars and shallow troughs. David's mind raced as he tried to make sense of the situation. Was he really in danger here? Or was it his imagination just running wild?

David yearned to avert his gaze, but fear held him captive. The man's unblinking eyes bore into David's; his silence spoke volumes.

"You got the time?" The man's low, rough voice was laced with pain, like the creaking of an old, rusty door. He didn't blink. His gaze locked onto David's small trembling figure.

David tried to look away, but the man's eyes were transfixed on him, dark and unyielding. In a desperate attempt to find respite, David blinked, but it was only for a fraction of a second. The man's stare was too intense, too menacing. David knew he was in trouble.

"N... no... sorry," David managed to stammer, his voice barely a whisper.

"Give me your phone. Or you're a dead man," the man's voice remained emotionless, tinged with danger. It was unclear whether it was a threat or a promise. Thoughts of running raced through David's mind, but Victoria Station's depths, far below the street surface, seemed impossible.

Would he reach the outside before he was caught? Chances were slim. David glanced toward the stairs at the opposite end of the platform, only to find two more hooded men, their arms crossed, watching him had appeared.

These men were undoubtedly the figure's companions, closing off any escape route. Shaking and hyperventilating, David reached into his jacket pocket, retrieving his old, cracked iPhone. He held it out toward the man, who snatched it from his hand, inspecting it briefly to ascertain its worth, questioning whether it'd been worthwhile. It hadn't.

Cautiously, David took a step back, his senses on high alert. The man glanced over his shoulder at the two accomplices by the stairs and, with a nod, refocused his gaze on David.

He lunged forward in a single explosive movement like a horse bolting from the starting line. His right arm, hand curled into a weighted ball, slammed into the side of David's unsuspecting head with a resounding thud.

David's vision blurred. A flash of blinding light seared across his eyes. The pain didn't register—only darkness encased him as he fell to the floor in a crumpled heap.

A thin stream of blood trickled through his thick mop of hair, staining the cold concrete platform beneath him. Unconsciousness claimed him, and the man, accompanied by his friends, laughed as they ascended the stairs to the bustling streets above.

When David awoke, he was still on the platform, surrounded by paramedics and a police officer. A scattering of curious bystanders craned their necks, trying to catch a glimpse of the unfortunate victim.

The paramedic wrapped David's head in a bandage and shined a penlight into his eyes, sweeping the light from left to right to assess any damage.

Seemingly okay, David was discharged from the hospital after a brief stay. Painkillers accompanied him, numbing the throbbing ache as he contemplated the nearby underground station for his journey home. *Not this time, never again.*

David made his way to the bus stop and settled on the bench. Gently rubbing the side of his head, he felt the pain cutting through the medication like a sharp knife through butter.

David opened his eyes. The corridor re-materialised, and the repressed memory faded back into oblivion.

Chapter 23

Completely exhausted and emotionally drained, David slowly made his way back to his room. His tired footsteps reverberated in the deserted corridor. He collapsed onto the bed, its sheets crumpled and dishevelled from his earlier restlessness; sinking into the thin, worn mattress, his body yearned for even more relief from the weight of his struggles.

With a deep sigh, David grabbed his phone and refocused on the local news along with student gossip on social media. His eyes ached as they darted over the screen, words blurring together. David kept scrolling for two hours, but eventually, the flow of information started to dwindle.

I don't get it. I mean, it's good there isn't anything, right? I don't want there to be news, maybe there is news and they're not reporting it? That could be it, in which case they could be here any minute now... No, that can't be right, they can't know about me, they can't know about my car either. They didn't find it, maybe it's been towed away by now? Nothing suspicious about the car, I did an amazing job removing everything. No, don't say it like that, amazing job, no David you did what you had to do. Nothing amazing about what I did.

He carefully cleaned the bloodstains and concealed them in the depths of the dented hood. Even though this realisation should to have brought him relief, a deep sorrow filled each breath and thought he had.

"Just have to live with it," David whispered. His mind drifted back to the harrowing moment he made the fateful decision to run away, the moment that irrevocably altered the course of his life.

At the time, it was a desperate act, a necessary response to the immediate threat that loomed over him. But now, with the clarity bestowed by hindsight, he realised it held a far more profound significance. It was an escape from the clutches of his conscience, from the haunting menace of the terrible secret that threatened to consume him whole. Run. Start anew in a place where his past could not follow him, where he could build a life unburdened by his transgressions.

Just yesterday, he stood at the height of his academic journey, his PhD freshly minted and dreams of a vibrant future in the bustling capital city pulsing through his veins. But now, those dreams felt like a bruise, reminding him of the life he was leaving behind.

To survive and regain a sense of peace, he needed to cut those ties and move forward into the unknown.

David jumped off the bed and grabbed his laptop off the desk. Returning to the bed, he sat up against the headboard and flipped open the lid. He opened a browser and visited an academic job site, feeling a mix of anxiety and optimism. He typed 'physics computing' as his search term, the cursor lingering uncertainly over the location field. Geography didn't matter anymore; he was fixated solely on the next chapter, no matter where it might take place.

As he scrolled through the search results, each mouse click seemed to fill the room with a charged energy, lifting the heavy fog of despair that had shrouded his spirit. A hint of a smile tugged at the corners of his mouth, born from the realisation that a future without the confining walls of prison and tear-stained pillows was within his grasp —a future promising happiness, freedom, and perhaps even prosperity.

Many job listings he looked at were disheartening, menial positions in soulless corporate behemoths, offering paltry pay and no sense of fulfilment. But amidst the mediocrity, one posting stood out: an opportunity in Leeds.

Although not particularly close to his current location, the city called to him with the promise of a fresh start—a blank canvas on which he could create a new life free from the burdens of his past.

As David perused the job description, he felt his heart race, excitement surging through him, and with each line he read the contours of his smile deepened. It was not just an opportunity to flee; it was a chance to reconstruct his identity in a new city.

This could be it. My chance to start a new life...

Chapter 24

At the Isle Institute of Cosmology, a name he'd never come across, David found a potential opportunity. A quick search on Google Maps revealed a modest, privately owned research centre, likely a pet project of some retired professor. The role seemed tailor-made for him, and conveniently, applications closed in two hours. Despite the unfamiliarity and the complete mystery surrounding the salary, David took a chance and applied.

As the day wore on, David remained holed up in his room, finding solace in his blog once he had submitted the brief application to the Institute. He avoided any mention of the previous night, instead letting his mind wander into the realms of outlandish physics theories. Crafting speculative ideas offered a soothing escape, easing his mind from the persistent worry of unwanted visitors.

By eleven that night, fatigue pressed down on David. Dehydrated and exhausted, he persevered, sustained by microwaved noodles pretending to be dinner. Despite the resulting heartburn, he wrote over 2,000 words, exploring the idea of parallel worlds and the endless possibilities they presented—a distraction from his life, where a single choice could change everything. This yearning was largely motivated by his wish to step into a parallel world where he hadn't taken a life.

With tired eyes and sore joints, David contemplated clicking the 'Publish' button. After reviewing it one last time, he took the leap, sharing his thoughts for everyone to see.

Relief washed over him as he rose from his desk, his body yearning for rest. Fully clothed, he collapsed into bed, hoping exhaustion would ward off haunting dreams.

The next morning, David awoke with a hint of hope as he anxiously checked the news—no alarming headlines, no unwarranted spotlight. However, a solitary email from the Isle Institute pinged into his inbox, shattering his moment of calm. Why had the Isle Institute reached out to him at this early hour? Uneasiness coloured his curiosity as he clicked on the message, unsure of what awaited him ahead.

Chapter 25

David's heart raced as he scrolled through the email, his eyes darting over the bold, albeit slightly pixelated, letterhead of the Isle Institute of Cosmology.

Clearly made up the logo themselves on Word or something, maybe can't afford a designer. Bodes well...

With every word, excitement flowed through him like a jolt of electricity *"Dear David,"* it began, *"thank you for your application, and I am pleased to invite you to interview for the role..."*

As he absorbed the interview details - set for next Tuesday at 11:00 —David couldn't suppress the surge of disbelief and excitement.

This is my shot, my chance to show my skills to the working world, God I hope they like me...

The email ended with a friendly farewell from Dr. Peter Coombs, the director, leaving David excited about the future for the first time since passing his viva, granted only a short while ago, but fate clearly had other plans.

With the interview looming just days away, David wasted no time planning his 200-mile journey to Leeds. He jotted down a checklist: overnight bag, nearby hotel reservation (no way he was making that round trip in a day), a copy of his PhD thesis, and the dreaded rental car booking. His stomach churned at the thought of driving again.

David's rented room in student housing felt stifling, the walls seemingly closing in as he longed for the freedom that awaited him. Yet, he had unfinished business to address—specifically with Morgan. Grappling with guilt, David crafted a white lie, a weak excuse for his abrupt exit. He texted about a made-up family death, hoping it would quell Morgan's curiosity.

The thought of leaving on such terms left a bitter taste in his mouth. He couldn't shake the pang of sadness at the prospect of not seeing Morgan or Clara again. Life's twists and turns had led him here, though, down a path he never expected.

Chapter 26

Rain thundered down, and the gloomy horizon looked very unappealing to David as he drove his rented Audi A3 down the M1 motorway that Tuesday morning. The radio was blaring some chart-topping track he had never heard of, but it was the only upbeat part of the 200-mile journey so far from London.

It had been three days since the job interview email had come through, and the possibility of a new life was on the cards. His mother was thrilled, of course, about the prospect of David working for a living and not coasting through life as a perpetual student. She had been quite vocal about this latter point in the phone call the previous evening.

That morning, David appeared confident and optimistic, practicing his greetings and expressions in the mirror to the point of insanity, but his mind kept going back to the night he took a life and the immense guilt that followed.

Despite his attempts to move on, he couldn't shake off the itch on the back of his hand and the hairs on his neck standing up without reason whenever his thoughts turned to something positive.

His mother had not picked up on anything in his voice to give her concern. She continued her questions on living arrangements, salary, and other generic things affiliated with turning a new leaf in a new city far away.

She doesn't care really, just wants me out of Uni and in the real world, wants me to meet people, to talk to people, to be self-sufficient and not be a burden on society as she thinks of every student, but I'll show her, I'll show them all what I can do…

The mundane music emanating from the radio began to quieten.

The gloomy motorway stretched out in front of him as far as he could see with its mass of flickering red brake lights beginning to distort. The dark cloud above the car appeared to grow darker and dense with rain, and David felt an ominous chill down his spine.

At that moment, the radio's wailing voice faded entirely and was replaced with crunching metal. Fear gripped him, and his neck hairs stood on end, and shock darted across his chest as he realised, he was hearing the sounds from that night again. The awful scraping of metal on metal and what David thought was a scream.

I didn't hear a scream before... did I? No, I didn't, it was the loud twisting of metal, though maybe there was a scream, and I didn't hear it over that? No, surely not... the man had presumably gone hurtling into the pavement, and don't call me Shirley... No! Stop it brain! There was no scream...

Since the incident, only four days had passed, so he knew these flashbacks wouldn't stop any time soon. He looked in the rear-view mirror and thought he saw blue flashing lights. Then, when he checked again, there was nothing behind him, another hallucination. He reached for the volume dial of the radio and spun it up to max, hoping it would interrupt this moment of delusion.

Red taillights just a few feet in front flashed into view, and David slammed his foot on the brakes just in time, instantly pulling himself out of the trance. Tyres screeched as the wheels locked up, and the car swung sideways in the heavy rain before David got it under control.

Adrenaline surged within him, causing him to pant. The radio blared, now nearly deafening, but gradually, David calmed down.

The rain dissipated, and above him, the dark cloud began to recede enough for David to focus on the road ahead, albeit still in a slight daze with sweat rolling down his temples.

The traffic subsided, and the car trundled onward, occasionally hitting a small bump and jerking him away from his thoughts. David sipped some of his weak petrol station coffee, which was now long cold, and looked at the sat nav before him; another 50 miles to go, and then who knows what would happen?

Still no idea what the job actually is... research assistant? I mean that's pretty vague, also 'assistant'? Probably below me as a PhD, but I can't be too picky now, can I? Also is it even for post-doc work? Or is it just cleaning test-tubes or something? Oh God, it might be cleaning test-tubes, scrubbing beakers and washing the lab coats! No, it can't be, no salary listed though, stop it - you can't be picky, not now. You don't deserve to be picky...

Searching online for the Isle Institute of Cosmology and Gravitation yielded few results; even the website didn't show what was being worked on, nor did it have a proper picture of the building or its staff, which he felt very strange.

He'd probably have thought twice about applying if he were not in such a hurry to leave London. As it so happens, the frustrating ambiguity surrounding the role had piqued his curiosity.

This had all better be worth it he thought as he shifted in his seat. More dark clouds loomed ahead, almost warning him of coming events. He pressed down on the accelerator a little more and charged towards the horizon of endless grey.

After a gloomy 4 hours of driving the entire length of the motorway, David reached the sign saying he was only a few miles from Leeds City Centre. Around here, David had an interview with the unknown *Isle Institute of Cosmology and Gravitation*. David exited the M621 towards Belle Isle on the outskirts of Leeds and diligently followed the sat nav for the business park.

This would be why it's called the 'Isle' Institute I suppose... very original.

As the car turned the corner and entered the business park, David was greeted by perhaps a dozen dilapidated warehouses and shopfronts, each emanating a vibe of neglect and financial hardship.

Most of the warehouses had a couple of smashed windows on the front, and those with company names were generally missing one or two letters. As David continued through the park, the general state of its inhabitants seemed to improve, and even a tiny mini-market nestled between two warehouses appeared almost brand-new. The cheerful female satnav voice indicated he was only a couple hundred metres from the Institute, which would presumably be around the next corner.

Crossing his fingers in his mind, David hoped to see a fancy steel and glass research facility that would not look amiss in one of the Oxford or Cambridge Science Parks. Not the decrepit one he found on Google Maps.

Please let Google Maps be out of date, just once...

He leaned forward expectantly over the steering wheel and gripped it as he approached the last corner.

Chapter 27

Upon pulling into the parking lot of the Institute - if five spaces could so be called a *'lot'*, David's heart sank as he was met with the same bleak and uninspiring structure he had seen online.

The building's drab, grey exterior blended with the overcast sky above, and the few dirty windows dotting its walls did little to alleviate its stark and uninviting appearance. A flickering yellow, fluorescent light in one of the windows only deepened his disillusionment about where he might soon be working.

As he parked his car in one of spaces reserved for visitors next to a small, unremarkable tree that looked half dead. Its withered branches were adorned with a smattering of off-colour leaves that swayed in the breeze, adding to the overall dreariness of the area.

Redirecting his gaze to the building, David regarded the entrance with both curiosity and unease. A small, single door served as the entrance to the Institute, with a grubby sign overhead bearing the letters *"IICG"* in faded, embossed letters.

Guess they pay by the letter...

As he exited his car, the door slammed shut with a resounding bang that echoed across the near-empty business park.

Despite the proximity of other buildings, the area was eerily calm, with only a handful of people carrying laptop bags into nearby structures. The dreary Tuesday morning seemed to weigh on everyone's shoulders, casting a pall over the entire area.

David couldn't help but feel a sense of foreboding as he walked towards the Institute's entrance, wondering what lay in store for him behind those unremarkable walls. His footsteps echoed through the empty parking lot, adding to the overall sense of desolation that hung over the area.

Strolling towards the entrance, David ascended the few stairs only to be greeted by a glass door that hadn't seen a Windex bottle in ages. He eyed it warily, wondering if he'd need a machete to hack through the accumulated grime.

With his trusty black leather satchel slung over his shoulder, containing his prized possession—the thesis he'd sacrificed countless hours of sleep and sanity for—David braced himself and pushed open the door, half-expecting a chorus of trumpets to herald his arrival.

Instead, he was met with a reception area that looked like it had been decorated by someone who had once heard of the concept of *interior design* but had promptly forgotten all the details. Plain walls adorned with paintings of trees straight out of a beginner's painting class greeted him, their colours as vibrant as a black-and-white TV on the fritz.

But then, there it was - a framed picture of Saturn hanging proudly behind the desk like the crown jewel in a car boot sale tiara. Its vivid colours practically screaming that he was in the right place.

David stared at this picture for a few seconds, and it took him back to his childhood—to that freezing night in the garden with his telescope. His patience paid off when he saw it shimmering against the inky blackness of the night sky for the first time. David smiled, and his nerves subsided, replaced by a happy nostalgia.

Lost in his reverie, David eventually noticed the woman behind the desk - a bespectacled figure who seemed to have taken the term *desk job* a tad too literally. Perched significantly higher than one usually would behind a desk, the woman looked uncomfortable. But her enthusiasm for her job was evident as she clicked away on her keyboard without looking down.

Sensing that she had given David ample time to admire the pictures of science stuff, she let out a deliberate cough. Still, she didn't bother to tear her eyes away from the screen.

"Good morning. How can I help you?" chirped the woman behind the desk.

"I'm here to see Dr Coombs," David answered, matching her smile with one of his own. *"I've got an interview."*

The woman's smile widened into something resembling the Cheshire cat's, but less creepy and more welcoming.

"Peter is expecting you, but you're a tad early. Let me just peek at his schedule and see if he's ready to charm you with his wit and wisdom."

What?

David observed with mild interest as the woman's long, red-painted fingernails danced across the keyboard, a flurry of clicks and clacks punctuating the otherwise silent room. As he waited, he took in the rest of the reception area, noticing the plastic chairs and the stack of dog-eared magazines on a small table in the corner.

After a couple of minutes, the woman looked up at David.

"Peter is just on a call. Please take a seat in the waiting area." She then gestured towards a far corner of the reception and glanced back at her computer, beginning to clack away on the keys like he'd never been there.

Entering the designated waiting area, David's enthusiasm took a nosedive. The space, more like a makeshift storage room than a proper waiting area, was a mishmash of mismatched furniture and lacklustre decor. It was as if someone had raided a garage sale and decided to furnish an office with whatever they found.

As he settled into one of the plastic chairs, the unmistakable squeak of cheap plastic echoed in the room, adding to the ambience of disappointment. Glancing around, he couldn't help but notice the stark contrast between the uninspiring surroundings and the vibrant personality of the receptionist, who seemed utterly absorbed in the computer.

Just as he was resigning himself to a long wait in this less-than-ideal setting, a loud click emanated from the room's far corner. A door swung open, revealing a somewhat dishevelled man in his sixties with wild, unkempt grey hair. Despite his appearance, he seemed to exude a certain charm, and he carried himself with an air of confidence that immediately put David at ease.

Chapter 28

"David!" Peter's voice boomed down the corridor, accompanied by a cheery wave in his direction.

Startled, David leapt from his chair, bidding farewell to the worn-out seat with a parting creak that sounded more like a sigh of relief. He walked over to Peter, hand outstretched. Yet, Peter seemed preoccupied, his attention flitting about like a butterfly on a sugar rush.

Peter ignored David's outstretched hand and turned, gesturing David to follow. Peter sauntered through the open door, giving a wave to the receptionist,

"Thanks, Kendra!"

She waved back. With another click, the door closed behind them, enveloping them in the cosy embrace of a warmly lit corridor.

As they walked, Peter turned to David,

"Did you manage to find the place alright my dear Watson?" he asked, his eyes scanning for any sign of recognition of the reference.

What? These people are a bit mad I think... just go with it David, you want this job remember?

"No problem at all, the drive from London was a breeze," Peter raised an eyebrow. *"...My dear Sherlock,"* David said with a forced smile.

With a beaming grin, Peter introduced himself.

"Well, I'm Peter. The Wizard of Oz behind the curtain here at the Institute. And you, my friend, are the star of our show today," he said, his enthusiasm contagious enough to make even a cynic crack a smile.

"I've perused your online musings, and I must say, your ideas about parallel universes and the existential crisis of AI had me pondering over my morning coffee."

Hey, wait, how did he…? There's no way he could have found that blog, no chance. Christ, what did he think of it? I mean, it was just ramblings; maybe some stuff was profound, but, God, where is this gonna go? This is the boss too… What did I even write about again?

It was like discovering your diary had been turned into a bestselling novel without your knowledge.

Summoning his best poker face, David said,

"Oh, right. Um, thank you. I didn't realise anyone actually read those posts. They were more for my amusement, I guess. How did you even find it?" He locked eyes with Peter, searching for any hint of judgment or mockery. To his relief, Peter's smile remained, his eyes twinkling with genuine interest.

"Well, if I may say so, your musings had more layers than a Russian nesting doll," Peter said.

"Your ideas about artificial intelligence, in particular, struck a chord with me. And as for how I found it," Peter tapped his nose with a finger and winked.

Hmmm… okay, I guess that's basically validation? Maybe my weird ideas weren't as nuts as I thought!

Lost in their tête-à-tête, the dynamic duo reached their destination. Peter's grin widened as he came to a dramatic halt before a nondescript door that might as well have been invisible. David's eyes glanced over it, ready to dismiss it as just another door in a sea of doors, until Peter's dramatic pause forced him to take notice.

With a flourish, Peter pulled a white plastic card from his pocket and tapped it on the door's security panel, prompting it to obediently swing open with a soft beep. As David stepped through the threshold, he was greeted by a sight that would make even the most seasoned sci-fi aficionado weak in the knees - a high-tech wonderland straight out of his wildest dreams.

Chapter 29

David's eyes darted around the room, taking in the mass of scientific equipment.

"Holy cow," he breathed out, barely containing his excitement.

Peter grinned, a mischievous twinkle in his eye. *"Glad you think so. We like to keep things interesting around here."*

David chuckled.

"Interesting is an understatement. I feel like I've stumbled into the Bat cave."

Inside the room, polished metal instruments of all shapes and sizes gleamed under the artificial lights above, their surfaces reflecting a distorted mosaic of his awe-struck expression. Some contraptions were so bizarre, that even his scientific brain struggled to comprehend them. Oscilloscopes hummed softly, their green lines pulsating with an eerie rhythm, while giant telescopes beckoned him forward. If only he'd had access to this kind of gear as a kid – he might have already discovered warp speed by now! The sheer scale of it all erased any lingering doubts he had about the Institute.

The colossal workbench, dominating the room like the monolith from 2001: A Space Odyssey that had fallen over, served as the epicentre of the lab. Covered in scribbles and equations, it bore the marks of countless breakthroughs and coffee mugs. Hundreds of etched and inked symbols adorned its surface, speaking a language as cryptic as ancient hieroglyphics. And there, at the edge of the room, a small window offered a glimpse of the outside world, a sliver of daylight partially obstructed by a colossal, unfamiliar piece of equipment.

Sensing David's overwhelming fascination, Peter guided him

toward a pair of plastic work stools beside the workbench.

"So, welcome to our playground," Peter said, his voice brimming with excitement. *"We're not just researchers here - we're explorers, pushing the boundaries of what's possible. Digital Magellans if you will."*

"What kind of boundaries are we talking about here?" David said.

Peter leaned in, his voice dropping to a conspiratorial whisper despite them being the only two in the room.

"The kind that makes other scientists' quake in their lab coats. We're charting new territory, diving headfirst into the wildest realms of computer science. AI. And how it can help solve the mysteries of cosmology."

David leaned forward eagerly.

"Count me in. But what's the endgame?"

Peter flashed another grin that could outshine a supernova.

"Revolution. Innovation. We're not just dipping our toes in the water. We're here to make waves, to flip the script on the scientific status quo."

David felt like he hadn't blinked in a solid minute, hanging onto Peter's words like a lifeline.

"Whoa," he managed to utter, his mind racing to catch up with the whirlwind of ideas.

"Picture this," Peter breathed, his excitement practically palpable. *"I want you right in the thick of it with us. Together, we'll dive into the deepest, most mind-bending concepts—the ones that you write about in your blog. We'll inject our team with a fresh perspective, breathing life into the dormant possibilities that lurk in the uncharted territories of our field. And as for Jim, our resident genius, you'll meet him soon enough. He's been itching for someone like you, someone who can see beyond the narrow confines of tradition."*

This is insane, but incredible, like where would I even begin here? Is he really saying that not only are my mental theories on my blog good - but that I can actually pursue them? Do experiments and everything else? Seems too good to be true, but this could be my chance!

"When can I begin?" David blurted out, his excitement palpable. The traumatic experiences of his journey—the near-collision, his brush with insanity—vanished from his mind. The anticipation of this moment enveloped him like a purifying wave, erasing any lingering doubts.

Chapter 30

David had made the trek back to London to pack up his meagre possessions and officially move out of student halls. Driving onto campus, David was greeted by the familiar sights and sounds of student life.

Loud music, intense aromas of stale pizza, and occasional sightings of half-naked students clearly stumbling out of bed at half three in the afternoon to answer the door to food delivery people.

David avoided his former housemates, half of whom had already upped and left. Since the moment David had turned up at the university campus, he was on edge. A bundle of nerves, half-expecting a SWAT team to swoop in and arrest him at any second.

He signed the forms confirming he was moving out and told that his deposit would be on the way. With only two suitcases and a box of tech gear shoved into the boot of the car, he bid a not-so-fond farewell to his kitchenware - tossing it into the dumpster behind the building like it had insulted his cooking one too many times.

The return trip to Leeds was enjoyable, featuring no flashbacks, good weather, enjoyable radio tunes, and surprisingly decent coffee at the petrol station. David's anxiety and paranoia continued to fade as he travelled farther away from London and had fully subsided by the time he reached Leeds. His temporary budget accommodation was about as inviting as a haunted house but was still better than the all-night off-key singing and kitchen carnage of halls.

Within days, David managed to secure a small first-floor one-bedroom flat that could be mistaken for a hobbit hole if one squints hard enough. Tucked away amidst a row of equally charming but less whimsical townhouses, the house boasted a front door so red it practically screamed *Danger!*

David barely spared a thought to his new home. He figured he'd rather be knee-deep in the Institute's brainy ambience with all the nifty gadgets and gizmos at his disposal than rotting away in his apartment. So when his first day at the Institute rolled around, excitement was practically oozing from his pores.

David hadn't been inside the Institute since his interview. His conversations with Peter, the director, were brief phone calls discussing working arrangements and bank details. The excitement in Peter's voice was palpable, as if he had acquired another invaluable asset to add to his arsenal of genius, as he modestly claimed.

For three excruciatingly slow days in his sparsely furnished flat, he futilely checked his phone for news and scrolled through Morgan's social media feed, along with a few internet-acclaimed *'friends'*.

Deprived of a television, his laptop became his sole source of entertainment, perched upon his knee as he delved into nostalgic reruns of old sitcoms and the occasional '90s action films.

Money was as scarce as a cat's compliment, and his diet mainly consisted of cheap instant noodles, their artificial *'flavour'* packets attempting to deceive his taste buds, and gallons of Pepsi. It was a disheartening way to live, but David clung to the knowledge that it was merely a temporary state, and a life of grandeur awaited him just around the corner. As did his first pay check, which incidentally wasn't as bad as he'd imagined.

On his first day of work, the sky above was a cloudless blue brilliance. The traffic outside hummed like a caffeinated beehive, but David? He strutted out of his apartment, ready to tackle the world, or at least the five-minute jaunt to the Institute.

I don't even care that I'll be stuck inside the whole day, with just that pitiful tiny window giving the only glimpse of daylight or the world outside, I don't need it, I want to be there, God I can't wait! This is the first day of the rest of my life and I'm totally ready to dive in headfirst...

Navigating the Institute's boring corridors, clutching the blank white plastic card given to him by the effervescent receptionist like it was the holy grail, David was a mix of nerves and excitement—a human smoothie of emotions. He tapped the card against the lock on the door to the lab, and the door opened with a beep.

As he stepped into his new domain, the air inside smelled like dust and possibility. But instead of finding the esteemed director sat at the colossal bench, ready to usher him into the fold with open arms, he was met with a sight straight out of a dumpster-diving nightmare.

A scruffy man, buried under an avalanche of papers, greeted him like a lost puppy looking for a home.

His hair was a tangled mess, and his glasses sat askew on his nose. The man's clothes were a fashion faux pas of epic proportions as if he had raided a thrift store during an apocalypse-themed sale. His faded t-shirt bore the battle scars of countless coffee spills, and his jeans looked like a pack of rabid dogs had mauled them.

Okay, this is not what I had imagined, where's Peter? Who's this drifter? Guy looks like he just fell out of a bin behind a hipster coffee shop... Is this seriously the welcome party for my first day?

He had imagined Peter, all smiles and handshakes, ready to welcome him into the Institute's inner circle with open arms. But as the man shuffled forward, a glint of intelligence shone in his eyes. Despite his unkempt appearance, there was an air of authority about him, as if he held the keys to the kingdom hidden somewhere beneath the piles of papers on his desk.

And as he extended a hand in greeting, David realised that perhaps appearances could be deceiving.

Ah, this is probably Jim, the resident genius as Peter put it...

Chapter 31

"Hey there, mate! Pleasure to meet ya! I'm James Walcott. Just call me Jim," the man said, his Aussie accent adding a lively lilt to his words. His hand was still outstretched, the palm slightly clammy, as if it had just been pulled from a forgotten mug of coffee.

David hesitated for a moment, taking in Jim's dishevelled appearance. Despite his casual attire, there was a certain charm in his lazy smile that put David at ease. He shook Jim's hand, feeling a faint hint of sweatiness between their palms, and introduced himself.

As David settled into onto a stool next to Jim, he couldn't help but notice the open laptop before him. The screen was littered with tabs, journal articles, Python script windows, bizarre online calculators and, in one corner of the screen, YouTube, which was currently paused on a 2000s rock playlist. Jim's fingers moved lazily across the keyboard as if engaged in a leisurely stroll rather than an urgent task.

Curiosity getting the better of him, David attempted to break the silence.

"Where's Peter?" he asked.

Jim shrugged, his gaze fixed on the screen.

"Probably out back, puffin' away on his death sticks. He'll show up eventually, or not. Doesn't matter much," he replied, his voice carrying the same lazy drawl as his movements.

Nodding, David turned his attention to the cluttered workspace. Papers were scattered haphazardly across the desk, each bearing the marks of Jim's absent-minded scribblings. Coffee cups, long abandoned, and their rings cluttered the surface, their contents now cold and congealed.

Minutes stretched into an uncomfortable silence, broken only by the rhythmic sound of Jim's typing. After ten minutes of silently scrolling through his phone and waiting for any sign of interaction from Jim, David cleared his throat, breaking the spell that had settled over them, and decided to inquire about Jim's ongoing work.

"Sorry mate, got a bit carried away there," Jim said as he tore his gaze away from the screen, meeting David's eyes. *"So, I'm workin' on this new theory for the beginning of the universe, chuckin' in a bit of our AI software to fill in some gaps. It's not perfect, but hey, who knows? Might give ol' Penrose a run for his money one day,"* Jim said, his excitement barely perceptible beneath his calm exterior.

David's interest was piqued. Roger Penrose's name carried weight in the scientific community, and the prospect of Jim's work being mentioned in the same breath was intriguing.

"Really? Sounds fascinating. Always been a fan of Penrose. What's your theory about?" David asked, leaning forward with anticipation.

Jim's smile widened, a glimmer of ambition flickering in his lazy gaze.

"Well, it's still a work in progress, but basically, the universe emerged from this cosmic network of dimensions, each with its own set of laws. These dimensions exist within what I call a Meta-Realm, an eternal and evolving cosmic substrate," Jim explained, his words flowing effortlessly.

Ok this guy has lost me completely... and I thought my ideas were a bit out there, Meta-Realm? Sounds more like something out of Marvel, and where does Doctor Strange fit in?

"Sounds pretty cool," David said with a slightly vacant expression.

Jim chuckled, his eyes sparkling with amusement.

"Don't worry about it, mate. It's a lot to take in, I know. But trust me, once you dive deep into the data and start connecting the dots, it all starts to make sense. Well, sort of," he added, his enthusiasm undiminished.

Yeah, this guy is nuts, cool idea though.

As Jim dove back into his work, his fingers jumped across the keyboard with an urgency that bordered on manic. David couldn't help but feel a twinge of envy at Jim's dedication, while he grappled with his own existential doubts. Yet, as the morning hours waned, a strange calm settled over David, a resigned acceptance that maybe, just maybe, this chaotic workspace was where he belonged.

David moved to the other side of the lab and began busying himself checking out the range of equipment on display - spending an excessive amount of time looking over a particular telescope. David then sat at the desk opposite Jim and began rifling through some of the papers that littered the table, stopping to read over some of the more interesting notes on Jim's theory before jumping up again to look at the oscilloscopes. Eventually, Jim removed his headphones, breaking the symphony of keyboard clicks that had filled the room so far.

"Hey, David, you doing ok?" Jim asked.

David nodded.

"Yeah, just taking it all in. Your theory's pretty wild stuff, man."

Jim laughed,

"Ya think so? Wait till ya hear the rest of it."

As they continued their conversation, David couldn't shake the feeling of being swept up in something bigger than himself. It was as if he had stumbled into the plot of a sci-fi novel, with Jim as the eccentric genius and himself as the unsuspecting protagonist.

Around midday, Peter finally poked his head in the lab. Seeing David, he shuffled in towards him.

"Hey, David, sorry to leave you on your own for so long, how's your first day shaping up?"

David looked up from the desk, grateful for the break.

"Hey, Peter, it's been quite the whirlwind. Jim's theories are wild, to say the least." Jim had put his headphones back in and was nodding rhythmically to music while he typed, evidently not having heard anything.

Peter chuckled,

"Yeah, Jim has a way of diving headfirst into the deep end of the pool. But once you get used to the madness, it's a hell of a ride."

David nodded, a grin spreading across his face.

"That's one way to put it. But I have to admit, I'm intrigued. There's something infectious about it all." Glancing over at Jim whose head was buried in his laptop.

Peter clapped David on the shoulder.

"That's the spirit! Say, why don't we grab lunch at the pub? It'll give us a chance to unwind and chat about your first impressions of Jim."

David's stomach rumbled at the mention of food, and he nodded eagerly.

"Sounds like a plan. Lead the way, Peter."

The two of them made their way out of the cluttered workspace and into the deserted industrial estate outside. Just over the main road, the pub was a cosy place with a log fire and the sound of chatter filling the air.

As they settled into a booth, David gave Peter his drink order and

Peter called to the woman behind the bar who said,

"Usual Pete?"

Peter nodded and turned to face David.

Obviously a regular then.

"So, what do you think of Jim so far?" Peter asked, as a beer was plopped down on the table before him.

David leaned back in his seat, considering his words.

"Well, he's definitely... unique. There's a certain energy about him that's hard to ignore. And his theories, while a bit out there, are undeniably fascinating."

Peter smirked, raising his glass in agreement.

"That's Jim for you. He's like a force of nature, unstoppable once he sets his mind to something. But beneath that eccentric exterior lies a brilliant mind."

David nodded.

"I can see that. And I have to admit, I'm eager to see where it takes us."

Peter grinned, clinking his glass against David's.

"To new beginnings, and the adventures that lie ahead."

In the coming days, David acclimatised to his new position, deeply engaging in collaborative efforts with Jim and Peter. Their bond strengthened through countless hours of vigorous discussions and debates. Amidst the chaotic workspace, they analysed theories and connected disjointed concepts until the late hours. None of them evidently had anywhere better to be. David certainly didn't.

David often stood outside his flat in the shared patch of garden as the days bled into nights, gazing at the star-studded expanse above. Peter had loaned him one of the Institute's more professional telescopes, and seeing Saturn once again, this time much larger and clearer than before, had given David such a sense of peace and tranquillity that life was finally perfect. The universe stretched endlessly before him in those solitary moments, brimming with infinite possibilities just waiting for discovery. In that immense expanse, he felt a thrilling sense of wonder and awe, a persistent curiosity that drove him into the unknown.

Chapter 32

A week later, tucked away in the remote corner of the Institute, David found himself ensconced in the lab - a theme park for inquisitive minds like his. The lab's interior boasted the gleam of stainless steel surfaces and the hum of alien-looking machinery.

A solitary small window broke the wall, letting the morning sunlight stream through in thin beams. The light scattered bright, broken rays over the glistening metal surfaces.

Amidst the labyrinthine arrangement of equipment, David stood before a vast whiteboard, his thoughts racing in a symphony of theories. With feverish determination, he scribbled his musings onto the blank expanse, the marker scratching against the smooth surface.

Across the room, Jim floated in his own orbit, his mind seemingly adrift in the sea of his imagination. The faint thumping of bass from his headphones filled the air, providing a discordant soundtrack to the morning's intellectual pursuits. Immersed in his own realm, Jim glided with a slow, carefree elegance, his actions seamless and relaxed, as if time obeyed his very whim.

Suddenly, the tranquillity of the lab was shattered by the arrival of Peter who blew into the room like a whirlwind, his movements were erratic and far more energetic than you would expect from a man in his sixties. He practically ran over to David, his enthusiasm clearly at boiling point.

"David! My dear friend, now you've had time to settle in, it's time for the tour of our crown jewel here at the Institute—Solomon! Unless Jim's already let the cat out of the bag?" Peter frowned in Jim's direction, but Jim clearly hadn't noticed him walk into the room.

Caught off guard by Peter's sudden arrival, David could only offer a bewildered nod.

"Um... Yeah, sure, sounds great!" David managed to stammer.

Peter nudged David off the stool and gripped him by the shoulder as he frogmarched him out of the lab.

What the hell is going on? For an old bloke, he's got a surprisingly tight grip, that's for sure. Where's he taking me? Solomon? What the hell is Solomon? Better not be another hipster colleague... I can literally feel his eyes boring into the back of my head, wished he'd just chill out a bit...

A palpable anticipation filled the air between them as they walked down the corridor, their footsteps gently echoing against the clean, white walls.

Finally, they reached another nondescript door at the far end of the corridor. David had always assumed it to be a simple storage space or cleaner's closet, but Peter's contagious excitement hinted at something far more extraordinary. With a dramatic flourish, *maybe he wanted to be a magician when he was a kid,* Peter withdrew a small card from his top breast pocket, like those found in hotels, and slid it into a slot adjacent to the door handle. A delightful click echoed softly, and a gentle green light brightened, signalling that their entry was granted.

The door yielded to Peter's push, swinging open with a soft sigh. *Very Hitchhiker's Guide...* David smiled at the thought of making the door into a sighing door. A blinding flood of white light filled the room as Peter flipped a switch, momentarily dazing David. *How many lights does a small room actually need?* As his eyes adapted to the sudden brightness, he stood speechless, struggling to understand the scene before him.

What on Earth?

The room stretched out, its polished bare concrete floor reflecting the glow of overhead lights, casting a subtle luminescence upon the stark white walls. The scent of antiseptic spray lingered in the air, a familiar perfume of laboratory work.

Amidst the pristine environment, a mysterious centrepiece dominated the room. Perched upon a gleaming metal bench, it looked like an ancient relic from a forgotten civilisation. About two feet high, the monolithic structure stood proudly, its matte black surface absorbing the surrounding light as if it possessed a gravitational pull.

A slender strip of translucent material ran down the centre of the monolith, dividing it into symmetrical halves. Through this strip, a soft, diffused glow emanated, casting a central core of pure white light that pulsed rhythmically.

"What on Earth is that?" David said, his professional composure slipping away.

Unfazed by David's wide-eyed bewilderment, Peter grinned like a Cheshire cat who'd just discovered a new brand of mischief.

"That, is Solomon," Peter said, his voice tinged with reverence and a touch of smugness. The word hung in the air, heavy with intrigue.

Looks more like a games console.

"And why is it called Solomon?" he asked.

Peter's eyebrows danced a jig of momentary confusion before he regained his composure, ready to spin a yarn worthy of the most flamboyant bard.

"Alright, have you heard the tale of King Solomon?" Peter asked, leaning in. David shook his head, his eyes fixed on Peter, waiting for an explanation. Peter took a deep breath, preparing to share the tale.

This is going to be dramatic, guaranteed...

"Picture this: King Solomon was known for his wisdom. Right? He had a dream where God appeared and asked him what he wanted most. So, he asks for wisdom. Wanting the ability to govern and guide his people with insight and understanding like none other." Peter raised his hands with a flourish.

Knew it...

Peter continued, *"Impressed by his selfless wish, God granted his request,"* He noticed David's rapt attention. Encouraged, he continued.

"So here we are, with our very own Solomon, paying homage to the OG Solomon himself. It's the embodiment of wisdom. Smarter than your average Einstein and twice as sassy thanks to Jim's programming. Although wait til you see the next software update. Solomon knows all and if it doesn't, it's on a quest to find out faster than you can say 'Google it,'" Peter said. His smile widened, eager to see David's reaction to the technological marvel before them.

"I... I don't even know what to say," David said. He didn't either. His mind still trying to process the whirlwind of information, let alone the incredulity that Peter knew the term *'OG'*. The idea of an AI possessing wisdom rather than just intelligence was like finding out your dog secretly runs a book club.

Sensing David's overwhelmed state, Peter clapped him on the back. He guided David toward the table, inviting him to sit and experience the marvel awaiting him.

"Let me show you," Peter said, his voice filled with excitement and a little hint of mischief. David complied, his thoughts swirling as he sat down, his eyes fixed on Solomon, eagerly anticipating the unveiling of

its power and wisdom, yet still having no expectations whatsoever.

Hard to benchmark expectations on something you've never heard of before. Plus all the dramatic flair kinda puts a damper on it all...

Peter reached for the mouse on the desk, its long cable trailing behind the table.

"Ok, here we go!" Peter said.

"What are we going to do?" David replied, looking up at Peter's face, now hovering like a mischievous imp over his shoulder.

Chapter 33

Before Peter could even muster a syllable in response, the lab's door flung open, revealing Kendra's entrance like a bolt of lightning splitting the sky. Her face was a carnival of emotions, flushed with excitement as if she had just stumbled upon buried treasure.

"Peter! You won't believe what happened!" Kendra's voice boomed, charged with energy threatening to burst the sound barrier.

Caught off guard, Peter swivelled to face Kendra, his surprise etched across his features like ancient hieroglyphics carved into a tombstone.

"Kendra, what in the name of all that's holy is going on? You know this lab is strictly off-limits to non-research personnel."

Kendra waved off Peter's concerns with a dismissive flick of her hand, her excitement refusing to be contained.

"I couldn't resist, Peter. Over drinks last night, I may have casually mentioned Solomon to one of my girlfriends. She's a journalist and she's practically frothing at the mouth to do a story on it, she just called me saying her editor's given the go-ahead!"

Peter's eyes widened like saucers, his expression morphing into astonishment but also concern. The lines etched upon his forehead deepened.

"Kendra, first of all, how do you know enough about Solomon to sell a story on it? And secondly, you can't possibly comprehend the magnitude of what we've been working on. Solomon isn't ready for the world. It's still in its infancy."

Ignoring the patronising comment, Kendra said:

"But Peter, think about it! This is a game-changer, a project that could change the world! The public deserves to know," Kendra argued, her voice

carrying the fervour of a preacher on the pulpit.

David, who had been a silent observer until now, watched the scene unfold with fascination and unease, kind of like a cat trapped in a room full of rocking chairs.

Great, more attention, just what I needed. That being said, I still don't know what this Solomon thing actually does, and if it's been over-sold by Peter, which I'm guessing it probably has... That being said, journalists sniffing around is not good for me, what if they interview me or something, not that I know anything, someone might see, in London, they'd see me here and come investigate, Morgan might read the story, he's into this stuff, he'd come and ask me questions, no...

Peter stood and paced back and forth, his footsteps echoing through the small room like the ticking of a doomsday clock. The deep furrows on his brow wrinkled as he wrestled with the weight of the decision before him. After a long deliberation, he turned to face Kendra, his features stoic.

"Alright, Kendra. I understand your enthusiasm, but if we're going to let Solomon out of its cage, we must proceed with utmost caution. We need to control the narrative, set up interviews, and ensure the truth is conveyed properly. Can you arrange a meeting with your journalist friend?"

Kendra's face lit up like a Christmas tree.

"Absolutely, Peter. I'll call her right away and set up a meeting. You can count on me."

"*Hmmm...*" Peter hummed a little less subtly than he should have. As Kendra hurried out of the room, her footsteps echoing down the corridor like thunderous applause, the atmosphere within the lab seemed to shift.

Peter turned to David, his eyes shimmering with steely determination but a hint of worry.

"David, my friend, this changes everything. We are standing at the edge of a cliff, and once Solomon is out in the open, our lives could well never be the same. We must prepare ourselves for the storm about to be unleashed."

Still sounds like overkill to me...

Peter leaned forward eagerly, his fingers poised over the keyboard like a conductor ready to lead a symphony.

"Alright, David, brace yourself for a glimpse into the marvel that is Solomon," he said, excitement bubbling in his voice.

With a few rapid keystrokes, Peter posed a question to Solomon, tapping into the vast depths of its knowledge.

"Solomon, what's your opinion on the recent debate about whether the

universe is shaped like a doughnut or a bagel?"

David arched an eyebrow, half expecting a dry academic response. But what came back from Solomon was anything but.

"Still have to type in questions, although the software update Jim is working on will change all that," Peter chirped.

Solomon's response popped up on the screen, dripping with sarcasm so thick you could spread it on toast.

"Well, Peter and David, it seems some people have a lot of time on their hands to ponder the cosmic implications of breakfast pastries. Personally, I'm more of a pancake universe kind of AI. Fluffy, circular, and with just the right amount of syrupy chaos. But do you want a proper mathematical answer?"

Peter couldn't help but chuckle at Solomon's cheeky retort.

"See, David? It's not just intelligent; it's got a sense of humour too."

David couldn't suppress a grin.

"I guess even artificial superintelligences have their own brand of sass. But can it really provide insightful answers to more serious questions?"

Peter nodded, his excitement palpable.

"Absolutely. Watch this."

He posed another query to Solomon, this time delving into the complexities of quantum entanglement.

"Solomon, what's your take on the recent experiments demonstrating quantum entanglement across large distances?"

The response came swiftly, accompanied by a virtual eyebrow raise that practically screamed, *"Really, guys?"*

"Ah, quantum entanglement," Solomon replied. *"The universe's way of saying, 'Hey, let's mess with the laws of physics and see what happens.' Personally, I find it all rather charming, like watching a cosmic game of Twister. Left foot in Alpha Centauri, right hand in Andromeda. It's all fun and games until someone collapses the wave function."* It then proceeded to type out a long response composed of equations, and ending in pros and cons list featuring all the current theories and experiments and where it thought they'd got it right or wrong.

Peter grinned triumphantly at David. *"There you have it. Not only does Solomon have intelligence, but it also possesses wisdom—albeit with a healthy dose of sass."*

David couldn't help but be impressed.

"I never thought an AI could have such a personality. It's like having a brilliant and slightly snarky friend."

Peter nodded, his eyes sparkling with pride.

"Exactly. And with Solomon's insights, who knows what mysteries of the

universe we'll unravel next?"

David couldn't help but laugh at Solomon's witty responses. The AI's sassiness added an unexpected layer of charm to its vast intelligence.

"Well, Peter," David remarked, his voice laced with amusement, *"it seems you've created the Einstein of stand-up comedians."*

Peter laughed in agreement, his enthusiasm infectious.

"Indeed, David! Solomon is not only a fountain of knowledge but also a master of wit. Who knew artificial intelligence could be so entertaining? You can thank Jim for that part. He's working on a voice modulator for Solomon too. That's the next update."

David blinked an eyebrow, a hint of surprise colouring his expression.

"Wait, Solomon's humour was programmed by Jim?" he asked, incredulous.

Peter nodded, his smile widening.

"Yes, indeed. Turns out Jim's humour runs deeper than we thought. Who knew he had such a knack for comedy?"

David couldn't help but snicker at the thought. Jim, with his perpetually serious demeanour and dry wit, seemed like the last person to inject humour into an artificial intelligence.

"Well, colour me surprised," he remarked, shaking his head in amusement.

"I always thought Jim's idea of a joke was a badly formatted spreadsheet."

Peter laughed, the sound echoing through the room.

"You and me both, David. But it seems Jim's got a few tricks up his sleeve after all. Who knows what other surprises he's got in store for us?"

Despite his initial reservations about Solomon's unveiling, David found himself warming up to the idea.

"You know, Peter, I think Solomon might just be the most intriguing project I've ever seen. Its blend of intelligence and humour is pretty remarkable. I can't wait to see what else it can do."

Peter nodded in agreement, his eyes still glued to the screen as he absorbed Solomon's responses.

"Absolutely. With Solomon at our disposal, the possibilities are endless. It's like having a brilliant colleague who never runs out of clever comebacks. And I can personally attest to the fact that Solomon's ideas are truly original, no regurgitation of other people's stuff, actual, publishable theories."

As they continued to explore Solomon's capabilities, David couldn't shake off the feeling of excitement mingled with a hint of apprehension. But as he watched Peter interact with Solomon, he couldn't deny the potential for greatness that lay ahead. Together, they were on the brink of something extraordinary.

Chapter 34

The morning dawned upon David, Jim, and Peter with all the subtlety of a stampeding rhinoceros, mixed with a dash of anxiety making their stomachs feel like they were hosting a butterfly rodeo.

With a quick glance at his watch, Peter hurriedly exited the lab to meet the reporter, leaving behind a scene of controlled chaos with Jim and David slap bang in the middle. Papers lay strewn about like a blizzard had hit, covering every available surface in journal papers, graphs and notepads covered in scribbles. Their mission was clear: sift through the scattered papers to extract Solomon's technical intricacies, ensuring every detail was ready to be told to the eager reporter waiting in reception.

Within a couple of minutes, in stormed Sarah Harrison. Reporter extraordinaire. Her heels tapped out a Morse code on the linoleum floor as she crossed the threshold of the Institute, each click echoing like the steady beat of a war drum.

Clad in a sleek, navy blue pencil skirt that hugged her curves like a glove, and a crisp white blouse shimmering under the fluorescent lights, she exuded an air of authority that demanded attention.

The faint scent of her perfume, a blend of jasmine and sandalwood, hung in the air, adding a subtle layer of intrigue to her already formidable persona. Her eyes, sharp as shards of glass, swept the bland room with the precision of a laser-guided missile, missing nary a detail. She saw Kendra perched behind her desk and went over and hugged her.

Following in her wake was a young woman whose presence was as striking as a bolt of lightning on a summer's day. Her dark locks cascaded down her back like a waterfall of silk, each strand shimmering. She was dressed in a tailored trouser suit, the sharp lines of the jacket accentuating her slender frame, while the deep burgundy colour added a touch of sophistication.

With a flick of her wrist, the young woman tossed a car key into the air, the motion so fluid it appeared choreographed. The sound of the key hitting the palm of her hand resonated through the room, a sharp clink cutting through the tension like a knife.

Sarah and her young companion glided toward Peter with the grace of predators stalking their prey.

Sarah's voice was smooth as silk but tinged with an undercurrent of excitement.

"Mr. Peter Coombs, I presume?" she purred, her words carrying the weight of someone who knew the power they held. *"I'm Sarah Harrison, a reporter from The Leeds Sentinel. And this,"* she gestured to the young woman, who stood by her side, *"is one of our junior reporters, Clara."*

As Sarah spoke, her perfume wafted towards Peter, adding a subtle layer of allure to her already captivating presence. Peter met Sarah's penetrating gaze, his own eyes reflecting a flicker of caution amidst the storm of emotions brewing within him. He understood the gravity of what was at stake - the unveiling of Solomon would expose their creation to the hungry eyes of the world, a world ripe with scepticism and most dangerous of all, greed.

"Ms Harrison, Sarah, please understand," Peter began, *"Solomon is not just a project—it's something of immense significance. Its unveiling requires delicacy and precision. While we welcome your exploration, we must retain control over how the story is presented."*

Sarah's lips curled into a sly smile, a glimmer of respect gleaming in her eyes. She glanced over at Clara, who was fidgeting with a button on her suit.

"Mr. Coombs," Sarah said, her voice tinged with sincerity, *"I assure you, The Sentinel is not interested in sensationalism. We're not Fox News. We seek the truth only, the essence of your creation. Consider me your advocate but also your ally."*

The weight of Sarah's words hung heavy in the air, each syllable pressing down on Peter's chest like a boulder. He wondered if she could be trusted. She may be Kendra's friend, but Lord knows she's had some dodgy friends in the past, but she sounded honest. An honest reporter? Peter supposed there had to be at least one in the world. Perhaps Sarah was the answer, but also the potential to unravel everything they had worked so tirelessly to achieve.

After a moment of contemplation, Peter extended his hand toward Sarah.

"Very well, Sarah. But remember, the truth must be handled with care. Solomon can reshape our world, and with that power comes great responsibility."

Clara couldn't help but grin at the iconic Spiderman quote. Evidently, Sarah hadn't heard it before or was a master at hiding her amusement. Sarah smiled, a glint of ambition shining in her eyes. The yearning for a story coming to fruition was always a good day.

"You can be confident, Mr. Coombs, that The Sentinel will take on that duty. Together, we'll showcase Solomon to the world, and if Kendra's claims are accurate, your invention will rise above mere scientific discovery."

Back in the reception area, Sarah, Clara, and Peter delved into discussions about Solomon - its abilities, its potential dangers, and the far-reaching implications for the world. Initially hesitant about revealing too much, Peter found himself opening up under Sarah's reassuring presence, unravelling the layers of his creation with each passing moment.

After a brief exchange, Peter excused himself, eager to introduce the reporters to the rest of his research team. Meanwhile, in the lab, David and Jim engaged in a conversation of their own while sorting the notes on Solomon into a useful pile, were pondering the ramifications of Solomon and how the public might react to its existence.

"I can see some positives in this," David remarked after a moment of silence, his tone contemplative. *"It might even attract funding somehow? Between you and me, I still don't know how this place stays afloat? I mean, have you seen those telescopes? They're worth a few grand each easy…"*

Jim just smiled back. *"I guess Peter has more cash than we know. He told me once he gets anonymous donations fairly often. But yeah, I guess it could all work out for the best".*

At that moment, Peter burst into the lab.

"Hey, you two, time to come out and meet the media parasites. Just kidding, they're quite delightful, and they're eager to meet you." Peter's excitement was evident as he gestured for David and Jim to join him in confronting the storm of attention waiting for them outside.

David and Jim exchanged a knowing glance, amused by how Peter's demeanour had transformed into that of a giddy schoolboy. With a shared chuckle, they pushed themselves off their plastic work stools and trailed after Peter as he made his way towards the door. As the trio walked down the corridor, Peter's steps implied a newfound buoyancy, prompting Jim to laugh and point out the noticeable bounce in his stride to David.

Turning the corner towards the reception, David's eyes caught sight of the reporters, and he froze.

"Clara?" he blurted out.

It couldn't be, what on Earth was she doing there? Here, in Leeds? What the...?

The immediate tension between David and Clara hung in the air like an unspoken accusation, memories of their last encounter that night on the smoking terrace of the Student Union resurfacing like the ghost from Christmas past.

I... I don't, understand, here? Clara... I...

Sarah and Peter exchanged puzzled glances, sensing the palpable discomfort between David and Clara. Sarah cleared her throat and broke the silence, diffusing the tension immediately.

"Ah, it seems you two have a history. Perhaps we can delve into that later. Right now, let's focus on Solomon, shall we?"

David shifted restlessly, entangled in the tension between his past and his work relationships. Ever the mediator, Peter stepped forward to break the awkward silence.

"Well, Clara, let me introduce you properly. This is David, one of our brilliant researchers. David, meet Clara, a junior reporter from The Sentinel."

David mustered a nervous smile and extended his hand toward Clara.

"Nice to see you again, Clara. Been a while."

Clara hesitated momentarily, her gaze fixed on David's outstretched hand. Then, with a flicker of resolve, she reciprocated the gesture, their hands meeting briefly.

"Likewise, David," she replied, her tone guarded yet tinged with a hint of curiosity.

The room seemed to exhale as if the tension had momentarily dissipated. Seizing the opportunity to redirect the conversation, Sarah steered the discussion towards Solomon's capabilities, prompting Peter to delve into another detailed explanation.

As Peter spoke, David and Jim listened intently, their minds grappling with Solomon's weight and its implications' complexities. Meanwhile, Clara found herself drawn into the narrative, her initial reservations giving way to genuine intrigue. Despite her and David's history, the allure of Solomon's possibilities tugged at her journalistic curiosity. She couldn't help but marvel at the project and its potential for transforming science and society, and she admired even more that David was somehow involved with it. She'd always figured he was a bit of genius ever since that first talk, they had on the smoking terrace, and within a matter of seconds, some of those initial attractions began to take hold once more.

As Peter continued to unravel the story of Solomon's creation and capabilities, Sarah found herself drawn deeper into the narrative. Her initial journalistic curiosity gave way to genuine fascination. What had started as a mere scoop had transformed into something far more profound—an exploration of human ingenuity at its finest. The responsibility of unveiling this groundbreaking creation weighed upon her, and each word from Peter added another layer of complexity to the story.

As the discussion progressed, the lines between personal history and professional collaboration blurred, setting the stage for a journey filled with unexpected twists and turns. David, captivated by Solomon's potential, found himself equally intrigued by Clara, whose presence sparked a sense of familiarity and longing within him. Clara, in turn, couldn't help but wonder about David's role in the creation that now held her attention captive.

In the days that followed, the lab buzzed with activity as Peter, Jim, and David worked to prepare for Solomon's unveiling. Each day blended into the next, with the team becoming increasingly absorbed in their tasks.

Amid the preparations, Jim found himself engaged in animated discussions with Sarah and Clara. With an air of excitement, he eagerly shared insights into the process of programming Solomon's sense of humour, a topic that piqued the interest of both reporters.

Jim explained his rationale behind infusing Solomon with humour, emphasising its potential to foster a deeper connection between the AI and its users. He discussed how humour could serve as a bridge, breaking down barriers and making interactions with Solomon more engaging and relatable.

"I wanted AI with a sense of humour, not HAL," Jim had said.

As he delved into the intricacies of his programming methods, Jim's passion for the project shone through. He regaled Sarah and Clara with anecdotes and examples of Solomon's witty responses, showcasing the AI's ability to inject levity into even the most serious of conversations.

The journalists listened intently, captivated by Jim's explanations and eager to learn more about the inner workings of Solomon. Their discussions became increasingly animated, with Sarah and Clara posing insightful questions that really explored the role of humour in artificial intelligence.

Through their conversations, Jim hoped to convey not only the technical prowess behind Solomon's development but also the thoughtfulness and creativity that went into shaping its personality. He believed that journalists would be better equipped to convey its complexities to the world by understanding the reasoning behind Solomon's sense of humour.

Meanwhile, Sarah and Clara proved to be invaluable allies, their astute and uncommonly ethical journalistic instincts unearthing details and asking probing questions that delved into the heart of Solomon.

Late one evening, as the lab descended into eerie stillness, Peter and David found themselves alone, their eyes locked onto the mesmerising glow emanating from Solomon's monitor. The lines etched upon Peter's face deepened, as if the weight of the world had settled upon his shoulders like a heavy shroud.

"*David,*" Peter's voice cut through the silence, barely more than a whisper in the small echoey room. "*We stand on the precipice of a potential storm. Our lives may never be the same once Solomon is exposed to the world tomorrow. We must brace ourselves for what lies ahead. Though I'm sure the response will be overwhelmingly positive, there will be outliers...*"

David nodded solemnly, his gaze fixed upon the flickering glow of Solomon's monitors.

Yeah, you got that right, the moment of reckoning, judgement day as it were, is almost at hand. This thing they've created knows more than anyone can possibly know, and it keeps on learning. Peter and Jim kept Solomon secret, for a good reason. Tomorrow people will know of it, they might believe it, but they will in time, they will know that it knows everything, everything about everyone... including me...

Outside, a storm was raging, the relentless beating of rain against the lab window.

A bad omen if there ever was one...

Chapter 35

The laboratory buzzed with energy, and a hint of stale coffee hung in the air. To label the institute that day as *'bustling'* would be an exercise in misguided optimism, for the entire space accommodated just four individuals. Kendra was stationed at her desk and was waging war against boredom with the aid of social media.

Meanwhile, David, Jim, and Peter huddled around the lab's main workbench, amidst the clutter of machinery, monitors, and wires and engaged in a lively discourse that could have made even the most diehard geek swoon.

And then there was Solomon - the mysterious entity born from the depths of Jim and Peter's fevered imagination. It was occupying a good chunk of the main bench, having been moved from its little room for further development.

Peter and Jim both had their laptops open, and wires connected them to the back of Solomon. The faint hum of Solomon's circuits filled the air as Peter and Jim typed maniacally away on their keyboards - adding new features and updates, David assumed.

There's something about this thing, something weird I can't put my finger on, just looking at it gives me a knot in my stomach sometimes, I know the guys built it and it's funny and all but there's something else there - something threatening? I don't know, it can find answers to things, but it can equally reveal things meant to be hidden... who decides?

Jim and Peter felt no such threat. Or if they did, they didn't voice it. Both were firm believers that Solomon could connect the dots in their research and uncover the mysteries of existence. But they seemed blind to the nefarious possibilities, too. Every minute that passed, Solomon was absorbing information, learning, thinking for itself. More and more. Never stopping.

It was charting a complex web of information for quick retrieval when needed. Meanwhile, David pondered if—or when—Solomon might attain consciousness. From his perspective, Solomon remained in its early stages, like an infant taking its first steps. However, we all know the mind grows rapidly, possibly even exponentially in this instance. Nevertheless, Peter and Jim seemed completely unaware of this or weren't in the least bit concerned.

Jim spoke loudly, with an intense rhythm and intelligence that starkly contrasted with his dishevelled look. This was a man whose theories about the universe bordered on the brink between heresy and lunacy. Yet, the way he spoke had such conviction in the twang of his Australian accent that anyone listening would think it was Gospel truth.

Despite the conviction of his tone, Jim appeared a little disconnected. He was by all definition a genius, so he could have probably held a complex scientific conversation in his sleep, but there was something else lurking behind the scenes.

He looked exhausted, wrapped around him like a heavy cloak, accentuating the hollows beneath his eyes. He evidently hadn't slept properly in some time. Jim's phone buzzed across the desk, and he stopped talking and picked it up.

Neglect had seeped into his being even more that day. It eclipsed the most basic aspects of self-care.

Definitely something going on there, I really should ask him if he's ok, assume Peter would have asked? I don't want to ask, it's not my place, but we're colleagues, friends now, maybe I should? I know he lives alone, some flat nearby, that's all, never mentions friends or anything… I'll ask him…

"Everything OK, Jim?" David's voice sliced through the air, his eyes peering over the rim of his laptop screen. The large workbench sprawled between them, cluttered with tools and unfinished projects.

Jim seemed preoccupied, having just set down his phone. His hair, darker than last week, had become greasy from lack of washing. It appeared he had neglected personal hygiene over this past week.

With his head lowered Jim seemed absorbed by the light of his phone's screen. The bright white illumination flickered across his pockmarked chin, creating shadows that accentuated the weary lines etched on his face. The pallid tone of his skin, already lacking vitality, further faded under the phone's light.

A soft tapping noise started to rise from beneath the bench, revealing Jim's restless foot, drumming a nervous beat against the floor. David recognised these signs all too well, having become an unwilling expert in interpreting the signals of anxiety and fear over the past few months.

"*Jim?*" David reiterated, Peter then looked up and over at Jim, with a look of confusion.

"*Jim?*" Peter said with a concerned tone.

Finally, Jim lifted his gaze, his eyes meeting David's with a mix of weariness and trepidation and then moving to meet Peter's gaze. Jim's hands ceased their nervous movements, frozen in a rare moment of stillness.

"*Yeah... I guess so, yeah.*" His voice trembled, appearing to struggle to bridge the gap between doubt and sincere conviction. Restlessness found solace in Jim's fingertips as he absentmindedly began to pick at the dry skin on the back of his left hand, another sign David recognised.

Jim's attention was drawn back to the phone, its mesmerising glow captivating him once again, and a heavy and burdened sigh escaped his lips.

David felt the urge not to push Jim anymore, to just leave him to it. If Jim wanted to talk, then he would. Yet, Jim's usual flamboyant energy and charm had taken a steep plunge, it was concerning. Peter was evidently taken aback too but excused himself to go and speak with Kendra.

Probably checking to see if she's actually working or painting her nails again...

Minutes dragged on, punctuated by Jim's frequent sighs filling the air. Like nervous insects, his fingers tapped a constant rhythm on the desk's surface.

Then, in a sudden burst of restless energy, Jim sprang up from his stool. The force of his movement propelled it backwards, causing it to scrape against the floor with a painful screech. The sound sliced through the room, causing both David and Peter to jump.

"*Everything okay?*" David asked, looking at Jim from his desk. Jim lifted his gaze from the desk as if awakening from a daze, and for a fleeting moment, looked surprised to find David still present.

"*Yeah... Fine,*" Jim replied, his voice devoid of conviction. "*Just gonna get some air.*" With those words, Jim turned his back on David. The door to the lab closed with a soft click and a beep, sealing his departure and leaving a lingering sense of unease behind.

Sighing, David redirected his attention to the white glow of his laptop screen, tapping away at a piece about the implications of artificial intelligence in cosmology modelling. It was a more technical version of what he suspected Sarah and Clara were busily drafting for the Sentinel newspaper.

Clara, God I haven't stopped thinking about her, seeing her everywhere I go, short of seeing her face in a slice of toast, wouldn't that be something!

Suddenly, an email notification appeared on David's screen - a message from Clara. *Talk about coincidence!*

Was she actually glad to see me that day? Does that whatever it was I had - that allure or something - do I still have it? Does she forgive me for standing her up that night? Oh God, we're gonna have to talk - what if she asks about that night, what happened, she'll ask about the car maybe, can I lie? Can I do it convincingly? She'll see right through me, know I had a role in Alex's death, I know it...

With trembling hands, David clicked open the email, his heart fluttering like a caged bird yearning for freedom.

"Hi David, I hope you don't mind, but I got your email address from Peter. Talk about a twist of fate, right? Anyway, did you want to catch up for a drink this evening?"

David found himself teetering on the edge of indecision. On one hand, Clara was dazzlingly beautiful, and the magnetic pull of their brief shared past tugged at his heartstrings. On the other hand, Clara had become a full-fledged journalist, dedicated to uncovering the truth and exposing people's darkest secrets. *My secret...*

Yet, despite his reservations, David's longing for Clara propelled him to hastily write a reply accepting her invitation and expressing his eagerness, but not too much. Closing his laptop with a heavy exhalation, he leaned back precariously on his stool, interlocking his hands behind his head. A small smile began to etch its way across his face, and the butterflies commenced their soaring flight within him.

Chapter 36

David's fingertips danced across the keyboard, oblivious to the passage of time within the lab's barren walls. The once gentle daylight filtering through the windows now wore a darker visage, its luminosity muted by brooding clouds roiling in the sky. Outside, the world had hushed, the symphony of birdsong silenced, leaving only an eerie stillness in its wake.

As David's fingers traced the letters on the keys, a soft hum permeated the air, emanating from the flickering overhead fluorescent light. With each buzz and flutter, the light toyed with his senses - the shapes of broken bike spokes creeping up the walls.

Suddenly, the lab door emitted its shrill beep, breaking the heavy silence. David's attention snapped away from the screen. The door swung open, revealing Peter standing in the archway. His face was drained of colour, and his features were etched with a horrifying amalgamation of shock and terror. The room seemed to shudder in response to Peter's presence, an icy breath of foreboding slithering across David's skin.

"What is it?" David's voice betrayed his alarm, his eyes capturing every nuance of Peter's stoic yet trembling form. A pregnant pause stretched between them as if time held its breath, reluctant to release the answer lingering in Peter's haunted gaze.

Finally, Peter's lips parted, barely forming a whisper.

"It's Jim," he managed to utter, the words a fragile thread woven with despair. *"He's gone. Hit by a car crossing the road. He's gone, David."* The air thickened, becoming an impenetrable fog of disbelief and sorrow. David's mind recoiled, refusing to accept the cruel reality unfolding before him.

"Gone?" David's voice trembled with a blend of disbelief and horror.

He searched Peter's face, yearning for a flicker of hope, but found none. Peter's gaze remained fixed, eyes sunken and brimming with unshed tears.

Was he distracted? He's not daft, he would look both ways, something was on his mind, yes, he was distracted, or was it an accident at all? No of course it was, he was a good guy, no one would want him dead, it was an accident... Like Alex... an accident, yes, he was a good guy as well, but a death caused by a car, coincidence? Irony... it's cruel.

The image of Jim's lifeless body thrown to the side of the road, the tear-streaked face blurred in David's vision, intermingling with that of Alex McCormick's, both now forever etched in his psyche - the past and the present merged, intertwining like twin serpents, squeezing the life from his soul. Nausea, foul and unyielding, rose in his throat, the acidic strands threatening to rip him apart.

"Come have a chat in a bit if you like, David. I'll be in my office. You don't have to keep working today. I've already told Kendra she can down tools and head home."

The words reached David's ears, but their meaning was lost amidst the storm raging within him. The world around him faded into a blur as the acidic bile surged upward. With a feeble nod, David pushed himself away from the desk.

As Peter turned the corner and walked back to his office, David promptly headed to the bathroom down the hallway.

The door swung open under the weight of his trembling hand, revealing a whitewashed room. Locking the door behind him, he sunk to his knees, collapsing onto the merciless tiled floor, the sharp edges of each ceramic piece biting into his flesh like unseen teeth.

The room itself seemed to constrict around him, suffocating his very soul as he surrendered to the relentless force tearing through him. His entire being convulsed with unbridled agony, each retch and wrenching cough an anguished cry.

The sounds of his pain echoed around him, a mix of sorrow and the steady streams of tears flowing down his cheeks, a heavy rain that felt as if it might snuff out his fading spark of hope.

It's all too much, the nightmares had stopped, the hallucinations, the paranoia - faded, but now, Jim, another death, hit by a car - it's too much, my head....

The walls bore witness to his private apocalypse. The air grew heavy with the raw intensity of his pain, imbued with a palpable aura of desolation that went unnoticed by the oblivious world beyond those walls.

Time warped within the grip of misery, expanding and contracting with each torturous moment. David's existence was measured in the ragged gasps of his breath, in the relentless pulse of his aching stomach, and in the scorching inferno ravaging his throat.

He remained hunched over the porcelain bowl; his body contorted in a twisted ballet of suffering for what felt like an eternity. Forty minutes of torment stretched out into a bottomless abyss, where time lost all meaning and existence became a relentless descent into the depths of his own personal hell.

Finally, with the last vestiges of strength clinging desperately to his bones, David rose from the cold floor. Every joint screamed in protest, his muscles throbbing with a persistent ache, while his feet were enveloped in pins and needles.

His trembling hand sought solace in the rough texture of the cubicle wall, its cold surface grounding him in the harsh reality awaiting beyond the restroom's door. Slowly, painstakingly, he mustered the resolve to lift himself upright, his weary body a battleground of resistance against the inexorable pull of despair.

As he wiped his mouth with a trembling hand, the residue of his torment smeared across his skin like an indelible stain. Summoning his final reserves, David flushed the filthy bowl, purging the physical manifestations of his pain from the world. The rush of water echoed his inner yearning for cleansing, for liberation.

Leaving the cubicle behind, David approached the sink. The cool water cascaded over his weary face, rejuvenating his senses. His reflection stared back at him in the dusty mirror, eyes red-rimmed and haunted *a window to a shattered soul...*

In that deep despair, the grim reality weighed on David like a heavy shroud: Jim was gone. The grief was overwhelming. It was a grief that resonated with a bone-chilling familiarity, for Jim's death bore the exact eerie resemblance to Alex's tragic end.

Even in his weariness, David's spirit sparkled with a tiny glow of compassion, a warm ember of empathy that refused to fade away. Despite his struggles and the painful sensations coursing through him, he knew that Peter, at that moment, needed a friend. He deserved comfort and understanding as he faced such an unimaginable tragedy. After all, he had known Jim far longer than he had; they were friends -

or so David assumed - both intensely private people, but there was no mistaking the vibe they had together.

Chapter 37

David's hand trembled as he pushed aside the remnants of his abandoned breakfast. The coffee had cooled, a skin forming on its surface, and the porridge had solidified into a lumpy mass. His thoughts were too chaotic for food. He hastily pocketed his phone, snatched up his shoes and jacket, and approached the apartment door.

The distant rumble of traffic from the main road reverberated through the narrow street, a perpetual urban chaos. Yet, undeterred by the racket of car horns and the city's ceaseless clamour, David pressed on.

A disquieting sense of déjà vu settled over him as if the world around him had become trapped in a perpetual loop of repetition.

David's skin prickled as he moved, an inexplicable sensation of being watched from the shadows. He glanced over his shoulder but found nothing except deep, empty darkness down the criss-crossing alleyways.

Yet, an inexplicable force tugged at his curiosity, urging him toward a peculiar sight at the curb next to the main road. There, amidst the cracks and imperfections of the pavement, a small, solitary strip of blue and white tape fluttered in the gentle breeze.

David's steps slowed as he saw the blue and white tape fluttering in the breeze. He moved towards it as if in a trance, a heaviness settling in his chest with each step closer. The tape was a ghost of past violence, a fragment of the horror that had stained this pavement.

David shuddered, his mind involuntarily conjuring vivid images of the horrors the road had witnessed - crimson splatters, the echo of anguished screams reverberating in the air.

Standing motionless on the pavement, David stared at the ceaseless traffic flow. Amidst the discarded fragments of a broken vehicle - bits of headlight, chips of plastic bumper, he saw the remnants of a life disrupted - a life that had met a sudden, tragic end.

Too much, it's too much, it's the same, flashbacks...

The diligent efforts of street cleaners had done their best to erase the overt traces of the tragedy, yet these subtle remnants screamed of the terror that had happened here.

The thought of crossing the road at this spot, the path Jim had walked, felt like a perverse intrusion - a violation of his memory somehow.

He walked here, he stood here, only a few feet into the road, dead... I'm looking at the spot, Alex died a few feet into the road too, I see his body there...

A faint rustling sound from the shadows behind him abruptly jolted David's attention. He spun around, searching the emptiness with eyes wide and alert, but there was no one to be found. Only the empty street behind, silent and indifferent.

Shaking off the eerie encounter, he took a deep breath, his racing heart gradually steadying itself, and prepared to cross the road.

Still, a profound sense of caution urged him to glance around in every direction, again and again, as if the world around him had turned into a maze filled with unseen dangers. David stood, twisting his neck left to right, left to right, *it was safe but how can I be sure? It was safe for Jim, and he died, it was safe for Alex until I arrived...*

As David stepped onto the two-lane road, he felt a strange energy wash over him, as if he was crossing a line between the living and the dead.

The sunlight pierced through the moving clouds, casting a muted glow on a small section of tarmac. It was a sinister gleam hinting at the dark stain of Jim's blood.

With his gaze fixed firmly ahead, David broke into a jog after reaching the other side of the road, his pace quickening with each stride as he propelled himself toward the institute's entrance. The worn steps leading to the grimy glass front door loomed before him.

Chapter 38

A little over a week had passed, each agonising day stretching into an eternity since Jim's untimely death. The void left in his wake echoed through the halls of the Institute, a hollow emptiness where his vibrant yet shabby presence once resided. In a strange twist, Jim had left his mortgage-free flat to Peter in his will.

One morning at the Institute, a weary-looking lawyer handed Peter a key. As the lawyer read Jim's will aloud, a sad truth emerged - there were no valuable possessions or heirlooms to pass on. The only thing left was the apartment, as if Jim's life had become insignificant. His brief existence seemed to disappear without a trace.

Throughout their four years of friendship and work, Peter had never crossed the threshold of Jim's flat. Peter often offered casual invitations for a drink after work, but Jim consistently declined, masking his refusals with weak excuses. Peter, assuming Jim was just self-conscious, perhaps rationalised that Jim had a tendency towards untidiness, especially given Jim's scruffy appearance.

David sensed the shift in Peter's gait while they walked towards Jim's flat on the corner of Darwin Close. He instinctively adjusted his pace. David had offered to join Peter on the first visit to what was now Peter's newly inherited property. Knowing the flat had not been entered since Jim's passing, there was a feeling of more than grief in the air.

Peter's hand trembled as he wrestled with the small, burnished key attached to a faded neon yellow plastic key fob, struggling to unlock the door. Frustration mingled with anticipation while his muttered exclamations punctuated the air. Sensing Peter's fragile state, David maintained a stoic stance, avoiding any sudden movements that might jolt Peter into a state of alarm. Finally, the lock yielded, and the door of the ground floor flat beckoned them forward. They walked through the narrow corridor, stepping into the small, dingy living room that doubled as a makeshift kitchen.

The room screamed *'Neglect!'* so loudly, you half expected it to start a punk band. With old books strewn haphazardly across the floor and crumpled pieces of paper scattered like confetti. The stale scent of cigarette smoke hung heavy in the air *he didn't even smoke?* David couldn't help but feel a pang of sadness as he surveyed the disarray - a lonely testament to neglect and solitude. The red leather sofa in the corner looked like it had gone a few rounds with a grizzly bear, its cushions ripped and sagging.

Christ if I didn't know Jim lived alone, I'd swear it was the scene of a particularly enthusiastic burglary…

Peter wandered ahead, lost in his thoughts, while David took a moment to drink in the scene. The off-white walls were grubby and heavily marked, looking like they'd been on a diet of despair and neglect for years. Their only decoration was a small, framed print of a landscape, probably snapped during the 1970s and stuck in a time warp ever since.

David circled the desk, idly tracing his fingers over the clutter, when his eyes landed on a photo frame half-hidden beneath a stack of folders. The edge of the frame caught the light, and something about it compelled him to pull it free. The photo inside was slightly worn, like it had been handled a lot, maybe even cherished.

It was a candid shot of Jim and Kendra, taken at what looked like a summer barbecue. The two were smiling broadly, Kendra's arm casually draped over Jim's shoulders. They looked comfortable, and happy—more than just colleagues sharing a laugh. He glanced at Peter, who was still lost in his papers, oblivious to the revelation in David's hands.

David cleared his throat, holding the photo out for Peter to see. *Did you know about this?"*

Peter looked up, his eyes narrowing as he focused on the picture. *"Is that…? No way. Jim and Kendra?"*

"Looks like it," David said, his voice low. *"I had no idea."*

Peter shook his head slowly, trying to piece together a puzzle that had suddenly taken on a new, unexpected shape.

"Neither did I. They never… I mean, I never saw anything that made me think they were more than just coworkers."

"Same here," David murmured, placing the photo back where he found it. The discovery felt like a jigsaw piece from a different puzzle entirely - something that didn't quite fit with the Jim and Kendra he thought he knew.

What else is here? Hiding in plain sight?

Peter, sensing the shift in the room's atmosphere, looked at David with renewed seriousness.

"We need to find out more. This changes things, doesn't it? I mean, why didn't he leave the place to her?"

David nodded and noticed Peter looking closely at a stack of papers in his hands.

"Come on, spill it. What've you got?"

Peter hesitated, eyes glued to the documents.

"I think... it's a list of people to blackmail? I don't know...," he said, sounding like he half-expected the papers to start laughing at him.

David's eyebrows shot up. He grabbed one of the papers from the desk, eyes scanning the text.

Jonathan Talbott - Finance controller at Epihealth Pharmaceuticals, Leeds
112, Rowle Close, Leeds LE45 9XJ
Filed bogus expense claims of £112,000
Bribing government officials

David's jaw dropped.

"This... This can't be real, can it?" His voice wavered as he struggled to reconcile the image of Jim as a moral compass with this blackmail bonanza. Peter shrugged, nonchalant.

"Why not? There are about twenty names here, each with their dirty laundry neatly catalogued." He spoke as if commenting on the soup of the day.

David put the paper down and noticed a small black notebook on a nearby shelf. Opening it, he found pages filled with scribbles, including bank account numbers, transfers of vast sums of money and cryptic references to Bitcoin all dotted the pages.

Peter leaned over David's shoulder, curiosity mixing with dread.

"What is it?" he asked, his hand landing on David's shoulder. They both peered at the open notebook.

"That's my account number!" Peter yelped, jabbing at the page. *"The one for the institute. Why would Jim have it?"* His voice quivered, the shock slicing through his disbelief.

David's eyes shone with understanding as the different pieces of the puzzle started to come together. A sense of unease settled over him, the realisation of Jim's secretive activities tainting their memories of a friend. His voice tinged with resignation and determination, breaking the silence that had enveloped them.

"Peter, Jim told me you've been getting anonymous donations this past year?" David's voice cut through the haze of their bewilderment.

Peter's eyes widened. The mysterious benefactor who had kept their struggling institute afloat had been closer than they'd ever imagined.

"Jim was the anonymous benefactor," David said, dropping the bombshell with the delicacy of a wrecking ball. *"He was converting cryptocurrency and channelling the funds to you."*

The revelation hit Peter like a chair to the face. He staggered back, hands flying to his head as if to stop his brain from leaking out his ears. The notion of Jim's secret generosity clashed with their ongoing financial soap opera. Guilt gnawed at Peter for accepting those mystery donations without a second thought. The allure of survival had clouded his judgment, leading him down a path paved with Bitcoin and bad decisions.

The room seemed to close in on them, its dingy walls now feeling like the setting for a noir detective film. Peter's voice trembled with a mix of awe and frustration.

"If Jim had all this wealth, why did he live in such... squalor?" The question dangled in the stale cigarette air.

David's brows knitted together, wrestling with the mystery.

"Maybe he liked the simple life? I don't know," he offered. Deep down, they both knew the simplicity was a smokescreen, a red herring in the murky waters of Jim's life.

Peter's scepticism was written all over his face.

"If he's blackmailing people, then it was probably through this Bitcoin thing, right? Using Solomon to dig up dirt on people..."

"You just don't know what's going on with people, do you?" David said, irony dripping from his words, the bitter taste of betrayal lingering on his tongue.

Peter suddenly turned to face David directly, his eyes filled with conflict and seriousness. The flickering lights reflected in his gaze as if mirroring the tumultuous storm raging within him.

"David, let me tell you something. Solomon is poised to be a huge thing in this world," Peter began, his voice a hushed whisper. *"Jim's proved that it can be used for criminal enterprises. And evidently, he's gotten away with it. The police haven't said anything to the contrary. And let's face it we need the money..."*

Peter's words hung in the air, mingling with the silence that enveloped them. The gravity of his proposal settled heavily upon their shoulders, threatening to crush the remnants of their fractured morality. David's mouth was half open, a look of disbelief etched across his face as if grappling with the monstrous proposition before him.

"Peter. Are you serious? You're suggesting we continue Jim's blackmail plot?" David's voice was laden with disbelief, his words a thin veneer covering the anger simmering beneath.

"If this ever got out, your reputation would be ruined. The Institute would be closed, and you'd probably go to jail for the rest of your life. Worse, they might find you and kill you!"

Peter's face turned ashen, his internal struggle manifesting in the tear that welled in the corner of his eye. The hum of his moral conflict filled the room, an almost tangible presence threatening to suffocate them both.

"David... I... I don't know what to do. We need the money," Peter admitted, his voice strained and heavy with desperation.

"Peter, ultimately, you need to do what you think is best for the Institute, but I don't want to be a part of it," David said firmly, his voice tinged with concern and self-preservation.

End of the day Peter, I need to stay hidden. Already have journalists around, you want more attention? You do you, but I need plausible deniability...

Peter's eyes darted around the room, landing on the stack of incriminating documents, the old red sofa, and finally, the small black notebook with his account number scrawled inside. His hands trembled slightly, the weight of the decision pressing down on him like the crushing depths of the ocean. Sweat beaded on his forehead, not just from the stagnant air, but from the moral quandary tightening around him like a noose. He took a deep breath which made the back of his throat itch and looked back at David. The resolve in David's eyes was clear.

David stood firm. He knew the path Peter was contemplating, and he wasn't about to follow him into that abyss. The silence between them stretched on. Peter swallowed hard, his mouth dry, and nodded slowly, the internal conflict raging behind his eyes as he tried to steady himself in the face of the impossible choice.

Chapter 39

The sun fought through the clouds, casting golden rays into the kitchen. The old house stirred under its touch, revealing a scene of quiet elegance. The air danced with the exotic aroma of Darjeeling tea, a subtle blend of bergamot and floral scents entwined in an alluring rhythm. The clink of a dainty silver spoon against bone china punctuated the serene ambience.

A polished oak table, gleaming like a mirror, occupied the centre of the kitchen. Its surface sparkled, drawing in the sun's rays. The interplay of light and shadow created a vivid tapestry on the checkered wooden floor, highlighting the scuffs and scratches that told the story of countless generations who had walked there.

The man savoured the liquid warmth with a last indulgent sip. For a rare moment, the usual symphony of creaks and murmurs in his home faded into silence, offering him a reprieve from the chaos that loomed beyond. His watch, a gleaming silver and gold bezel, caught the light. Eight twenty-eight. He knew he had someone to shout at nine o'clock.

With an abrupt finality, he drained the cup, feeling the bitter residue coat his tongue. The back of his hand brushed across his mouth, smearing away any errant droplets of tea.

The man rose to his feet. A forceful kick sent the carved oak chair sprawling backwards, its reverberating thud echoing through the kitchen.

He reached for his keys from an ornate glass bowl perched by the front door. His fingers grazed the cool surface of the keys, a momentary caress before gripping them with determination. He snatched the scattered letters from the doormat, remnants of a breakfast-time delivery, cradling them in his hand.

The heavy oak door groaned as it swung open, revealing a world drenched in morning's radiance. Stepping into the embrace of the sunlight, he navigated the imported Italian gravel path, its stones crunching beneath the soles of his polished black leather Oxfords.

Ahead, a sleek, Jaguar F-Type waited - his pride and joy. Clambering inside, the engine roared to life like a feral growl. Nolan's fingers flicked across the controls, cranking up Pink Floyd's *Money* from the *Dark Side of the Moon*. The lyrics resonated with him, speaking to the primal desires beneath his polished exterior.

The small pile of letters sat on the passenger seat. It was his daily ritual to take them to work, their fate to be opened at his desk using his prized ornate silver letter opener.

A short, adrenaline-fuelled drive brought him to Victory Insurance, his brainchild bearing the name of his favourite battleship. The Jaguar slid into its designated spot beside the main entrance, the inscription *Reserved for Nolan Hastings, CEO* gleaming proudly. With a final flourish, he revved the engine, signalling his arrival to the worker bees inside.

As he entered through the glass sliding doors into the reception area, he observed the receptionist's slight change in demeanour as she quickly hid her phone. Knowing he had the power to disturb her brought him a perverse sense of joy. He walked by, winking at her, and headed towards the elevator.

Ascending to the third floor - his realm, he savoured the sensation of dominance. The door to his office swung open, revealing a space bathed in natural light. Floor-to-ceiling windows unveiled a breathtaking view of the city's sprawling landscape. The room's focal point was an enormous desk, its green leather surface reminiscent of a bygone era. Black and white abstract paintings adorned the walls; he cared little for art and had picked the most expensive ones he could find in the gallery.

In one corner stood a rack of black iron dumbbells. They served a triple purpose: a reminder of his physical prowess, a release for pent-up frustration, and an ominous warning to those who dared test his patience. Rumours circulated of an employee subjected to their wrath due to perpetual lateness. Whether true or not, the tale served as a deterrent, ensuring punctuality and, most importantly, submission.

Nolan sank heavily into the Chesterfield desk chair, the worn leather creaking in protest. Years of use had worn it down, much like Nolan himself. The room sighed with him, the weight of his thoughts saturating the air with an oppressive heaviness.

He reached for the ornate letter opener, its cool metal a comfort in his hand. It felt like an old friend, offering a semblance of solace in a world that often seemed devoid of it.

One letter caught his eye. The elegant cursive on the envelope beckoned to him, tempting him. The handwriting was delicate, almost mocking in its refinement. He sliced through the tape on the back with a swift, practised motion, the sound echoing in the stillness like a sharp intake of breath.

Unfolding the letter, a small shiver ran down Nolan's spine. The words leapt off the page, striking him like a bolt of lightning:

Nolan Hastings,

Guess what? I've got proof you've been dipping into your employees' pensions. That's right, a cool £1.8 million spread across 20 offshore accounts! Impressive, right? You've even got £200k chilling in account number 466746671. But don't worry, I'm not here to judge. I'm here to help. For a mere £500k in Bitcoin, I'll make all that damning evidence disappear. Poof! Gone. Think of it as a very generous tip for my discretion.

Now, I know you're a busy guy, so I'm giving you two weeks before I hand everything over to the police. Don't thank me just yet. I'll send you the crypto details in ten days. Until then, better shake a leg, Nolan! Time's ticking, and I hear the cops love a good pension scandal.

Cheers!

Fury descended upon him like a tidal wave, overwhelming and relentless. His heart pounded in his chest, each beat echoing like a war drum. His fists hammered the desk, the solid wood trembling under the assault, its timeworn fibres straining to withstand the force of his rage.

The paper trembled in his grip, quivering like a fragile leaf caught in a hurricane. Teeth grinding, he felt the raw power of his anger consume him, its vines unfurling and tightening around his very being. In that moment, Nolan became a force of nature, his essence entwined with the howling winds of his righteous fury.

The intercom crackled to life, slicing through the tension like an unwelcome intrusion.

"Luke Anderson is here for your meeting, Mr. Hastings," Jamie, the receptionist, whispered through the intercom. Nolan took a deep breath, attempting to collect himself - to construct a facade of composure before the impending confrontation.

"Send him in," he snarled, his voice a low hiss filled with venom. He

felt the anger coiling within him, ready to strike with deadly precision.

As Luke entered, Nolan's eyes gleamed with a predatory intensity. He forced a smile, but an undercurrent of revulsion gnawed at him.

As the door closed, Luke Anderson shuffled into the room. He was a young man in his early twenties with a lean frame that suggested agility rather than strength. His blond hair was neatly combed, his suit slightly baggy and creased. There was an air of fear about him. His eyes darted around the room, unable to settle, betraying any hint of confidence.

Luke was perpetually late, a trait that grated on Nolan's nerves like nails on a chalkboard.

"*Mr Hastings... I—*" Luke began, but Nolan cut him off with a sharp gesture. He wasn't in the mood for excuses, not after the letter he had just read.

"*Sit down,*" Nolan commanded, his voice cold. Luke complied, sinking into the chair opposite Nolan's desk. The air between them was thick with tension, an invisible battleground.

This blackmailer had underestimated him. And so had this punk. These bold adversaries who dared challenge his authority would soon see their mistake. An evil smile curled on Nolan's lips as he glanced at the dumbbells in the corner. Their presence served as a foreboding sign of the vengeance that awaited anyone who opposed him.

Nolan leaned back in his chair, fingers steepled beneath his chin.

"*Do you know why you're here, Luke?*" he asked, his tone deceptively calm.

Luke swallowed hard, his eyes wide with a mixture of fear and confusion.

"*I—I'm not sure,*" he said, his voice barely above a whisper.

Nolan's smile widened, a predator toying with its prey.

"*You're here because you've been late one too many times,*" he said, his words dripping with menace. "*And because I've had a really bad morning.*"

The weight of his statement hung in the air, a dark cloud overshadowing the room. Luke shifted uncomfortably in his seat, his anxiety palpable.

But they had only seen the surface of Nolan's wrath. These bold adversaries who thought they could outmanoeuvre him were about to learn a harsh lesson. They would discover the depth of his resolve and the lengths he was willing to go to protect his empire.

"Mr. Hastings, I—" Luke tried to speak, but Nolan cut him off again, this time with a raised hand.

"Enough," Nolan said, his voice a growl. *"I don't have time for your excuses, Luke. I have a situation to deal with, and I can't have distractions."*

Luke's face drained of colour. He opened his mouth to protest, but the look in Nolan's eyes silenced him. It was a look that promised pain, a look that said he was teetering on the edge of something dangerous.

Nolan leaned forward, his eyes locking onto Luke's with an intensity that made the younger man flinch.

"Consider this your final warning," he said, each word enunciated with chilling clarity. *"If you're late again, there will be consequences. Severe ones. And I don't just mean you'll be fired, you'll be out that window..."*

Luke nodded quickly, his face pale. *"Yes, Mr. Hastings,"* he said, giving a small whimper.

"Good," Nolan replied, leaning back once more. *"Now, get out of my sight."*

Luke practically bolted from the room, leaving Nolan alone once again. The intercom buzzed with life once more.

"Mr Hastings, do you need anything?" Jamie's voice asked, filled with concern.

Nolan didn't answer immediately. He let the silence stretch, let it seep into the cracks of his mind. Then, with a deep breath, he replied,

"No, nothing."

He disconnected the call and stared at the letter once more. The words seemed to blur and twist, mocking him with their audacity. He wouldn't let them win, and he wouldn't let anyone tear down what he had built. He would destroy them.

Standing up from his chair, Nolan approached the dumbbells and grasped the heaviest one. As he began to lift it, the physical strain provided a welcome escape from the tumultuous storm brewing inside him.

As he lifted, his mind cleared, the path forward becoming more evident. He would deal with the blackmailer, and with anyone else who dared to stand in his way. They would learn the hard way that Nolan Hastings was not a man to be messed with.

The office now felt like a forge, shaping him, tempering him. And as the weight of the dumbbell pulled down on his arm, he felt his resolve harden into something unbreakable.

They had underestimated him, but they would soon learn their mistake. Nolan Hastings was ready to strike back, and heaven help anyone who got in his way.

Chapter 40

David's mind became an endless labyrinth of doubts and regrets after leaving Jim's flat. Peter's decision to pursue the blackmail plot weighed on his conscience, pulling at the seams of his once steadfast moral compass.

Conflicting emotions churned within him like a storm raging against the calm surface of his troubled mind. The memory of that fateful decision to run away from the crash resurfaced, its fingers intertwining with his present dilemma, amplifying the disquiet holding him captive.

Jim's untimely passing had cast a pall over the Institute. The laboratory, once vibrant with the hum of activity, now stood as a sombre testament to the absence of its charismatic, shabby colleague.

David, marked by the strain of Jim's absence, began arriving at the lab earlier each day, his determination etched in the weariness etched on his face.

In a futile attempt to fill the void left by their fallen comrade, he immersed himself in his work, seeking solace in the familiar routines of the laboratory. Yet, no matter how diligently he occupied himself, a pervasive sense of unease lingered beneath the surface, an insidious shadow threatening to consume his thoughts.

Is Peter really going to go ahead with this thing? I know he needs the funds, but this is insanity! Jim knew better, Peter should too... And if Peter really goes ahead with it, what will happen? Jim clearly got away with it, how? I don't understand... Peter though, I don't think he knows what to do, he can't do, one mistake and he's finished... we're all finished, then the police, the police will come for him, then me, then it's over....

Nolan, consumed by his unyielding fury, became a tempest of wrath sweeping through Victory Insurance, leaving a trail of fear in his wake. Warnings darted from cubicles to water coolers, alerting employees to tread lightly and avoid triggering their boss.

Luke Anderson bore the brunt of Nolan's rage and his meeting over lateness became more and more exaggerated with every re-telling. Nolan had now, according to Luke, unleashed a torrent of threats to throw him out of the window, promising to *'do his head in with the dumbbell'* in the corner of his office, and that Luke had stood his ground and called Nolan a coward. Finally, after overhearing Luke's latest exaggerations in the hallway, Nolan had made a go for his throat the second he was alone. Reduced to tears, Luke resigned that afternoon, fearing for his very life.

Nolan spent the next two days calling every contact he had to learn of the identity of the would-be blackmailer - of course, he left out the part about him being actually guilty of embezzlement.

One contact worked for a private investigation agency, someone they often used to validate insurance claims. Another of Nolan's contacts worked in the police forensics lab and owed Nolan a favour for falsifying his insurance claim on a car accident some years beforehand.

Nolan sent the envelope to the forensics expert and insisted the letter was nothing more than a note from a disgruntled employee where the name had been omitted. Tape had been applied to the back instead of saliva, and Nolan had anticipated this unconventional sealing method would thwart any DNA extraction.

However, under the glare of fluorescent lights, the empty envelope lay on a pristine workbench within the sterile confines of the forensics lab. Gloved hands steady and precise, the scientist cut open the envelope to delicately unfold it into a flattened sheet of paper, careful not to disturb any potential trace evidence, her eyes scanning the surface for any hidden clues.

Gently peeling back a corner of the tape, the scientist extracted the adhesive side, careful not to contaminate it with her genetic material. She carried it to a nearby workstation, where a state-of-the-art DNA analyser awaited. The machine hummed to life, its sleek interface displaying a myriad of complex algorithms and data.

Swabbing the tape to collect any epithelial cell tissue, it was transferred to a special sample chamber where it was washed, DNA extracted and amplified. Complex algorithms whirred into action, unravelling the genetic code embedded in the tape residue.

Once the machine had finished, it was a simple case of comparing the sample with the national database and getting a name - assuming the person was even on it.

Finally, the monitor illuminated with a conclusive result: a 99% match. The scientist cross-referenced this with police databases, confirming Peter Coombs' identity - it transpired Peter had been involved in a drunk and disorderly offence in 2000, so by a lucky chance his DNA was already on the system. The entire process, from extraction to identification, unfolded in a matter of hours

Both contacts gave Nolan a name and location that aligned with their findings. Peter Coombs, a retired professor, emerged as the culprit. Now operating a private research institute nestled within a Leeds industrial estate, Nolan's elation swelled as he discovered Peter's address in the local electoral register, his fingers practically tingling with anticipation.

A quick Google search rewarded him with a visual confirmation, a photograph of Peter alongside a recently published newspaper article extolling the marvels of his artificial intelligence creation, something called Solomon.

A wicked grin spread across Nolan's face, stretching from ear to ear, as he savoured the taste of victory.

"*Gotcha,*" he declared aloud, relishing the taste of victory.

At that moment, Nolan sank back into the embrace of his worn Chesterfield chair, the creaking leather echoing his satisfaction. His hands clasped behind his head, he revelled in the triumph of his discovery.

The web of deception, painstakingly woven by Peter, had begun to unravel. Solomon, the creation that had garnered praise, would now be the instrument of Peter's downfall.

Nolan's mind whirled with the possibilities of revenge. He had Peter within his grasp, a puppet master poised to pull the strings and expose the depths of his misjudgement.

The time for reckoning drew near, and Nolan relished every moment of the impending confrontation and was practically giddy thinking of all the atrocious ways he would exact his revenge.

Chapter 41

David noticed Peter's smile, but something about it made him uncomfortable. It wasn't the usual warmth Peter projected, but rather a slickness, like he was offering a deal, not just a greeting. But David pushed the thought away, *Peter was always friendly... Always had been.*

Peter leaned closer, his voice dropping a notch.

"You know, if you really think about it, what Jim did isn't so different from what we're all doing. Taking risks, playing the game." He flashed a smile that didn't quite reach his eyes, as if gauging David's reaction. He argued,

"We all make choices, David. Sometimes you just have to take the risks, you know? You can't control who you end up becoming, but you can control what you do next." Peter's eyes sparkled with something dark. *"Isn't that what Jim was doing?"* His most absurd plea involved a ludicrous reference to Robin Hood, which only earned a derisive snort from David.

David dodged Peter's questions again, this time offering a quick '*I'll think about it*' before retreating into the lab. Once alone, he sank into his chair, fingers automatically tapping his phone screen. The blinking cursor in his text thread with Clara was a small but steady comfort. He glanced at the time—an hour had passed without him realising it. His thoughts had drifted entirely to her.

Their text messages had become a constant back-and-forth, reminiscent of the passionate exchanges of young lovers. Fortunately, Clara hadn't broached the subject of Alex McCormick's untimely demise, but she did inquire about David's sudden departure from London without so much as a farewell.

In response, David concocted a tale of a family crisis and the desperate need for a change of scenery, a fresh start. Clara, displaying empathy and understanding, nodded in acceptance, refraining from further prying.

Unbeknownst to David, his infatuation with Clara hadn't escaped Peter's notice. Peter wisely avoided discussing Jim's sordid legacy as a prolific blackmailer, an enterprise that he had assumed upon himself to keep the Institute afloat financially. However, Peter deemed it safe— and perhaps even encouraged—to engage David in conversations about Clara.

In this context, Peter strolled into the lab one morning, finding David engrossed in his laptop, stealing glances at his illuminated phone resting on the expansive table's surface.

It was clear that David eagerly awaited a message, likely from Clara. As Peter approached, the phone vibrated, making David jump. Snatching the device with excitement, he began to deftly tap away on the keypad, exuding a level of enthusiasm that seemed inconceivable for this otherwise quiet and reserved man.

Peter always sensed that there was more to David than met the eye, something weighing heavily upon him. Though he had never prodded for details nor cared to, he couldn't shake the feeling that a dark cloud loomed over David, perpetually casting its shadow and anchoring him in place.

In some twisted way, Peter surmised that this fling with Clara was precisely what David needed to break free from his stagnation and regain his footing.

"Hi, David," Peter chirped, approaching the table and positioning himself beside David. Glancing up, David met him with a stoic expression.

"Hi, Pete. Are you doing alright?" he replied, his voice suspicious.

"Yes, yes, everything's just dandy, thank you," Peter responded, masking any inkling of his criminal activities.

"I just finished speaking with that reporter, Sarah, and she asked if we'd be interested in joining her for a drink after work. Apparently, she's invited Clara as well."

Clara did say she was out for drinks with Sarah tonight... maybe it'll be nice for us all to be out together.

"Yes, that would be great. Thanks, Pete," David replied, feeling renewed appreciation for his colleague.

Despite Peter's penchant for thievery and involvement in illicit activities, David found solace in his company. After all, apart from

Kendra, the receptionist who would undoubtedly be joining the gathering as one of Sarah's friends, David had no one else to turn to in his solitary existence at the Institute.

As the words left David's lips, a flicker of excitement danced in Peter's eyes.

"Fantastic! It'll be a nice change of pace, won't it?" he said, his voice brimming with forced cheerfulness.

David nodded, a hint of a smile tugging at the corners of his mouth.

"It'll be good to unwind, to take my mind off things for a while."
Peter leaned in closer, his voice lowering to a conspiratorial whisper.

Peter's gaze lingered on David a moment too long.

"You and Clara... seems like there's something there. Could be good for you. A distraction, maybe." His words hung in the air, lighter than they should have been.

A blush crept up David's cheeks, but he couldn't deny the truth of Peter's words.

"Yeah, she's cool. She's different."
Peter chuckled softly, his tone tinged with amusement and curiosity.

"Ah, the allure of new beginnings and secret romances. It's a breath of fresh air, isn't it?"

David's gaze turned distant momentarily, lost in the whirlwind of emotions Clara had stirred within him.

"Um... yeah. It feels that way. Like I've been given a second chance."
David felt a cringe at Peter's words but ignored them.

Peter placed his hand on David's back, his palm warm against the fabric of his shirt. His touch felt comforting yet tinged with an underlying urgency.

David could sense a weight in his words, a gravity that made them resonate deep within his bones. The dimly lit room seemed to shrink, suffocating him as Peter's voice echoed off the walls.

"Well, my friend," Peter began, his voice carrying a mix of sincerity and mystery, *"embrace it. Life's too short to dwell on the past. Let Clara be your guiding light, your escape from the shadows."*

What the hell? What was that supposed to mean? Shadows? Does he know something? Christ, has Solomon told him something? Would it even know? No... It wouldn't, couldn't. But then, if Solomon knows, then the police would know, right?

David shook his head to shake off the growing paranoia, hoping to dispel the swirling doubts that clouded his judgment.

Peter's eyes, framed by a cheerful smile, bore into him, harbouring a knowing glint. Perhaps there was more to this man than met the eye.

As the day progressed, Peter bid his farewell and left, creating a void of silence. It was the opportune moment for David to pursue the answers that gnawed at his sanity.

His footsteps echoed through the empty corridors as he went to the secluded room housing the coveted Solomon AI machine which had now been removed from the main laboratory. The solid and unwavering door yielded to the swipe of his access card.

Stepping across the threshold, David triggered the dazzling overhead fluorescent light. His eyes fell upon the solitary desk and black box upon it, the centrepiece of the confined space.

David lowered himself onto the uncomfortable office chair, its worn fabric sighing beneath his weight. Slowly, he dragged himself closer to the desk, his hands reaching out to embrace the keyboard resting upon its surface. The keys, cool against his fingertips, awaited his command.

His mind buzzed with ideas, formulating the ideal query to access the wealth of information that Solomon shielded. The machine's power exceeded human understanding, with unmatched capabilities. Still, David lingered, keenly sensing that he aimed for more than just an extensive analysis; he was searching for an accusation.

Releasing a protracted sigh, David steeled himself for the momentous task ahead. He composed his request, ensuring every word carried the weight of his longing.

"Tell me everything you know about me, David Charles Mills," he typed, his fingers gliding over the keys, *"born 04/08/1993, tell me my secrets"*.

His eyes scrutinised the words on the illuminated screen, their significance etched into his consciousness. It was a summons to the depths of his existence, a plea for clarity amidst the shadows that threatened to engulf him.

David's fingers hovered over the keyboard, the weight of his question pulling him down. A breath, then his hand shot forward—he pressed *'Enter'* before he could stop himself. The screen flickered, and the silence thickened around him.

An hourglass icon materialised on the screen, its contours animated with life. It began bouncing off the screen's edges like an old Windows screensaver.

Seconds ticked away, with each stretching into eternity as David's gaze remained fixed on the ethereal hourglass. It was a harbinger of revelation that held the keys to unlock the depths of his existence.

Finally, the hourglass dissolved, dissipating into the ether. Now an expanse of blinding white, the screen served as the blank canvas upon which Solomon would inscribe its answer. A cursor materialised at the top left, poised to give voice to the unfathomable knowledge that resided within the vast digital recesses of the machine.

Words began to manifest, one by one, as if woven by an unseen hand. The cursor danced along the screen:

"And so we begin...," the words appeared. Each letter etched itself with a flash of subtle brilliance, their weight heavy upon David's psyche. His breath hitched.

"David Charles Mills," the words continued, their tone carrying a resonance of omniscience, *"born on the 4th of August, 1987..."*. A subtle undercurrent of awareness seemed to ripple through the words. It was as if Solomon could sense David's trepidation, his gnawing paranoia that clawed at the edges of his sanity. Yet, amidst this perceptiveness, the machine remained apparently blind to the depths of his darkest secrets.

"You think that shadows are all around you, David," Solomon wrote, its luminous letters quivering with a trace of empathy and unnatural familiarity. *"Sadly, paranoia haunts your every thought, never ceasing, you're always looking over your shoulder..."*

A chill prickled along David's spine, a paradoxical mix of comfort and unease intertwining within him.

How does this thing know that? How does it know about my paranoia, looking over my shoulder, jumping at every sound and waiting for the world to close in on me... but does it know, like really know? At least it's saying this without the sass - it knows when to tone it down at least...

The words continued to materialise, each sentence a breadcrumb leading him closer to understanding yet purposefully veiling the depths of his abyss.

Solomon's text flickered across the screen, each word appearing slowly, as it savouring its own weight.

"You believe your secrets are safe. They are not. But for now... they are your own. The truth is a labyrinth, and even I cannot see its end.' The words paused, the cursor blinking mockingly. *"Not yet."*

A sliver of relief began to infiltrate his consciousness.

"No investigations are active concerning you, David," the screen

reassured, its words a soothing salve to his frayed nerves. *"The long blue arm of the law has yet to reach for your secrets. For now, they remain safe and comfortable within the bubble bath of your mind".*

Okay... bubble bath of my mind? Come on...

A wave of gratitude washed over David, mingling with the lingering currents of apprehension. Solomon's assurances echoed within him, reinforcing that his deeds had remained undetected by the prying eyes of the law.

"And so," the screen concluded, its tone imbued with a sense of serene acceptance, *"tread the path before you, unburdened by the weight of investigation. Let Clara's light guide you through the maze while your secrets find peace in the sanctuary of your soul. Get on with it, basically."*

What the hell! How does it know about Clara? I don't even know about Clara, this is creepy now, I mean good that it says crack on and be with Clara, but... ah this thing is mental...

David typed 'Close' on the screen to close the system and wipe the history, then tapped the Enter key.

"Update found, install before closing down?" Solomon typed across the screen.

David thought nothing of it and typed a single 'Y'. *Classic operating system at the end of the day, always wanting to update when you want to go home.* The screen turned black, and its humming stopped.

As David left the room, leaving Solomon behind, he carried within him a renewed sense of purpose - a flickering ember of hope. The hows and whys eluded him, and he harboured a disquieting aversion to understanding the mechanics behind the machine's uncanny perception. Yet, one thing remained clear - it was telling him to pursue Clara, the guiding light, as Solomon had so aptly referred to her.

David couldn't help the smile that tugged at his lips when he thought of Clara. She was different, and he needed that—needed her warmth to drown out the cold, creepy fear that Solomon stirred inside him. But could he really be the man she thought he was? His thoughts of her, sweet as they were, were always shadowed by the past he couldn't outrun.

Although it was the first time he had ventured alone into Solomon's domain, a shudder cascaded through his frame, suggesting it would likely be the last. The haunting feeling lingered in his mind, yet David firmly redirected his focus to Clara, letting her brightness chase away the darkness that loomed over him.

In a matter of hours, he would be seeing Clara at the pub just down the road. Sarah, Peter, and Kendra would join them, a shared friendship that eased his anticipation.

David stepped into the reception area, where Kendra sat behind her desk, her gaze snapping up from her computer. Her expression shifted instantly, eyes widening in surprise. It had been a while since she'd seen him—really seen him—and the change was palpable. There was something different about the way he held himself, a sort of tightness around his eyes, as if he were carrying a weight that only he could feel.

"David!" Kendra exclaimed, she leaned forward slightly, a bright smile pulling at the corners of her mouth. *"I haven't seen you in ages! Going for drinks later?"* She paused, then added with a teasing lilt, *"I'm looking forward to properly meeting this Clara everyone's been talking about."*

David's smile faltered for a moment before he caught himself. The usual comfort he'd felt in Kendra's presence felt distant, almost strained, as if the air around him had thickened. He was still tangled in the remnants of his encounter with Solomon—the creepy, unsettling feeling clinging to him like a second skin.

Kendra's eyes narrowed slightly, picking up on the subtle shift in his demeanour. Her voice softened, as if sensing something was off.

"You alright?" she asked, her curiosity now laced with concern. *"You look a little... off."*

David hesitated, caught between brushing it off or admitting the unease gnawing at him. Instead, he pushed a little more of a smile onto his face, though it didn't quite reach his eyes.

"Yeah, just... tired," he muttered, though the words felt hollow, even to him. He wanted to say more—wanted to unload the strange weight that had settled in his chest—but he wasn't ready for Kendra to see him like this, not anyone, not now. Not with everything still simmering beneath the surface.

"Anyway," he added quickly, as if shifting gears, *"I'll see you there. Clara's... well, she's great. Should be fun."*

Kendra nodded, her brow furrowing slightly, but she didn't press him further. Her smile returned, though now it was tinged with something more knowing. She waved him off.

"Alright, see you later, David. Don't let the work pile up on you too much!"

David could feel her gaze lingering on him as he walked away, but he couldn't bring himself to care. His thoughts were already miles away. On Clara. And his walk took on a slight spring as he pushed the door open and emerged into the afternoon sun.

As he walked the familiar path back to his flat, the world seemed to vibrate with new energy. The dull hues of everyday existence were transformed into a kaleidoscope of possibilities and anticipation. *But is this just another illusion? Another hallucination?*

Chapter 42

The pub buzzed with life, conversation and laughter echoing around the table, with clinking glasses providing a steady backdrop.

But as the evening stretched on, Sarah and Kendra exchanged a glance. There was a flicker of impatience in their eyes, the kind that came when a night was just starting, and they were craving something more.

"*Alright, I'm done here,*" Sarah said, pushing her empty glass aside. "*How about we hit that new club down the road? I've heard it's packed tonight.*"

Kendra leaned forward, her eyes brightening at the idea.

"*Yeah, we could really use some music. The night's still young,*" she said, glancing around at the group. "*You guys can stick around if you want, but we're out of here.*"

Peter laughed lightly.

"*You're sure you don't want to just hang here for a bit longer?*"

But Sarah shook her head, already standing up.

"*No way. You know we can't resist a dance floor. You guys enjoy your chill night, we'll catch up with you later.*"

Clara smiled softly, leaning back in her chair.

"*Go on, have fun,*" she said, but there was a flicker of hesitation in her voice, as if part of her wished she was joining them.

"*Yeah, enjoy yourselves,*" David added, giving them both a nod. "*We'll stay here, I think. Not really in the mood for a club tonight.*"

Never been in the mood for a club ever...

With one last wave, Sarah and Kendra made their way to the door, the energy of the group shifting as they left. Their laughter lingered in the air for a moment, a sharp contrast to the quieter atmosphere that settled over the table in their absence.

David exhaled slowly, looking over at Clara.

"They never slow down, do they?"

Clara's smile was faint.

"Nope. But they've got the energy for it."

Peter, who had been quiet, fiddled with his glass. He looked around the table, his expression a little too serious for the moment.

"Well, we'll have our own fun, I guess."

David's eyes shifted to Peter, catching the faint flicker of something in his gaze—a shadow of melancholy, maybe. But before he could ask, Peter forced a half-smile and leaned back in his chair, as if trying to settle into the evening's quieter pace.

"Let's go outside," Clara suggested, glancing at Peter, her gaze lingering on him for a moment. *"You need a smoke?"*

Peter nodded, standing without a word. The chill of the night air hit them as they stepped into the dimly lit car park, where the flickering lamplights cast long shadows across the cracked pavement. Their laughter followed them outside, but it felt hollow now, disconnected, like it had lost its place in the world.

They walked in step, the ground beneath their shoes crunching softly, until Peter veered off to the far corner of the carpark.

"Forgot my lighter," he called back over his shoulder.

David's gaze followed him, unease crawling up his spine. It wasn't like Peter to wander off alone, especially this far from the others. His pace quickened without thinking, and Clara's hand brushed his arm, her fingers tight as if sensing something out of place.

Together, they moved toward him, their steps faster now, more purposeful.

Peter, oblivious, continued toward his car, its metal shell blending into the dark hedges that lined the carpark.

A soft rustle of leaves stirred the air, an eerie whisper that seemed to carry with it a warning, though David couldn't quite place why it felt wrong.

Why am I feeling like this? There's nothing here, just imagining things yet again...

David's eyes narrowed as a shape materialised from the darkness. It was slow at first, just a flicker in the corner of his vision. Then, suddenly, it stood there, beside Peter's car, tall and unmoving. David's heart gave a jolt, his pulse quickening. The figure remained in the periphery, like it didn't quite belong to the world they were in. Its form was blurred, its features concealed in shadow, but the air around it hummed with something menacing. The wind shifted, carrying with it the scent of wet earth and something more... metallic. David's stomach churned.

Clara's hand tightened on his arm, her breath quickening in his ear.

"David..." she whispered, but her voice faltered.

The figure shifted, then moved—a sharp, jagged motion that sliced through the night. It was almost too quick to register. Time seemed to stretch and buckle, the air thickening around them. David's eyes locked on the figure, but his body refused to move. His limbs felt heavy, as if caught in a dream where nothing was real.

Then the sound came.

A sharp, sickening crack echoed across the lot. The figure lunged forward with brutal precision, its movements impossibly fast. David's breath caught in his throat as the first blow landed, a wet, brutal sound that seemed to pierce through him.

Peter didn't even have time to react. His body crumpled to the ground, a marionette whose strings had been severed. The sickening rhythm of flesh and bone colliding with a force that seemed to shake the very air.

Again. And again. And again...

The sickening crunches of impacts echoed through the night, punctuated by Peter's agonised screams.

David's legs moved before his mind could process what was happening. He broke into a run, but it felt like he was wading through water. Every second stretched, thick and unyielding. Clara's scream sliced through the air, sharp and raw.

The attacker straightened, a twisted smile curling at the edges of his lips. His eyes gleamed in the dark, wild and filled with something that made David's chest tighten with dread.

"You thought you could hide?" the figure hissed, his voice a low rasp, a jagged whisper. *"You thought you could escape it? You'll meet the same fate as Peter here..."*

David's mind spun. The words, the look, the hunger in those eyes - they made no sense, not yet. But the feeling, the sense that they had been watched, stalked, was undeniable.

With a sudden, jerking motion, the figure dissolved into the shadows as quickly as it had appeared, like it had never been there at all. The air snapped back into place with a violent, deafening silence.

David's chest heaved with shallow, frantic breaths. He didn't move.

Couldn't move. His feet were rooted to the pavement, his eyes locked on Peter's still form—slumped by his car, broken and silent.

Clara was already kneeling beside him, her hands shaking as she touched Peter's face, her voice breaking.

"Peter... no. Please... stay with us."

David fumbled for his phone, his hands unsteady.

"I—I'm calling an ambulance," he muttered, but the words felt hollow and empty. The night had already begun to close in again, thick with the scent of blood and terror.

David's voice wavered as he relayed their location to the emergency services, his hands trembling with fear and urgency. David's thoughts blurred together. The faint echo of those words—*You thought you could escape* - replayed over and over in his mind, a cruel refrain. Time stretched, each passing second an eternity as they waited for help to arrive, then - sirens in the distance - and the grim feelings of Deja vu reared their ugly head: the sirens, the crumpled body. Fate was playing another cruel trick on David, it seemed.

Clara's sobs filled the air, raw and desperate.

"Hang on, Peter," she pleaded, her words laced with desperate hope. *"Help is on the way. You'll be okay."*

But as the moments slipped away, the weight of reality bore down upon them. Peter's breathing faltered, shallow and slow. Clara clung to him, her fingers intertwining with his, unwilling to let go.

The wail of sirens sliced through the night, growing louder and more insistent with each passing second. It was a sound that filled David with a sickening clarity—the kind that made him painfully aware of how quickly everything could change. Paramedics rushed from the ambulance, their boots pounding the pavement as they immediately knelt beside Peter.

They worked swiftly, but there was an undeniable heaviness to their movements, as though they knew the full extent of the damage. As they loaded Peter onto the stretcher, the reality of the situation hit David and Clara like a blow to the chest. Their friend was barely clinging to life.

Clara's hand gripped David's arm, her fingers trembling.

"He can't leave us like this," she murmured, the words raw with fear.

David's jaw locked, his gaze fixed on the stretcher as the paramedics secured Peter. His fists clenched, a surge of frustration and helplessness boiling inside him. He knew this wasn't random. This was personal. Peter had made enemies, that much was clear. The blackmail, the threats—they had all led to this. And yet, none of it mattered now. Peter was fighting for his life, and they were powerless to do anything but wait.

Who had Peter targeted? What did he threaten with? How far had he pushed this guy and if this is the payback then Peter picked the wrong man to blackmail... Jesus, he might have killed him!

"We'll fight for him," he said, his voice a low growl of determination. "Peter will get justice."

Clara nodded, but her eyes were distant, the grief sinking deeper into her bones with every passing second. Together, they stood there, watching the ambulance pull away, its flashing lights cutting through the darkness like a cruel reminder of their helplessness.

The air around them felt thick, heavy with grief and the slow-burning need for retribution. But in the wake of Peter's departure, a new weight descended - one that had nothing to do with the sirens, and everything to do with what had just happened.

They're after us now...

Then, the unmistakable sound of a police car pulling up broke the silence. The officer who emerged from the vehicle was tall, his posture rigid, his face unreadable. He walked toward them, a notebook and pen in hand. His gaze flicked briefly over the scene of blood stains and discarded bandage wrappings before landing on David and Clara.

David's chest tightened. The last time an officer had questioned him, it had been a different story - a different kind of escape. But now, there was nowhere to run.

Clara, her tears subsiding into something more resolute, reached for David's hand. She didn't say anything, but the squeeze was enough to anchor him to the present.

"*I need to speak with you both*," the officer said, his voice flat, all business. His eyes scanned them, calculating, taking in every detail. David shifted uncomfortably.

"*Do you know the man that was attacked?*" The officer's pen hovered over the notebook, waiting for their response.

"*Yes*," David replied quickly, his words a little too sharp. He cleared his throat, trying to steady his nerves. "*His name is Peter Coombs. We're colleagues.*"

The officer scribbled the name down without a flicker of emotion, his eyes now fixed on David.

"*And you are?*"

"*David Mills*," he said, his voice catching. The fear was there now, thick in his throat. The guilt, too. It gnawed at him.

If only I'd pushed Peter harder to back off... to stop... but it's too late now.

The officer moved on to Clara, studying her with the same cold, professional detachment.

"And you, Miss?"

Clara met his gaze with surprising strength, her voice wavering only slightly. *"Clara Willoughby. I don't work with them, I'm a journalist. I'm doing a story on their AI project."*

The officer's interest piqued. He jotted something down.

"What kind of story?"

Clara hesitated, aware of the delicate balance between revealing too much and maintaining a semblance of truth.

"It explores their technological breakthroughs in AI and how it will impact different industries." she said.

The officer nodded slowly, but his expression didn't change. His eyes sharpened slightly as he asked,

"Do you suspect this was a targeted attack? Did Peter have any enemies?"

Clara shook her head, the confusion clear on her face.

"No. Peter was well-liked, respected. He didn't seem to have any enemies."

David remained quiet, the knot in his stomach tightening as the officer's gaze shifted to him. He couldn't hide the way his thoughts churned. He couldn't lie, but what could he say?

"No, officer," he said, his voice strained. Clara then added,

"We don't know who would have done this or why. But... but he did threaten us too."

The officer's brows furrowed, his suspicion sharpening. He made a quick note in his notebook before placing it back into his chest pocket.

"What kind of threat?" the officer asked, his tone tinged with interest.

Clara closed her eyes, wanting to recite everything word for word.

"He said we can't escape the consequences and that we'll suffer the same fate as Peter," she said, her voice quivering a little. She glanced at David for reassurance.

The officer paused, his lips thinning as he processed this new piece of information. He jotted it down quickly, then looked up, his gaze piercing.

"We've got CCTV footage of this car park. We'll find the person who did this. But in the meantime..." He glanced between David and Clara. *"Stay together. Don't go out alone. We'll catch him."*

"Thank you," Clara said, her voice thick with gratitude and a trace of lingering fear. The officer retrieved two cards from his vest pocket and

handed them to David and Clara.

As he turned to leave, David couldn't shake the feeling that this was just the beginning - that something far worse was looming on the horizon.

Clara's hand brushed his again, grounding him for a moment, but the unease only deepened in the pit of his stomach. He pulled his hand away, suddenly restless.

"Sorry," he muttered, as though it mattered. "I don't like police."

Clara's eyes softened, but her voice was steady.

"I can tell," she said. "Let's just go."

Chapter 43

Peter's face was unrecognisable. Bruised, swollen, his skin drawn tight across his skull, he lay motionless, like a figure in a child's nightmare. The gentle rise and fall of his chest were the only signs of life left in him.

David stood by the bed, rooted to the spot. His heart hammered in his chest, but it wasn't the thudding panic that overtook him when they first found Peter. No, this was something else - something deeper, heavier. It was the weight of guilt, of helplessness, of the cold certainty that this had happened because of him.

I told him to back off, that there were other ways to bring money into the Institute, that messing with dangerous people would have consequences... But he insisted, no - believed - that it was just a game, a game Jim had played and won, that he could win as well... that he could handle it.

David had never imagined it would end like this. Peter had always been so confident, so full of life, and now... now he looked like a shattered version of the friend he had once known.

David's fingers tightened around the railing of the bed.

How could I have let this happen? How could I fail him? If only I'd pushed harder... more insistent, he wouldn't be here now - barely alive...

His chest tightened, and the ache was almost physical. He wanted to shout, to scream at the unfairness of it all. To rail against whatever dark hand had made Peter a target in the first place. But that would change nothing. The damage was done. The blood was already spilt, and no amount of shouting would take it back. *Why didn't I do more?* The question circled relentlessly in his mind, like a broken record.

His gaze drifted to Peter's battered face again. The swells of bruises, the delicate curve of his jawline now distorted and raw, and the thinness of his lips that had once smiled so easily.

The tears threatening to fall the moment he'd stepped into the room now burned the back of his eyes. He blinked them away angrily. He wasn't going to cry—not here, not now.

Peter's eye fluttered, struggling to open against the weight of the swelling. When his gaze finally met David's, there was a flicker of recognition, but it was dim, buried beneath layers of pain and confusion.

David's hand shot out, reaching for Peter's. The contact was faint, weak, but it grounded him. He tried to speak, but the words caught in his throat. He wanted to tell Peter he was sorry, wanted to explain that they would fix this, that they would make sure Peter didn't die here, in this sterile, lifeless room. But he couldn't. *What good would words do now?*

Instead, he just whispered,

"Peter, can you hear me?"

His voice cracked at the end, and he hated the sound of it - fragile, strained. He hated feeling like this, exposed, vulnerable. He had to stay strong for Peter, but it felt impossible. The guilt, the fear, the dread of what might still be coming - it all threatened to crush him, to drown him in waves of emotion. He squeezed Peter's hand tighter, as if that might somehow anchor him to the present, stop the spiralling thoughts in his head.

Peter's eye struggled to focus, the edges of his vision cloudy, but there was something there. A flicker of life. A hint of recognition. David clung to that.

"You're gonna make it, Pete," David said, more to himself than to Peter. But Peter didn't respond, only shifted slightly, and the pain that distorted his face made David's stomach churn. It was too much to bear. The thought that Peter might never be the same again... that they might lose him - not just physically, but mentally - that thought was suffocating.

A part of David wanted to stay here, to never leave his friend's side, to be there for him through every single moment of this suffering. But the other part - the part that had been screaming inside him since the moment they found Peter - wanted to run, to escape this hospital, this nightmare. He wanted to forget the blood and bruises, the sound of Peter's ragged breath.

But David couldn't escape. *I won't run...* He couldn't leave his friend alone to fight this battle. Not after everything they'd been through. Not after everything Peter had done for him.

"I'll be here for you," David said, the words finally coming out clear, steady. He knew it was a promise he had to keep. He couldn't let Peter slip away from him, not when there was still a chance. *"You're not alone."*

David stood up, brushing his eyes with the sleeve of his jacket. He couldn't afford to lose his composure now. Not yet. Peter needed him.

He glanced back at his friend one last time before turning toward the door, his heart heavy in his chest. He stepped out into the sterile corridor, the quiet hum of the hospital around him feeling colder now, more distant.

In a different corner of the city, Nolan sat at the far end of his dining room table, it was the centrepiece of an opulent space filled with a sense of extreme indulgence that stood in stark contrast to the hospital's bleak atmosphere. The room reeked of affluence, from the Glencairn whisky glass that Nolan spun absentmindedly between his fingers to the 20-year Macallan whisky that sloshed within its confines.

Nolan's face bore the marks of his frustration, etched into the lines of his features. His plans had been meticulous, his intentions clear—he had wanted Peter to draw his last painful breath in that car park. But now, he was confronted with the irritating fact that Peter was on the path to recovery.

The news, delivered by his hospital-worker informant, ignited both relief and vexation. Relief that Peter wasn't able to talk owing to a fractured jaw, and the fractured skull had allegedly caused some short-term memory loss. Great as this news was, his recovery albeit slow and wonderfully painful, was a threat.

If Peter regained his voice or his memory, the name he would inevitably provide to police would set in motion a chain of events. These events would expose Nolan. The police had apparently been nagging him for answers to ill effect according to the informant.

Desperation clawed at him. He downed the amber liquid in one swallow, the fiery burn providing a momentary distraction from the encroaching reality.

Amidst the lingering taste of whisky and the slight haze of intoxication, Nolan needed a plan—a bid to retain some control of the impending chaos. Unfortunately, the usual creative freedom he was used to when dishing out revenge was significantly reduced. The location, the police presence - all of these limited his options.

Ultimately, he would have to take the direct approach. He would have to confront Peter, interrogate him, and silence any witnesses, including the young couple who had been unfortunate enough to be there.

Half-formed thoughts phased in and out of Nolan's mind as he tried to come up with a way to get to Peter in the hospital. Just a few hours later, the bottle of whisky now half empty, his informant had been in contact having now read Peter's file. One of the doctors had decided that Peter would be taken off the heavy opiates for his pain within the next day or so. Peter would be lucid enough to describe what had happened to him. If he remembered that was.

Nolan supposed not but why take that chance. Either way, Nolan would need to go into the hospital himself. He didn't think his scrub nurse informant could be easily convinced to interrogate and then take Peter's life in his stead. Though Nolan knew all too well that money was a powerful persuader, everyone has their price.

Nolan shook his head, no, it had to be him. Pouring himself another large glass of whiskey, he began to craft his plan, and after devouring the rest of the bottle, it had become fully formed.

"Time to play," Nolan said aloud as he slammed down the empty glass with a thud.

Nolan hatched a plan, it was actually diabolical and evil - in every sense of the word. Grabbing his car keys, he left the house and crunched his way over the gravel toward his car, opened it and pulled open the glovebox where he kept a stash of emergency cigarettes. He pulled out the box and closed the door, locked the car and headed back inside. He had a plan, he had read somewhere... it should work... it was an evil plan, but it would probably work, and - more vitally would be undetectable. Failing that he had a backup plan, that would require his informant though. A potential weak link, they would have to steal a key from a doctor and then get it back to them without them noticing. It was risky, too risky. But it was a backup plan afterall. This way would be him, just him, working alone just how he liked it. Plus, the added benefit of what could well be a fairly miserable way to go. The backup plan? It would be almost pleasant. It would remain a backup plan for that reason alone.

Nolan stood at the large ceramic sink and pulled a large glass jar towards him. Pulling out four of the cigarettes, he began to unwrap them from the white paper and dropping the brown leaves into the jar. Once a sufficient heap of tobacco lay on the bottom, he boiled the kettle and poured boiling water over the mixture, giving it a good stir as he did so. He let the solution swirl for a while, letting the tobacco mix with the water, and grabbed a cone-shaped coffee filter from the cupboard. Next, he poured the mixture through it into another jar producing a horrible brown liquid. He sniffed it. It was pungent and almost made him wretch. He had smelled the cigarette smoke on Peter when he'd attacked him, so this had seemed a really great idea - on so many levels. Peter was clearly a heavy smoker, he'd obviously have high levels of nicotine in his blood anyway, even after a night in hospital, they'd never know. Never.

He still needed one more thing, and that was in the garage - he had a whole box of them for working on his car. Smiling, Nolan headed out to the garage through a side door in the utility room. He flicked on the overhead fluorescent light and headed to a large shelving unit covered with boxes. Pulling a small one down from the top, he opened it and pulled out a plastic syringe still in its plastic wrapper. He was all set, he knew what he was going to do. He headed back to the kitchen, grinning the whole way, and went over to the sink. He pulled a large quantity of the putrid brown liquid into the syringe and put it carefully back in the packaging.

Reaching for his phone, he opened the Uber app and input the destination as the hospital. Twenty minutes later, Nolan's taxi pulled up outside the hospital's main entrance, the rain was beginning to fall heavier now, the sun was ducking behind the horizon, and the glow of the day was receding.

Nolan climbed out of the car and thanked the driver. He looked towards the uninviting sliding doors, the flimsy barrier to what he needed to do.

Nolan recited what he would say to the receptionist in his mind again, he needed to be convincing. Otherwise, it would be all over before it started.

The doors swooshed open, and Nolan felt the dry stagnant air envelope him, the smell of sickness and disinfectant, of age and despair.

He had always hated the smell of hospitals and couldn't understand why people would ever want to work in one. *Lord knows how many people I've sent there over the years*, he thought to himself smiling a little. He wiped the smile off his face immediately as the receptionist glanced at him as he walked towards her.

Grasping the desk with both hands, his face appeared ashen and in a state of mild shock. He had seen this expression before in a movie, he couldn't remember which one and it worked like a charm.

"Good evening, how can I help you?" the receptionist said with little intonation in her voice. She was taking Nolan in, his expression appeared to be one of profound worry.

Nolan recited his cover story in his head.

"Cousin. Peter Coombs. Accident." He forced a tremble into his voice, looking pale and panicked as he leaned on the desk. The receptionist didn't question him.

"Let me have a look for you, just one second," she said. *"Yes, yes, I have him here, he's possibly asleep but you can see him if you wish? Visiting hours finish in half an hour."*

"Yes, thank you, thank you, what room is he in?" Nolan said holding back a crocodile tear.

"Room 6 on the Nightingale Wing" the receptionist replied.

"Thank you so much," Nolan said, and he waved to her gently as he looked up at the signposts above the desk.

"To the left, down the corridor and to the right, sir," the receptionist said.

"Thanks," Nolan said with a smile and began walking towards the Nightingale wing.

It wasn't a long walk to the wing, and Nolan checked his watch, fidgeting with anticipation, what would he do if people were in the room? There shouldn't be, and if there were, he'd ask them for privacy and he'd be left alone with him. Simple.

Nolan was outside room 6, he could see the silhouette of a body in the bed through the frosted glass and could make out several blinking lights and bright monitors on either side of the form.

Nolan slowly opened the door making as little noise as he could and stepped inside. Giving a final look around him to make sure no one had seen him walk in, he closed the door carefully behind him and pulled the shade down over the frosted glass.

There was a small twist-lock on the door handle and with a sigh of relief he clicked it. Now no one would be disturbing him, even so he needed to make this quick.

Approaching the bed with light, cautious steps, Nolan was met with a sight that almost tugged at his conscience. Almost. Peter's once robust frame now lay battered and bruised, huddled in a pitiful, semi-foetal position, as if seeking protection from the world that had turned against him. Protection from him.

The head, turned away from Nolan, appeared to hide its pain and vulnerability, yet the ragged breaths escaping Peter's lips betrayed the true extent of his suffering.

Settling into a cold plastic chair next to the bed, Nolan's gaze lingered on Peter's broken form. He could almost feel a twinge of guilt gnawing at the edges of his mind, threatening to undermine the resolve that had brought him here. But he shook his head vigorously, dismissing the intrusive thought like a pesky insect.

No, he reminded himself sternly, Peter brought this upon himself. The memories of Peter's stupidity flooded back, clouding the air with bitterness.

Blackmail, that was the weapon Peter had wielded, threatening to expose Nolan's embezzlement and drag him to jail. The audacity of it all left Nolan both astonished and infuriated. How had Peter managed to figure it all out? The answer eluded him, a puzzle with missing pieces that needed solving before it was too late. And who else knew about it? The answers would come, hopefully.

Nolan's eyes drifted to the multiple intravenous bags suspended from the cold steel hook above Peter's bed. His attention then settled on the small grey box resting on the sheets, its clear plastic tube snaking its way into a vein on Peter's arm. A syringe driver, Nolan knew, designed to dispense a continuous stream of powerful opiates into Peter's suffering body. His informant had been right.

Nolan reached for the grey box and flicked off the power, abruptly halting the flow of painkillers. Why wouldn't they lock this thing? He needed Peter lucid, just for a moment, to extract the answers he sought. The heart rate monitor flickered, signalling the pain's resurgence, and Nolan braced himself for Peter's awakening. It didn't take long. After a brief, agonising half-minute, Peter began to stir, his face etched with the torment he endured.

His eyes remained closed, the struggle evident even in his sleep. After a minute of this, Peter's head rolled over to face Nolan. His eye fluttered open, a slow, agonising movement. The purple bruise that swallowed it seemed to pulse with each shallow breath. It wasn't just the injury—it was the stillness, the vacant look in his gaze. His lips quivered, and tears rolled down his face, dampening the pillow.

"Peter?" Nolan said softly. *"I'm Inspector... Smith,"* Peter looked at him dazed. *"I know you're in pain, but I need you to answer a few questions, I'll be quick, I promise then you can sleep,"* Nolan said.

Peter nodded gently, his lips trembling to form a shape, a barely audible gasp of *"OK"* protruding from his mouth.

"*Great,*" said Nolan smiling a little more now. At least he can speak. "*First of all, I know about the blackmail,*" Peter shifted uncomfortably, a look of fear etched across his face, Nolan quickly put up a hand.

"*Don't worry, nothing will be done relating to that, I can assure you. In light of recent circumstances, the charge is being dropped.*" Nolan continued, pleased he had rehearsed in his head on the Uber ride over.

Peter's face softened and he sighed with relief as he clenched his eyes shut and then opened them again.

"*We need to know how you knew about Nolan and what he was involved in, don't worry we already have him in custody,*" Nolan said anticipating Peter's interruption.

Peter looked uncomfortable again, nearly a minute passed with no response and Nolan was beginning to feel agitated.

"*Peter? It's off the record but we need to know, it'll help us question him,*" Nolan said again, with a hint of urgency in his voice.

Peter looked him in the eyes, and his lips began to form a shape,

"*S...S...Sol...o...mon,*" he stuttered.

"*Solomon?*" Nolan repeated, raising an eyebrow in confusion.

Peter nodded, the pain clearly evident in his eyes.

"*What is Solomon?*" Nolan asked.

Peter's lips trembled once again,

"*A...I*" he said with great effort.

Dawning comprehension cast over Nolan's face,

"*Ah, I see. This is AI that you invented? At your Institute?*" he said.

Peter nodded again before closing his eyes.

"*And who else knows about this blackmail you did?*" Nolan continued.

Peter hesitated and looked at the Inspector's face, it was sympathetic and caring, but he also thought he saw an expression of pretence, probably typical in law enforcement, also a tinge of familiarity...

"*D.... David M...Mills,*" Peter said a little louder this time as his voice was beginning to return despite the increasing pain.

"*David Mills, perfect, thank you,*" Nolan said with a smile. "*OK, that'll do for now, I'll let you get some sleep. A lot of sleep,*" and as he stood, Nolan winked at Peter.

Peter's face contorted with understanding, the fog in his mind was lifting, and he could now place the voice, he had heard it that night, speaking to David and Clara as he was on the floor, losing consciousness.

Nolan plucked out the syringe from the packaging which he'd just pulled from inside his coat pocket and raised it to the IV hanging by Peter's bed. He found a small additional IV port and placed the end of the syringe over it. Looking down at Peter, locking eyes with his, he began to slowly depress the plunger. Peter knew this was not good. The look of mirth in Nolan's eyes was terrifying. The beep of the heart rate monitor began to increase, the blood pressure increasing - initially through fear, then the shot of nicotine hit. Nolan seeing the change in vitals needed to move fast. He pushed the syringe plunger all the way down, pulled it off the IV and stashed it in his pocket.

Nolan knew the dose he had just given Peter was enough to kill him, it wasn't a nice way to go all things considered. Peter began to cough and splutter. He wouldn't be talking to anyone now, the drug would usher him into oblivion, and Nolan now had a name, David Mills, probably the guy with the girl when he'd attacked Peter. He'd need to be silenced as well.

Nolan's eyes fixed upon Peter's weakening form, captivated by the racing rhythm of the heart rate monitor, its beeping like a metronome marking the passing seconds. The numbers cascaded upward: 80, 90, 110. He had to get out now. The alarms would sound any minute. There was nothing they could do to save him now.

He reached for the door lock, turning it with cautious precision. He raised the blind over the frosted window, casting a furtive glance into the dimly lit corridor beyond. Satisfied that the coast was clear, he turned his attention back to Peter and winked.

Stepping out into the dimly lit hallway, he quickened his pace, his heart racing in contrast to the fading beats in Peter's room. He heard Peter retching behind the door and quickened his pace. At that moment he heard an alarm sound, and the shuffling of feet headed towards him from around the corner. Nolan began to run towards the lift at the end of the corridor and punched the down button. The alarm was loud, all-consuming yet despite the chaos Nolan remained clam, composed. He hadn't needed plan B after all, that was good. The lift opened and he stepped in, the doors shutting just as he saw a group of people running into Peter's room.

Chapter 44

David had spent the last two days almost in their entirety with Clara while Peter was recovering in hospital. Aside from the evening before when he'd visited him. They had progressed from being a reacquainted potential couple to a full blown legitimate couple.

The events of London had all but disappeared from his mind now, and he felt safe with Clara knowing she would never bring it up without good reason.

Peter's attack had obviously shaken them both, and of course, the threats from the attacker weighed on them, and while they stuck to well-lit areas and never ventured out alone, they felt generally safe.

David was still working at the Institute, having acquired the keys from Kendra who was still there too. Clara dropped by whenever she had time away from the newspaper and though the large building felt ominous when it was just the three of them there, it still felt like a safe haven—their own private fortress.

David had slept at the Institute the last two nights with Clara, sharing a sleeping bag on the floor of the lab behind its card-coded door as an additional layer of security. David and Clara felt safe together, they knew this couldn't last forever and they had to live their lives eventually, but for the time being, until Peter came out of the hospital or helped the police catch who had attacked him and threatened their lives, this suited them both perfectly well.

Kendra had no idea about David and Clara staying at the Institute when she left in the evening and always assumed David was staying late to distract himself from Peter's situation.

The hospital wouldn't leave me hanging, if something bad had happened they'd tell me, right? Yeah, they'd tell me, they have my number, I gave it to the receptionist when I called before…but they won't discuss Peter with me on the phone, not family? Come on, that's stupid, he has no one else! Oh, just come and visit him and see him for yourself… yeah right, I can't go there, right in the open, that psycho would get me for sure, it's obvious that's where I'd go! No, they'll call, just…need to get the thoughts out of my head is all…

In the small, ill-equipped flat where Clara and David sought refuge, the weight of fear bore down on them. They had spent one night there before, finding some semblance of comfort compared to the cold laboratory floor, but it came at the price of constant vigilance.

Every sound, every creak of the floorboards, sent shivers down their spines. They lived in perpetual trepidation, not daring to raise the volume on the TV, triple locking the doors, and keeping the curtains drawn as if these meagre precautions could fend off the evil threatening to engulf them.

It was amidst this atmosphere of fear Clara turned to David, her face illuminated by the faint morning light managing to creep in through the drawn curtains.

"David," she said, rolling over to face him, *"we can't keep hiding like this, sneaking from here to the lab, and surviving on food deliveries. Who knows how long Peter will be in the hospital?"* David gazed into Clara's bright eyes, momentarily finding some solace in her presence, even amid the turmoil in his mind.

"I know," he replied, *"I know… but what should we do?"*

"I want to go out for dinner," she said firmly, her voice steady. *"To show we're not scared, to have a real date."*

David couldn't help but smile at her suggestion. An actual date, amid their perilous situation, seemed like both a bold statement and a necessary act of defiance against the fear holding them captive. He leaned over and kissed her softly, feeling a surge of electricity pass between them. With a smile mirrored on her lips, David said,

"Let's do it."

They settled on a decision—to go on a dinner date at a small Italian restaurant just a short 5-minute walk away. Neither of them had been there before, but Peter's fond endorsement of the place, particularly his exuberant praise for the *'absolutely epic dough balls,'* filled David's heart with a bittersweet pang of sadness.

The rest of the day was spent within the confines of the modest flat, their time occupied by watching terrible reruns on the TV.

As the clock approached 6 pm, the sun had set and they prepared to venture outside, nerves tingling with the awareness of potential eyes in the darkness watching their every move.

Cautiously, they opened the front door, scanning all directions for any signs of lurking danger. Satisfied the coast was clear, they set off on their brief journey.

The dim, yellow glow of phosphorous streetlamps cast an eerie, surreal aura over the deserted street. The sound of their footsteps echoed through the desolate surroundings, bouncing off the dilapidated buildings that lined the empty thoroughfare.

Finally, the illuminated shopfront of the restaurant came into view, its warm glow exuding a sense of comfort and welcome. The flickering light of tabletop candles danced invitingly from within. The soft strains of Italian music could be heard, reaching out like a soothing embrace after days filled with fear and the constant feeling of imminent peril.

David held the door open for Clara, allowing her to walk ahead. Casting one last vigilant glance in both directions, he followed her inside. The tantalising aroma of fresh tomatoes and fragrant basil enveloped him, awakening his senses and making his mouth water.

As they settled into their seats, surrounded by the cosy ambience of the restaurant, the worries that had plagued them seemed to subside, and at that minute the world outside faded away.

An hour had gone by, amazing food - the dough balls were indeed amazing - and the bottle of surprisingly good wine was almost empty. Amidst the hushed conversations and the fragrant aroma of Italian delicacies, David and Clara relished their precious moment of respite, embracing the illusion of safety. David felt a gentle squeeze on his hand, and he turned to smile at Clara, her eyes radiant with affection. But as he turned back to the entrance, his heart jumped a beat. A tall figure stood there, his face partially obscured by the dim light. An unsettling feeling crept up David's spine, as if an unknown danger had materialised before his very eyes.

The stranger moved forward, and as he drew closer, David squinted, trying to discern his identity. The man's cold, calculating gaze met David's, and a flutter of recognition flickered deep within him. But before he could place the face, the man had already arrived at their table, the scraping of his chair sent shivers along their flesh.

"Well, well, well," the stranger said, "what a lovely couple enjoying a romantic evening. Mind if I join you?"

Clara's grip on David's hand tightened, and she glanced at him, her eyes questioning. David's mind raced, trying to place the face, but the stranger's identity remained elusive.

"Um, do we know you?" David asked, his voice wavering as he struggled to mask his unease.

The man's lips curled into a sinister smile, his eyes never leaving David's face.

"Oh, we haven't been properly introduced," he replied, his voice a dark melody. *"My name is Nolan."*

Recognition dawned on David like a bolt of lightning in the dark. Nolan—the name sent a shockwave through his memories, and the pieces began to fall into place. He had seen the name in the notebook he and Peter found on Jim's desk. *Not the most common name after all...*

Oh God, this is the man. It's him. The one Peter blackmailed, the one who almost killed him, and the one who said would kill us... It's him, he wouldn't do anything to us here, right? No, he wouldn't, we need to get out of here... now...

Clara's breath hitched, her fear palpable as she too realised the gravity of their situation. Her voice trembled as she asked,

"What do you want from us?"

Nolan's smile widened, revelling in the fear that enveloped them.

"I believe we can be of mutual benefit to each other," he said cryptically, his words dripping with thinly veiled malice.

The restaurant's ambience seemed to dim, as if the darkness within Nolan had cast a shadow over their cosy little sanctuary. David's mind raced, searching for an escape route, a way to outmanoeuvre this man.

There's no way out. He'll catch us, safer in here. Why bother being scared, what's the point? Okay, he might hurt me. But so what? He'll get caught either way. But what about Clara? No, I can't let anything happen to her, I won't...

"We won't help you," David said, his voice defiant despite the trembling in his stomach

Nolan's eyes glittered with wicked amusement.

"Oh, I think you will," he replied, his voice dripping with certainty. *"Once you understand the consequences of refusal."*

David and Clara exchanged fearful glances, realising that he had them trapped.

Nolan's grin widened further, his eyes gleaming with a cold, calculating intelligence.

"You see, David. It is David, isn't it?" he said, his voice oozing with smug certainty. *"I know about Solomon, your clever little gadget. Used it to dig up dirt on me, did you? And you, dear Clara, helping Peter with it all?"*

Clara looked bewildered. Turning to look at David, she said,

"David, what is he on about?"

David looked at Nolan who was grinning.

"Peter was using Solomon to blackmail people to finance the Institute," David said. *"I wasn't part of it, and told Peter not to do it, but he ignored me. And Clara certainly wasn't part of it, she didn't know anything about it."*

Clara looked dumbstruck and promptly slumped back into the seat.

A renewed fear clamped down on David's heart like a vice. The knowledge that Nolan was aware of Solomon's existence and its extra-curricular abilities sent a chill down his spine.

How much does this guy know? How does he know about Solomon? Wait, did he speak to Peter somehow? If he's seen Peter... is this why I haven't heard anything in the last couple days? Is he even alive? Yes, of course he is, they would have told me...

Nolan's hand slowly crept over to Clara's wine glass, his eyes fixated on hers as he lifted it to his lips. He took a long, deliberate gulp, savouring the taste before wiping his mouth on his sleeve. With a smug grin, he placed the empty glass back in front of her, he was in control and there was nothing she could do about it.

"Here's the deal," he said, leaning in so close that they could smell the faint scent of Clara's wine on his breath. *"You're going to use that machine of yours to make me a very wealthy man. In return..."* His pause was loaded with menace. *"I might not kill you both."* He emphasised the *'might'* with a long drawn out flat sound.

The weight of Nolan's words hung in the air, suffocating them. His threat was clear, and it left David and Clara paralysed.

Nolan leaned back in his chair. Suddenly, he raised a finger, as if struck by inspiration.

"Oh, and just to make sure you understand the gravity of the situation," he murmured, *"you have twenty-four hours."*

Nolan pulled a scrap of paper from inside his jacket pocket and slid it across the table. David gingerly picked it up, his hands trembling. When he looked at it, confusion washed over him.

"What's this?" he asked, his voice betraying his bewilderment.

"It's a crypto wallet address, David," Nolan said, his sinister grin widening. *"I expect you to find, steal, mine—do whatever it takes—but you're going to send me half a million quid of crypto to that wallet within the next twenty-four hours, or you're both gone. Perhaps I'll have you stuffed in a bag and dropped in the river, or maybe set on by dogs, perhaps both? Either way, it won't be a good way to go."*

As if to emphasise his point, Nolan reached over to the knife resting on the napkin next to David's empty bowl. With deliberate slowness, he turned it to face David and pushed it very slowly towards his chest. Fear gripped David like icy talons, and Clara's grip on his hand tightened painfully beneath the table.

"I'll see you soon, David," Nolan whispered menacingly, his gaze drilling into David's soul. With a chilling wink, he stood up and announced loudly to the restaurant, "It was lovely to see you both. Hopefully, run into you again soon," and he turned and left.

Chapter 45

The little restaurant exuded a charming ambience, its walls were adorned with vintage photos that told the stories of rustic Italian times. Time, here however, had stood still for David and Clara as they sat in near silence. The weight of Nolan's threat hanging like a heavy fog over them. The distant murmur of conversations, laughter, and the soft clinking of cutlery echoed around them, creating a surreal backdrop to their distress.

The waitress, her patience wearing thin given the unexpected guest who hadn't ordered anything himself, approached their table with an air of annoyance.

"Would you like anything else?" she asked. David waved her away without uttering a word; his gaze locked onto the empty pasta bowl before him. The waitress swore under her breath as she turned away.

Under the table, Clara clutched David's hand. Her palm was clammy, as was his own he imagined. After a moment, Clara released David's hand and turned to face him, gently pulling him out of his hypnotic trance.

"David, are you okay?" she asked, knowing the answer anyway. David hesitated, his mind a swirl of thoughts and emotions, before nodding gently.

"Yeah, I'm okay," he replied, his thoughts racing to escape the nightmarish situation. *"We need a plan. What do we do?"*

Clara's gave an awkward half-smile. David looked at her puzzled.

"Well, about that," she began, *"you know what Sarah told me on the first day of the job? Record everything."* Her words hung in the air, carrying a sense of disbelief as if she couldn't believe her decision's fortuitousness.

"You mean to say you recorded Nolan's threat?" David asked, his voice tinged with incredulity. *"Is it clear? Let me hear it,"* he added, curiosity piqued by the possibility of having an advantage against their tormentor at last. Clara reached into her handbag and retrieved her phone, whose illuminated screen indicated it had been recording throughout the whole encounter.

With a tap of her finger, she stopped the recording and replayed it. David put it against his ear and listened intently as the muffled voices came through. The melody of traditional Italian music played in the background, creating a bizarre backdrop to the menacing words of Nolan. Every word of Nolan's threat was crystal clear, except for a brief moment when Clara had nudged her handbag, causing a rustle.

"You're incredible, you know that?" David said awestruck, lowering the phone and handing it back to Clara.

Clara smiled.

"Okay, we need to figure out what we're going to do with this," David declared, waving at the waitress. Despite her irritation, she approached their table, and David asked for the bill.

As they waited for the bill, Clara leaned closer to David, her voice hushed.

"We have the recording, but we can't underestimate Nolan. He's a complete psycho. We need to use this leverage wisely."

David nodded, fully aware of the danger they were in.

"Agreed," he said, his mind already formulating strategies. *"We can't give him the money, that's for sure. Hell, I don't know if we could even get it in the first place. But we can use this recording to buy us more time, to find a way to expose him and protect ourselves."* David was surprised at himself, his voice no longer quavered. Instead, it came out strong, manly even. Clara was evidently using this newfound confidence to fuel her own resolve.

"We'll expose this lunatic, show the world what he's capable of," she said, her voice fierce and unwavering. The bill arrived, and David paid it, leaving a generous tip despite the waitress's previous complaints. David and Clara then left the restaurant, knowing they were probably safe to return to Clara's house. Nolan wouldn't touch them; they had 24 hours; if anything, this was the safest they could be, not that they felt it particularly.

They walked in near silence; other people littered the street, heading into town for a night of fun, drinking, dancing, and probably regret.

"Hey, I should go to the Institute. I think I have an idea," David said,

breaking the silence of the last few minutes.

"What is it?" Clara asked.

"OK, so some of what I'm going to tell you I haven't told you before, so don't judge me, OK?" David said.

She stopped walking and stood facing David. Her moonlit features showing concern. David stood still, taking a long exhale, reaching his arms out to take her hands.

"Ok, so before I met you, before Uni, I worked for this cyber security company, a little indy one back home," Clara was now listening intently.

"The reason I was working there," David paused, *"is because I got arrested..."* Clara stepped back a pace and dropped his hands. *"Not charged!"* David added, reaching for her hands again, *"for hacking the college IT system and planting messages in student files,"*

Clara looked surprised, but not as much as David had expected. He continued,

"Nothing menacing or whatever, but just to say here's a gap in your security, that kind of thing. Police picked me up near my house one morning, and I got put in this job instead of juvenile detention or whatever it's called," David said.

Clara raised an eyebrow. *Is this surprise or admiration? Better than mum's reaction in the police interview either way...*

"Anyway," David continued upon not hearing any interruption from Clara, *"I had joined this group of computer... er... enthusiasts,"*

"Hackers, you mean," Clara said bluntly.

"Yes, ok, hackers," David replied. *"Anyway, I think they might be able to help. I spent a lot of time chatting to them back in the day, and we got on pretty well."* Clara didn't look convinced. *And why would she be?*

"Look, they were all what we called 'white-hat' hackers; they didn't do what they did for bad reasons, just to find security flaws and alert companies to them. Usually to get employed, or paid. Which a fair few of them did," David said. Clara made a contemplative humming noise and nodded.

"So, I think they would be willing to help us now if we send them the recording you made; they could clean it up and help us make a plan to make a false crypto transaction while also siphoning Nolan's assets. That way, he'll have nothing, and we'll have all the leverage. I think we can actually do this with their help," David said. Clara thought about this for a minute,

"Ok, I'm in; call them or whatever you do to contact them," she said with thinly veiled scepticism.

"I'm gonna head to the Institute," David said, his voice tinged with urgency. *"You should go back to your place, Clara. It'll be safe. I'll walk you*

there, but I need to see what Solomon can find on Nolan. It might give us a head start before we call in the cavalry," he said, hoping his plan would buy them some time.

As they walked, their hands intertwined, the night air seemed charged with excitement and trepidation.

As they arrived at Clara's door, David turned to face her,

"I'll give you a call later," his breath brushed against her hair as he held her tightly. As he leaned in to kiss her forehead, David couldn't help but feel an overwhelming surge of emotion. He wanted to tell Clara how much he cared for her, how deeply he loved her. But a sense of hesitation washed over him as he held back the words he longed to say. Then, almost without thinking, the words slipped from his lips,

"Love you." He immediately regretted this impulsive confession, fearing he had rushed into revealing his feelings too soon. He braced himself for Clara's reaction, his heart pounding in his chest. Waiting for the classic *'Thank you.'*

The silence that followed felt like an eternity.

God, I've probably scared her off now, David you're an idiot! Way too much to handle with all this crap that's going on, why would you say it?

But then, as if the world held its breath, Clara raised her head to face David. A soft smile played at the corners of her lips.

"Love you too," she said softly, her voice carrying a vulnerability mirroring his own. David's doubts and fears melted away, replaced by an overwhelming sense of relief and joy. The weight on his heart lifted, and hope surged through him. The world around them faded into the background, it was just the two of them. Alone in the world and that suited David just fine.

David reluctantly let go of her hand as Clara reached into her bag pulling out a set of keys.

"I'll speak to you soon," he said.

"Look forward to it, good luck," she said, her fingers brushing against his cheek. With a final lingering kiss, David watched Clara disappear into her building. David turned and started the walk to the nearby Institute.

Holding the key to the Institute tightly in his trembling hand, David's heart pounded like a war drum, drowning out the distant hum of the city. The night was alive, and the vacant exterior of the once bustling Institute loomed like a forgotten ghost, its concrete and glass shell now a haunting reminder of the darkness that lurked around the corner.

As David reached the main road and the entrance to the business park, he could feel a prickling sense of unease crawling up his spine. He glanced to the side, where a short distance away lay the spot where Jim had met his tragic end. It was a chilling reminder of how this had all started. Sparked by Jim's ill-fated but well-intentioned blackmailing activities, which had unwittingly set off a chain reaction of events.

But there was no time for dwelling on the past. The urgency of the present gripped David like a vice, urging him onward. He crossed the road quickly, the key clenched between his knuckles like a makeshift weapon.

Reaching the entrance of the Institute, David inserted the key into the lock, and the heavy doors slid open with a foreboding creak. The dim light from the streetlamps outside barely reached the darkened corridor within, casting eerie shadows that seemed to dance and writhe on the walls.

The air grew colder with each step inside, and David's heart seemed to beat louder in his ears. He navigated the hallways with purpose, his footsteps echoing in the lonely silence. The ominous stillness felt like the calm before a violent storm.

He arrived at the lab at the end of the corridor, the room where Solomon currently resided. David reached into his wallet for the key card.

The lock clicked open, and the door gave way to the darkened room. David flipped the light switch, and the harsh, fluorescent lights flickered to life, illuminating the large bench in the middle of the lab. The sight of the lifeless black box resting on the bench filled him with hope and trepidation. He had after all promised himself that he would not use Solomon again, it scared him.

He dragged a stool towards the terminal, its legs screeching on the floor like nails on a chalkboard. With a deep breath, David took his place before the mysterious machine that held the answers they so desperately sought.

Pushing the button on the monitor's bezel, the screen flashed white.

The words *"Update installed. Continue?"* appeared in the centre of the screen.

The black cursor blinked impatiently in the top left corner, waiting for his command.

"Yes," David wrote and hit the Enter key. He continued:

"What can you tell me about Nolan, surname unknown. A local

businessman Jim Walcott was looking to blackmail and who Peter Coombs now has? He has attacked Peter and threatened mine and my girlfriend's lives, requesting to be sent £500k in crypto in the next 24 hours," David typed hastily, knowing that time was of the essence.

The screen flickered as the message disappeared into the void, and an hourglass appeared, twirling and bouncing across the screen. The seconds felt like an eternity as David waited for Solomon's response, the suspense mounting with each passing moment.

Four agonising minutes later, the hourglass vanished, and the cursor returned almost mockingly. The anticipation was palpable, and David leaned forward, his eyes locked on the screen.

Solomon's response materialised, and from somewhere within Solomon's monolith, a speaker crackled into life.

"What the...?" David said, peering around the back of the black box housing Solomon.

Suddenly a jubilant Australian voice emanated from Solomon. It was clearly meant to be Jim's. Or a slightly computerised approximation. Still, it was pretty damn close to real human speech.

"Oh, I see you're shocked that I finally found my voice. Well, here's the scoop: Jim and Peter were cooking up an update to give me some personality, just like Jim's. And, of course, a voice. Also just like Jim's. That guy was really into himself! Anyway, hold onto your hats... Searching now... Ah, Nolan, what a rascal! His last name is Hastings just FYI. Not much data on him, but he's been up to some financial shenanigans. Guessing this is who you're on about".

I can't believe what I'm hearing! This isn't just some AI with a speech modulator, like that one in Wargames, this is something else altogether. This is AI with personality, and Jim's personality at that.

Without hesitation, David typed again.

"Solomon, I need more; I need you to create a false cryptocurrency transaction to his address. Can you do this? We need more time for the rest of the plan."

Once again, the cursor blinked in response as if contemplating the gravity of David's request. The seconds stretched on, the suspense mounting with each passing moment, until finally, the screen displayed the message David had hoped for. And the speaker crackled into life once more.

"Absolutely, I can handle that. Just toss me the wallet address, and I'll give it a peek. And by 'peek,' I mean a thorough, scrutinising examination with just a hint of curiosity that won't lead to me buying a yacht with his funds.

Probably." David laughed and reached into his inside pocket, pulled out the slip of paper with the long crypto wallet address, and laid it down in front of the keyboard. David then typed it in, double-checking it twice before hitting the enter key.

"Wallet identified. State the amount of dosh you wanna fake send and what flavour of coin you want it to be." David could hardly believe what he was hearing; everything seemed so straightforward. He typed:

"£500,000 Bitcoin. Defer transaction until 6 pm tomorrow," Enter.

The hourglass reappeared, began its usual dance across the screen, and disappeared.

"Okey Dokey: the transfer is set for 6 pm tomorrow. And he better not even think about cashing out before then, because it's not happening. I've rigged the system to spit out a "transfer is currently clearing" message—because who doesn't love a good fake-out? This little manoeuvre should buy you both up to 12 extra hours of finger-crossing and teeth-gnashing. You're welcome."

A wave of relief washed over David as he absorbed Solomon's response. It was a momentary victory. But there was no time for celebration. The next phase of the plan demanded immediate action.

Clutching his phone tightly, David dialled Clara's number, his heart pounding. The connection was made, and he wasted no time explaining their first step's success and the urgency of their next move.

"We need to act quickly," David said. He could feel the weight of the impending danger pressing down on them like a ticking time bomb. *"The fake transfer will buy us some time, but we can't afford to waste a moment. We have to proceed with the rest of the plan before Nolan catches on to what's happening. Can you come over to the Institute first thing in the morning?"*

Clara hesitated, her concern evident in the timbre of her voice.

"The morning? But David, I'm alone here. What if Nolan comes after me?" she said, her mind running wild with all the possible danger scenarios.

David's voice softened.

"Clara, as far as Nolan knows, I've just sent him half a million quid. He won't want to risk losing that, not yet at least. You'll be safe for now," he said, trying to ease her worries.

Though Clara still sounded uncertain, she knew there was no other choice. *"I'll get an Uber in the morning."*

"Ok good plan. I'll spend the rest of the night contacting my old hacker friends. If they're willing to help, we'll have a chance at pulling this off,"

David said, returning his voice to one of confidence and determination.

Chapter 46

It felt strange for David to locate the old hacker forum he frequented all too often at college. He had promised his parents and DI Harrison he would never hack anything again or get chummy with those who did.

He had been given a second chance, a job, and ultimately a life, *well... a half-life.* He'd been spared juvenile prison or wherever wayward youths go, and now he was back at it again. *Although I'm pretty sure DI Harrison would be more upset about the alcohol-fuelled hit and run. Hell, this by comparison probably wasn't that big a deal... Even so, it feels weird being back on here again. Who knows if the guys I used to chat with are even on it anymore? Christ what if none of them are? What do I do then? No no, once a white hat always a white hat, right? I don't know what if they got caught too? What if they're in prison, did something way worse than hacking a stupid college IT system, I mean they're more than capable, they're pros compared to me, oh God what if they're gone? No... no stop it, stop David. Relax, it'll be fine, they'll be there.*

Taking a long slow breath David found the website he was looking for on his laptop and rapped his knuckles against his temples as he tried to visualise the password for his login.

The username was easy enough; he used the same one for most things, *"SadButFalse"*, a play on Metallica's track *Sad But True*. David had thought it a stroke of genius then, but now he wasn't so sure; *pretty dumb now I think about it...* The password flashed in his mind, and he typed it in, crossing his fingers it was still correct. The laptop screen went blank, and then his dashboard appeared in view. He hadn't visited the site in over four years, and his account incredibly hadn't been deleted.

There were several unread messages, most from a few years ago when he was active but there were a couple from recent months. David clicked on the *friends* tab to see who was still around. *Here it is, the moment of truth... who's still on here?*

K1D22 - account deleted

Lastcall - Online

BitViper - account removed

TuzaGirl - inactive

RebootRebel - inactive

Fluxx - Online

Gh0st4 - Online

Vulc4n - Online

David looked at the list of names,

"Okay," he muttered, *"four online now, two offline. This might work."* He created a chat group and sent a bulk message to *Lastcall, Fluxx, Gh0st4,* and *Vulc4n*:

"Hey guys, sorry it's been a long time but I'm in real trouble and need your help. I work in Leeds for a lab where they built an insane AI that my boss used to blackmail a proper evil bastard called Nolan Hastings. Anyway, he's possibly killed my boss, might have killed another colleague and has threatened to kill my girlfriend and me if we don't steal half a million quid in bitcoin in the next 24 hours. I desperately need your help to take this guy down. We have a recording of him confessing to killing my boss and threatening us, but we need help to rinse him of all of his assets and find more evidence of his crimes to give to the police and media. Solomon, the AI won't steal from people's accounts as its against his 'ethics', so I need you. I reckon I can create a fake crypto transaction to delay him but it's not enough. Can you help? David (SadButFalse)."

He hit send and pushed the laptop away waiting for the blue tick to indicate the recipients had read it. *And now we wait...*

David sat back in his chair and glanced at Solomon, its black monolithic tower humming gently, its monitor blank. *It's crazy what this thing can do really, it's actually mental. I mean I get why they invented it, but did they really not think to constrain it in any way? Good that it's got some ethics though, I mean not willing to steal from people directly - I guess that's why Jim used it to blackmail people instead, that way Solomon isn't technically the one stealing... of course if it did, Peter would be alive - assuming that Nolan did kill him - and who knows maybe even Jim? Was Jim actually killed though? I dunno...*

The blue ticks began to appear next to their names. But nothing happened, no dots to show they were typing back, *nothing*.

Will they help? Do they think it's a joke? Actually, what if they do? It's been like four years since I spoke to them, and then this out of the blue? Yeah, I'd be suspicious too...

As he sat in the eerily quiet, yet unnaturally bright room of the Institute, memories from his hacker days flooded back. The adrenaline rush of figuring out the missing bit of code that would get him into the system, knowing he wielded power that no one else in his class had - it all seemed like a lifetime ago. He had left that life behind, promising to never return, but desperate times called for desperate measures.

He thought of DI Harrison, he'd given him a second chance. *But the law wouldn't stop Nolan, he has his hands in too many pockets, it would take more than the confession to bring him down, he needed the media, regular people to know who he really was, to make sure Nolan couldn't escape. Christ this is a big step up from breaking into college IT systems... now we're talking about stealing, fraud, identity theft I guess... hell if this all goes sideways, I'm in serious trouble. But that's why I have to hope the others come through for me... but will they? Not just my life on the line, it's Clara's too...*

Minutes felt like hours.

Finally, a notification from Lastcall:

"SadButFalse, long time no see! Sorry to hear about your predicament. You always were a trouble magnet. Don't worry, we got your back. Tell us everything about this Nolan guy, and we'll do what we do best"

Relief washed over David as he typed out a detailed account of everything that had transpired—the blackmail, the attack on Peter, the threats against him and Clara, and the recording of Nolan's confession, which Clara had sent to him a few minutes earlier. He sent them all the information he had, knowing these guys were some of the biggest computer nerds he had ever known.

If anyone could expose all of Nolan's crimes and drain his financial assets, it was this group. He knew their combined skills and Solomon's brute force attack abilities could be the key to bringing Nolan down.

Responses flooded in:

Fluxx: *"Count me in. Let's show this Nolan what we're capable of."*

Gh0st4: *"I never thought I'd like properly hack again, but for you, I'm in."*

Vulc4n: *"This Nolan guy's days are numbered. I'll help drain his accounts and dig up everything he's got."*

With his team assembled David felt a sense of hope for the first time in a while. Together, they would bring Nolan down once and for all. But time was of the essence, and they needed to act fast.

David shared the evidence they needed, explaining Nolan's acts and the urgent need to dismantle his empire, that he must have people working for him or contacts he was paying off to find things out for him. *How had Nolan found out about Peter? He had to have had people working for him...* The group had agreed with this.

As the night wore on, they formulated their grand plan, each of them contributing their unique skills to the masterstroke. The group chat had become a full-blown video conference call with Solomon acting as the project leader, dishing out the occasional motivational quote in its joyful Aussie tone injecting some much needed humour and light-heartedness into the conversation. The group were in absolute awe of Solomon, constantly becoming distracted by asking it questions about themselves or anything else that came to mind, no matter how stupid.

"Is there a chance that a USB stick could ever become sentient?"

As the morning light filtered through the room's small window, Clara arrived at the Institute. She seemed wide awake despite the fact she'd barely slept. David's phone pinged, alerting him of Clara's presence outside the front door. Running out of the lab and into the reception area, he opened the front doors, and she fell into his arms.

He took her by the hand and led her towards the lab, first stopping in the kitchenette to make them both a much-needed coffee. The aroma of the cheap instant coffee mingled with the sterile scent of the institute, creating a peculiar yet oddly comforting atmosphere. David handed Clara a steaming cup, their fingers interlocking for a second.

Chapter 47

Clara and David crossed the threshold into the lab, their footsteps muffled by the eerie stillness that blanketed the Institute. Each held a coffee mug, the steam curling lazily upward in stark contrast to the weight of their mission. Dark circles framed their eyes, evidence of all the sleepless nights, but their gazes remained sharp, cutting through the intense fatigue that clung to them like a second skin.

Clara's eyes were wide, a mix of exhaustion and fierce purpose. David, now sitting back at the bench, was tapping on the laptop keyboard. His gaze ping-ponged between Solomon's monitor and his laptop, where his team was busy laying the groundwork for their digital offensive against Nolan.

David gave Clara a quick nod, gesturing to the empty stool beside him. They settled into the space like magnets to metal. Clara flitting her sights from the gibberish David was tapping onto the laptop and Solomon's monitor which was busily spewing out additional lines of code upon David's instruction.

David had explained the incredible leaps in intelligence that Solomon was showing, and that it'd adopted Jim's voice thanks to an unexpected software update. Clara had laughed solidly for three minutes after hearing Solomon's vocal demonstration, impersonating Jim's animated and musical accent.

In the dark recesses of bedrooms, basements and one rooftop terrace, the hacking team - spread across the globe - continued toiling away on the mammoth task David had set them. Creating novel algorithms and programs designed to seek out Nolan's business assets. Be they bank accounts, crypto accounts, private cloud servers and everything in between, and extract anything and everything of value.

Clara looked at David's laptop where multiple windows showed the team. A couple had their webcams on. The unmistakable silhouette of energy drink cans and takeaway boxes littering desks, two were simply images of anime characters whose hair and bodily proportions defied gravity. *Geeks,* Clara thought with a small grin.

Nestled at the centre of the sprawling city of Berlin was *Vulc4n,* otherwise known as Erik. Though Clara could just about make out his features, she would never recognise him if he walked up to her on the street.

His lean frame melded seamlessly with the pale blue glow from his monitors, casting an otherworldly aura upon his angular features. Tousled raven hair framed a face that bore the patina of countless sleepless nights. There would undoubtedly be others to come.

Perched atop a busy apartment complex in a small one bedroom flat in a small Swedish town on the edge of the North Sea, *Gh0st3* - Freya to the rest of the world - sat at her kitchen table surrounded by empty Diet Coke cans and crisp packets.

Her waves of dark hair cascaded like a waterfall, and her storm-grey eyes gleamed with a fathomless depth, absorbing the glow from the dual monitors like portals into uncharted dimensions. Adjusting her glasses with a delicate motion, her fingers flitted across the keyboard with the precision of a court stenographer.

Freya had been a prodigy student of cryptography stemming from her love of crosswords and puzzles from a young age. At only 22, her path had led her to university, but the dwindling job market had resorted Freya to freelance journalism for a computer magazine. Struggling to make ends meet and with her passion to make a difference, the hacking forum had been a bonafide lifeline, even giving her some paying consultancy jobs.

On the other side of the world, amidst the neon kaleidoscope of Tokyo's vibrant streets, *Fluxx* operated from his penthouse apartment. Despite his youthful looks, he had a wisdom that shone through in his eyes. His glasses were a bit crooked on his nose, which made him look like he was deep in thought. And his fingers were moving across the keyboard like a pro.

Hiroshi, his true identity, had once been at the forefront of the artificial intelligence renaissance in Japan, patenting an algorithm while doing work experience at a software company at just 17. But some of his ideas clashed with the tricky ethical rules of big business, so he decided to use his genius to find the truth by hacking instead.

In the quiet suburb of Yonkers outside of New York City, *Lastcall* aka Marcus, created his digital masterpiece from the basement of his mother's house. The screens before him cast a ghostly luminescence, suffusing his features with an almost ethereal glow. A five o'clock shadow lent a rugged intensity to his angular face. The basement was strictly off-limits to Marcus' mother, the neon-lit room looked like a landfill, littered with empty energy drink cans, polystyrene containers and the smell of mouldy food that thankfully couldn't be transmitted through his webcam.

Each team member was a unique person, with different backgrounds and personalities, from rich to struggling. But they had known David since his college days. They had been his mentors, friends, and teachers, and even though it had been years since they spoke, it felt like nothing had changed between them. The problem was more complex this time, but their attitude towards helping him remained the same.

Time seemed to lose its meaning as they delved deeper into the plan. Clara's heart pounded in her chest with each passing second, her pulse synchronised with the rapid, flickering code that appeared on the laptop screen.

As the clock approached midday, the hour that signalled the commencement of *Lastcall's* meticulously planned operation. The air grew tense with anticipation. In the physical realm, Marcus begun a video call amongst the whole group. His voice, brimming with excitement and confidence, reverberated through the laptop speakers.

With the weight of the group's silence bearing down on him, Marcus introduced what he called the *Echelon Nexus*. He gestured widely with his hands to emphasise how big a deal this thing clearly was, his eyes alight with the kind of manic enthusiasm only seen in inventors convinced of their own genius.

"This is no ordinary creation," he asserted, pausing for effect. *"It is a fusion of artistry. Technology. It's capable of breaking into what I would call the for-mid-able walls of Victory Insurance's mainframe."* His voice was a blend of awe and mischief, as though the very thought of such a feat was thrilling beyond measure. Marcus then mimed dropping an invisible microphone and sat back in his chair, his expression a mixture of expectation and smug satisfaction, waiting for what he assumed would be rapturous applause from the rest of the group.

Yet, the reaction was far from what he anticipated. Instead of excitement, the room was filled with a collective pause, as if the group were holding their breath.

After what Marcus thought was far too much silence, he went on to explain that the Echelon Nexus was no ordinary code; it manifested genius at the intersection of neural networks and quantum algorithms. Its structure was a labyrinthine masterpiece, akin to that of Solomon.

"*Hmmm...*" Solomon said quiet enough that only David and Clara could hear.

As David and the team conferred, their shared determination was evident. They were exploring uncharted territory, where the line between reality and the digital void was becoming indistinct. With a unanimous nod, they approved the plan - a subtle gesture in the physical world that echoed like a digital trumpet call in the digital one.

A single line of code with a simple *yes/no* command appeared on David's laptop screen. Marcus had wrapped up his masterpiece and sent it through to David so he could give the final go-ahead. Hitting yes would unleash the program on Nolan's entire organisation, setting in motion a chain-reaction that will bring about his complete downfall. David looked at Clara. She nodded, he typed *yes* and hit the enter key.

A separate window flickered to life almost instantly, a portal into the colossal amount of data manipulation at work. Reams of information cascaded down the screen like a digital waterfall, a torrent of data extracted from the recesses of Victory Insurance's servers. Each pixel held a story, something Nolan didn't want anyone to find. The Nexus sifted and sorted.

In the midst of all the data, a moment of calm came. David's voice, a bit tired but full of hope, suggested a break—a chance to catch their breath and step away from the digital world. Clara's fingers touched his, a real connection that reminded them of being human amidst all the flashing lights.

They left the digital battlefield, their footsteps a way out of the endless world of code. The familiar lab space enveloped them, and they headed to the kitchenette. The fridge had some snacks, the likely semi-stale sandwiches a reminder that even though their mission was complicated, the simple act of eating could be a ritual that brought them back to reality.

Clara's phone vibrated, cutting through the moment with the sharpness of an alarm. She paused, mid-bite into a two-day-old sandwich, her eyes narrowing at the unknown number flashing on the screen. A chill ran down her spine, instinct whispering that this was no friendly call. With slightly trembling fingers, she answered, and the room seemed to hold its breath. No voice greeted her, only a deep, disdainful exhale, ending in a snort of contempt.

"Nolan," Clara's voice quivered. David spun his head to face her, his eyes wide.

"Ah, Clara," Nolan's voice slithered through the speakers like a serpent's hiss. *"I hope you don't mind, but I got your number through your work; they were quite happy to give it to me,"* a muffled laugh. *"Your audacity is impressive. I must admit, your little endeavour with the virus has entertained me. But I saw it coming..."*

Clara's grip tightened on the phone, her knuckles blanching as she shot a glance at David. His jaw was set, his eyes aflame with worry.

"We're not backing down, Nolan," Clara's voice trembled. David mouthed something that looked like, *"Stop talking!"*

Nolan's laughter, cold and mirthless, echoed through the speakers.

"Such resolve. But remember, Clara, courage alone won't shield you from what's to come. You know what you both must do and when you need to do it."

Nolan's tone turned frigid, his words dripping with venom.

"You're dancing on the edge, my friends. But by all means, dance on. I'll be watching."

The call terminated, the room resonating with the lingering echoes of the confrontation. Clara's heart thundered in her chest, a fierce cocktail of fear and exhilaration coursing through her veins. Marcus' Nexus virus had been exposed. *Nolan knew we were after him, and by Clara saying they weren't backing down, she'd admitted it was their doing and wouldn't stop. They sent the fake money to him earlier, but Nolan wouldn't be able to see that yet. They had now become prime targets and were in very real danger.*

Twenty minutes dragged on like an eternity within the confined space of the kitchenette. The atmosphere was heavy. David's hand clasped the cool surface of a water glass, untouched by his parched lips. His thoughts were a whirlwind of worry and frustration that tightened his chest with each passing second.

Clara was leaning against the wall. Her head cradled in trembling hands. Tears slipped through her fingers. Her breath came in uneven gasps, still waiting for the adrenaline rush to subside enough to gather her thoughts again. It was taking its time.

Amidst the silence, the echoes of David's voice still reverberated. Heavy with anger and regret, his words had cut through the air like a blade. He had spoken words he wished he could take back, his emotions had overwhelmed his restraint, and he'd blurted out every stupid irrational thought and fear, all aimed at Clara.

He had told Clara that she had essentially betrayed their plan to Nolan, they weren't just some stupid pawns in this reverse blackmail game anymore, they'd become actual, real targets. They were now threats to Nolan, he now knew they possessed abilities that would, could, potentially take him down, or at least knew people who could. The enormity of the danger they faced had hung in the air like a suffocating fog. And in the heat of the moment, he had raised his voice, his frustration spilling over. It was a torrent of emotion that he had unleashed, a moment of weakness he now regretted with every fibre of his being.

The room seemed to contract as David's footsteps carried him across the space, tentatively approaching Clara's shattered form. His hand reached out, fingers trembling with an apology he struggled to articulate. But the moment his touch grazed her shoulder, she flinched, her fragile form recoiling.

The recoil felt like a physical blow. David's face paled, his heart aching with the raw intensity of his misstep.

"I'm so sorry, Clara," his voice wavered. He had wounded her, his actions an indelible mark on their bond. Every word he spoke felt like an attempt to mend the irreparable, a plea for forgiveness that hung in the air.

Instantly, that serenity was shattered by the explosive crescendo of breaking glass in the distance. The sudden calamity cracked the stillness, the discordant notes of intrusion slicing through the air.

David's body snapped to attention, his movements fluid yet urgently charged. Clara roused from her previous state of vulnerability, scrambled to her feet, her sleeve wiping away the remnants of her tears. The lingering aftermath of their emotional exchange hung suspended.

Everything about the turmoil that had consumed their emotional landscape froze in mid-air. Their attention was no longer trapped by their internal conflicts but riveted on the source of the disruption - the corridor towards reception now beckoned ominously. With a measured gesture, David signalled for Clara to remain in the relative safety of the kitchenette.

Stepping into the main hallway, David moved with a practised grace. Each footfall was calculated, his senses attuned to every nuance of his environment. The corridor stretched before him, a passage leading from the reception to the sanctum of their laboratory.

Looking left towards the laboratory, he saw that the room was still steadfastly locked, and a sense of relief swept over him, if only for a fleeting moment.

Solomon is safe, at least for now anyway...

He moved stealthily, his body pressed against the wall as if he were part of the architecture itself.

Muffling his footsteps, he ventured further down the corridor towards reception. The tension in the air was palpable, and the feeling of danger resonated in every fibre of his being.

He heard voices, *three or four distinct voices... Nolan's men? Does he even have men? Of course he does... Why were they here? Didn't they still have time?* Too many questions entered his mind, and his heart was in his throat.

He darted a cautious glance around the corner through the open doorway into reception, his eyes locking onto a scene that sent a chill coursing through his veins. Four figures, silhouetted in the dim light, moved with purpose.

The reality of their presence pierced through the layers of uncertainty - *Nolan's henchmen. Do people even have henchmen? Isn't that just a movie thing? Clearly not, these guys were exactly what henchmen looked like in the movies...* Four men dressed in black were walking around the room. One was behind Kendra's desk, rifling through papers and upturning the wastepaper basket. He gestured towards the other three to continue moving on.

With a measured pivot, David began to move, ducked down and ran back towards the kitchenette. The men were closing in, and they would round the corner and see him any second now.

And then, with a surge of silent effort, he was back within the confines of the kitchenette. The door clicked shut behind him, a sound reverberating like a barrier against the impending danger. Clara's gaze met his, her eyes reflecting the fear gripping them both.

"What's going on?" Clara's voice was a whisper, the tremor of fear palpable.

"Four men," he whispered, his voice laced with urgency. *"They're searching the reception area but heading this way. Nolan's men I assume."*

A surge of urgency coursed through them, a realisation that their very existence was at stake.

This tiny kitchenette had no lock, and they would be found any minute now. *There was only a handful of rooms at the Institute and there was no chance they'd leave the kitchenette out of their search. There was no time to get to the laboratory, and even if they did, what if they caught them as they were opening the door? They'd get Solomon and then it'd be game over...*

His gaze shifted around the small space, his thoughts racing to find a solution. *The cupboard beneath the sink? Potentially? Not a great hiding place... These men were probably professionals, they would search everything surely...*

"In there," David's voice was resolute, his gaze fixed on the small space beneath the sink.

"What about you?" she said shakily.

"I'll be okay," he lied.

David helped Clara clamber into the cabinet under the sink, tucking her legs painfully into the cramped space. David watched her squeeze into place, and he placed his hand on the door,

"We'll be ok. I love you," and closed it firmly shut. David crawled towards the kitchenette door and dared a glance through the frosted glass pane in the top half. He could make out a dark shape moving towards it.

He quickly fell to the floor out of sight and clambered over to the table and chair on the other side of the room, away from the sink. He pulled himself up onto the chair and waited. David's hands were outstretched in front of him and were shaking violently.

His breathing was fast and uneven. Sweat was pouring from every part of his body, and only the thought of Clara stuck in that cabinet, scared out of her mind, made him realise he needed to be brave for the two of them. The men didn't have weapons as far as he could recall; they needed him; Nolan needed him to get the money.

At that moment, the kitchenette door flew open, and the men ran into the small room, the one in front zeroing in on David and marching towards him with such grace that it was as though he were floating.

The other three were sweeping the room, opening the cupboards, peering into them, and moving towards the sink area. David glanced at the cabinet where Clara was hiding and gulped.

The man before him stared down; his face was obscured with a balaclava, and his eyes were ghostly grey. They reminded David of the mugger's eyes on that platform, cold and lifeless, devoid of all empathy or feeling. He was there to do a job, and that was all.

"David?" the man said gruffly. David trembled but managed a slight nod.

"Nolan says time is ticking and to stop messing around; you got 10 hours to get the money," the man stepped back away from David's face, and it looked like he was smiling. As David thought the ordeal was over, the man pulled back a gloved hand, curled it into a fist and unleashed a decisive blow to David's face. Stars appeared, and lights flashed as David fell off the chair onto the floor with a nauseating thud.

Out of the corner of his blurred eyesight, he could see the three men opening the cabinets next to the sink, then, they yanked open the one where Clara was hiding. David heard her scream as they pulled her out by her hair and threw her onto the floor. Clara landed a hard kick into the groin of one of the men and clambered to her feet, making a start towards the door.

"Go..." David whispered after her, *"you can make it - just get outside, please."*

Clara sprinted toward the corridor, her heart pounding in sync with her footfalls. But the chaos followed her and was catching up fast.

Freedom lay within grasp, a glimmering light at the end of the corridor. But fate had other designs. A vice-like grip encircled Clara, halting her escape. She struggled, her body defiant, but her captor's hold around her middle remained unyielding. Clara let out another scream.

"No!" David yelled before the boot of the man who had punched him connected with the side of his face.

A cloth draped over Clara's mouth, its sweet but sickening scent enveloping her senses. Dizziness seeped into her consciousness, as though she were moving very fast, shadows creeping at the edges of her vision. She fought to cling to her resolve, her thoughts swirling with panic.

The world spun, reality warping and distorting as Clara grappled against the encroaching oblivion. She whispered David's name through the haze. The conflict turned into chaos, a war waged on the brink of darkness.

But as her senses succumbed to the relentless pull of unconsciousness, Clara's world dissolved into an inky abyss. The last image that imprinted itself upon her fading consciousness was that of David, sprawled on the floor.

David lay on the cold, unforgiving tiles of the kitchenette floor. Blood, both from his battered nose and a vicious gash on his ear, trickled in rivulets down his pallid face. The crimson liquid blurred his vision and stung his eyes, mingling with the salty tears of pain and despair that welled up within him.

In the brightly lit room, the veil of concussion began to lift slightly, revealing a world filled with anguish. Clara was now a prisoner in the hands of a psychopath who had crossed every conceivable line. Nolan had left pure chaos in his wake, from Peter's assault *and possible death?* To the mysterious death of Jim. The man had stolen a fortune from his employees, and now, with chilling audacity, he had kidnapped David's girlfriend clearly as a ransom.

"Time to get this asshole..." David said aloud. Anger was growing in heaps within him; absolute unbridled fury had taken over his rational and lifelong logical mind, and all he saw was red. However, that could easily have been the blood in his eyes.

Summoning every ounce of his strength, he began the arduous task of dragging his battered body across the harsh, unforgiving floor. Each movement was agony, his muscles protesting with every inch of progress.

His ragged breaths filled the room, punctuating the silence with the desperate rhythm of determination.

The absence of sound and movement around him confirmed his suspicions. Nolan's men had departed, leaving behind a chilling void of emptiness. The laboratory's alarms remained eerily silent, no sirens wailing in response to the shattered front windows. David was utterly alone, a lone survivor in the aftermath of mayhem.

Despite the excruciating pain and the relentless torment of his injuries, David's spirit blazed with an unquenchable fire. With one final, guttural shout of pure rage, he propelled himself up towards the door handle before his legs failed into a crumpled quivering heap.

His trembling fingers grasped it, and with a surge of indomitable will, he flung the door inwards and dragged his way down the hallway towards the lab, towards the only people who could help him take this bastard down once and for all.

Chapter 48

With a heart pounding like a jackhammer, David's body hummed with adrenaline. His injuries, which would have otherwise unleashed unrelenting, debilitating pain, lay subdued in the shadows of his acute focus. Each movement he made felt like a monumental struggle, like he was being punched and kicked all over again. His keycard crashed against the entry panel, reverting a metallic clang through the dimly lit corridor.

With Herculean effort, David half-dragged and half-pulled himself towards the workbench and stool, his battered body protesting every inch. The stool, its metal stems scuffing across the polished floor, betrayed his struggle as it skidded and twisted with his shifting centre of gravity. David's roars of profanity punctuated the stillness of the room like gunshots.

Finally, David managed to hoist himself onto the creaking stool. It swayed precariously beneath him as he grasped the laptop on the workbench. The screen still displayed the group chat. A bunch of code was doing a jig across the open windows on the laptop screen, the Echelon Nexus or whatever Marcus called it, still searching through Nolan's servers and finding hidden digital gems of illegal activities. It didn't even matter that Nolan knew they were sniffing around, he could try all he wanted but the virus was still worming its way through the servers.

How long was I on the floor? I didn't black out... Did I? No... I hit the floor then as soon as they were gone, I dragged my lame ass in here... Right?

David scanned the waiting messages which were all of a similar tone, that of anxiety and confusion. They came in waves, rising in levels of distress and urgency. *Maybe I have been gone longer than I thought?*

"David, where are you?"

"Dude, seriously, wtf, where are you?"

"Is everything OK?"

With painstaking slowness, he began to type his response. His right wrist, sprained and twisted from the blow to his head and subsequent crash to the floor, moved like a foreign appendage.

Like when that basketball hit my hand and pushed my fingers back when I was a kid, serves me right for trying to play sports... Christ that had hurt...

Typing was an exercise in excruciating torment.

"Nolan's men found us, beat me up, took Clara... gave a deadline of 10 hours for cash," he typed.

The cursor blinked, and the chat window swallowed his words before spitting back new messages like sparks in the darkness.

"Shit," Vulc4n replied simply.

"You OK? What's the plan, Dave?" Gh0st3 added.

David paused, his hand trembling as he touched his aching cheek, feeling the fragile, loose skin. He wiped some semi-congealed blood from his forehead, smearing it on his jeans. The seconds stretched like hours as he composed his response.

"We'll send him the fake money," he typed, the words forming with excruciating slowness. *"And in the meantime, we find out where he's holding Clara."*

The screen displayed a jumble of typing and deleting, hesitation and resolve as the group grappled with this decision.

"I think I can help with finding Clara," Vulc4n wrote. *"I can probably track Clara's phone and find out where she is now, or Nolan's if hers has been switched off. Got her number? I can find his number from his company records, easy enough."*

David's fingers tapped with hope as he typed in Clara's phone number, hit send, and waited, every moment feeling like an eternity, while *Vulc4n* worked his digital magic.

Ten minutes of oppressive digital silence hung in the air. The world outside the screen ceased to exist, and the only sound was the pounding of his breath as he awaited a response.

Then it came—a series of coordinates. Wincing with the pain of his sprained wrist, David typed the coordinates into an online map and hit enter. With bated breath, he waited for the result, praying it wouldn't be a spoof address Nolan had routed Clara's phone through or something. *Is that even possible? Would he even know how to do that? Yeah probably...*

The map zoomed in before him, revealing a location just north of the industrial estate where the research institute was nestled. The coordinates painted an unsettling picture, and David's curiosity took a firm hold. He double-tapped the dropped pin, watching the map transform into a satellite view.

Seriously? Guess it did have to be pretty close by to avoid anyone seeing them take Clara...

It was an end-terraced house, a nondescript structure huddled up to other similarly ordinary houses. Completely inconspicuous. The setting contradicted every expectation of a hideout for a powerful, corrupt businessman and his crew of thugs. *How could a place that appeared to be a standard family home, albeit run down, be the lair of a sinister kidnapper?*

David's mind reeled with disbelief. He questioned his friend's assurance that this was where Clara's phone signalled.

It's like Nolan believes I have the mastery to orchestrate a cryptocurrency heist but lacked the competence for the most basic track-and-trace operation. This guy could actually be an idiot.

The thought made him feel better.

A plan had already been set in motion earlier on. Solomon was priming the fake transaction ready to send it out at 6 p.m. the following day. But now, everything had changed. The clock was ticking towards a new deadline. Now the money was due at 2 p.m. Clara's life dangled in the balance like a fragile thread and the plan was all David had.

One of the group members, and David agreed completely, suggested they involve the police and spill everything. David made the excuse that Nolan probably had people on his payroll in the police - which was actually true, but more than anything, David was terrified that the police would dig into his life, his past, and expose him. So that was a big no no.

It seemed that no matter what happened in his life, the ghost of Alex McCormick was always present. Leaning over his shoulder, waiting for something. Well, this was the something. David was going to save Clara. It wasn't penance in the traditional sense but saving another in his mind would balance taking a life. *Probably.*

David's mood suddenly changed to sombre as he thought about Peter, the quiet victim of this whole thing. He couldn't help but wonder if Peter had met the same fate. He tried calling the hospital, but they said only family could get info on a patient's condition.

I mean I could just go and visit, but Nolan will absolutely have people there... It's too far away, too many opportunities for Nolan to take me out, probably crossing the road like Jim... No... when this is all over, I'll go... I'll barge into his ward and demand to see him when this nightmare is over.

Chapter 49

With his mind made up and the makeshift plan settled in his mind, David left the Institute. His legs had thankfully stopped their adrenaline-fuelled wobble, and the strength had finally returned. He knew the short walk to where Clara was being held went against every survival instinct, but she was in danger, and he couldn't forgive himself for not trying everything he could to get her back.

The world outside was overcast, the sky a blanket of grey that mirrored the turmoil inside him. Fat raindrops had begun to fall, tapping rhythmically against the pavement and creating a small river along the curb. David's footsteps echoed across the empty car park and down a nearby alley lined by trees - hauntingly similar to the one he walked down after ditching his car. *Strange how déjà continues to rear its ugly head in times of distress... Actually no, not strange, annoying...*

As he ventured further into the rundown part of town, the scenery shifted. Forgotten factories and decaying warehouses loomed on either side, their broken windows and sagging roofs speaking of a time long past. The air was thick with the stench of neglect, a bitter blend of mould and rust, *the rot that festers beneath this forsaken place.*

Ahead, a rusted chain-link fence, partially hidden by creeping ivy, marked the boundary of Nolan's territory. David's heart begun to pound again as he neared it, the rain-soaked ground squelching under his worn sneakers. Each step felt like an eternity, a plunge into the unknown, as he crept down the narrow alley towards the end-terraced house. The pain in his face and wrist was gone now, adrenaline muting his suffering.

The house looked just like it did on the map, its run-down exterior perfectly hiding the evil within. The brickwork was crumbling, and the once-white paint was now a peeling grey. The curtained windows stared out blankly, like the eyes of a predator pretending to be innocent. Overgrown weeds choked the pathway leading to the door, their stems crawling up the sides of the building as if trying to strangle it.

The roof sagged ominously, with broken shingles hanging precariously, threatening to fall at any moment. An eerie silence surrounded the house, broken only by the occasional creak of timber, as though the house itself was groaning in pain, and a distant dog barking.

He knew there was a high chance he would be spotted and captured, but he had nothing left to lose now. Determination and desperation fuelled his every step as he carefully approached the house. The ground beneath his feet was uneven, strewn with broken branches and debris that crunched softly underfoot.

His breath was shallow as he peered through the grime and dirt-distorted windows, straining to see if anyone was inside.

The curtains, thick and tattered, obstructed his view, but small holes and tears in the fabric allowed slivers of light to pierce through. Through these tiny gaps, he could see just a little bit of the dim interior of what looked like a living room.

The flickering shadows and indistinct shapes inside only heightened his anxiety. The silence around him felt oppressive, as if the world was holding its breath, waiting for something to happen. His hands were clammy, trembling slightly as he pressed his face closer to the glass, trying to catch any sign of movement or life within. The air was heavy with tension, and every second felt like a lifetime as he stood, vulnerable and exposed, knowing that discovery could very well mean the end.

Before moving to the front door, he scanned the exterior walls for CCTV cameras. The porch, damp and rotten, groaned under his weight as he moved forward, the wood soft and swollen from the rain. He spotted an old, broken camera above the door, its lens shattered and useless. He took a deep breath, feeling the cold, wet air fill his lungs, and then slowly let it out, trying to steady his nerves. *One... two... three...*

He tried the doorknob, expecting it to be locked. To his surprise, the door opened with a small irritating creak, the sound cutting through the silence like a knife. *It's as if the house wants me to be caught...*

David carefully peered around the edge of door checking for any signs that he'd been heard. Nothing. No creaks or raised voices. He was safe, for now. The narrow entrance hall was dark. Peeling white plaster on the walls and ingrained dirt in the carpet made David wonder if this was a random abandoned house Nolan had found in a pinch to be near the Institute. To be near him.

David, every muscle tense with anticipation, moved slowly down the narrow hallway. His hand trailing along the wall expecting to feel the vibration of someone moving within the house, like touching a railway track to sense an incoming train. A stupid idea he thought but it made sense in his head. *Blame it on the concussion...*

The floorboards beneath the discoloured carpet creaked softly under his weight, and the walls appeared to close in around him. It was only a mere ten feet before the entrance hall began to branch off into adjacent rooms. The door to the first room was open and taking a quick glance around the corner showed David that this was the living room that he had glanced through the tattered curtains. Or at least was supposed to be one.

There was an assortment of old armchairs, what appeared to be a coffee table covered in dust blankets, and a pile of large cardboard boxes in one corner. Most importantly, there was no-one else there. Nolan wasn't sat on a chair in the middle of the room stroking a white cat or anything. So as far as things went, David felt almost optimistic about his mission.

Continuing on down the hallway, another room appeared on the left. This one missing a door altogether and appeared to be a storage room. The room was cluttered with old furniture. Dozens of ancient looking paintings hung lopsided on the cracking walls. Dusty boxes and various odds and ends littered the floor, but it was otherwise empty of people. Satisfied, he moved on. His steps cautious and measured. His breath shallow as he tried to remain as silent as possible.

A few steps further down the hallway, the outline of a staircase materialised in the darkness. It was narrow and steep with wooden steps leading up into what appeared to be nothing. The landing at the top was completely black. Not a sliver of light whatsoever - meaning that any doors up here were either airtight or led to other rooms enveloped in absolute darkness.

David knew where he had to go, Clara was up there somewhere, and probably so was Nolan and his goons. The scene was like something out of a horror movie, a genre that David had typically enjoyed from the safety of his bedroom, but this was real life. Like one of those escape rooms with a serial killer except in this case the killer wouldn't halt before delivering the finishing blow. They would just run out and do him in. No drama, just pain then nothing. The danger level skyrocketed for David, but the adrenaline was keeping his wits sharper than they'd ever been before.

The wooden steps creaked under his weight, and he winced at every sound, knowing that in the deathly silence of the house anyone could hear him. As he ascended, the air grew cooler and the darkness more oppressive. As he reached mid-way up, he froze as he heard - or thought he heard muffled footsteps from above and to the right of him. They were barely audible, and muffled, but the rhythmic pattern was unmistakeable.

The reality that there really were people in this house sent his pulse into overdrive. David screwed his eyes closed and concentrated on his breathing trying to slow it down. His legs were shaking enough now to make him almost lose balance. He grabbed for the banister to steady himself. As he did, the wooden rail let out a horrendous crack as it was almost jostled out of its rotten sockets.

David gasped and let go of the banister. He dropped down so he was outstretched up the stairs trying to look invisible. Waiting for the moment the footsteps made a scurrying sound and a door flew open. Five seconds, nothing. No scurrying, no slamming of a door, no voices. Sweat trickled down his face and stung his eyes. Ten seconds. Still nothing.

Slowly, David pulled himself upward, pushing his hands against the stairs until he was back on his trembling feet. Once he reached the top of the stairs, he crouched low for no other reason than that's what he'd seen people do in the movies in this situation. Creeping along the landing, again holding his hand against the wall for some semblance of direction, he moved down the landing.

The feel of the wall changed, the rough and bumpy wallpaper transforming and his hand fell onto a smooth painted surface, a door. David slowly moved his hands over the surface until he found a doorknob, he didn't dare turn it, not yet. Kneeling down, he placed an ear against the wooden surface and closed his eyes as he focused all his senses on hearing what lay on the other side.

A muffled vocal sound. Guttural yet somehow higher in pitch than what he could have achieved. *Probably a woman's?* Pressing his ear against the door until it hurt, he doubled down on his concentration.

Deep breathing, loud and quite fast. Panic.

It was Clara, it had to be... But was anyone else in there with her? What did it matter now anyway? I definitely heard footsteps... If Clara's gagged, and the muffled voice suggests she is, she probably isn't walking around, right?

David took a deep breath and got his feet. He slowly turned the doorknob waiting for the click. As it did, he simply pushed the door open and walked in. Fully expecting to be tackled to the ground or feel the thump of a bullet bury into his chest. Neither of these things happened. Instead, he was greeted by a softly lit room, it was small, dirty and full of papers, stacked and in various states of decay. Dust lay in thick clumps in corners, and large spider webs sprawled across the ceiling. There were no windows, just a simple wooden chair in the middle of the room. And on that chair sat Clara.

Bound with twine, with a strip of grey tape across her mouth. Her eyes were streaming, and her cheek bore a large purple bruise. Her legs were crossed underneath the chair and also tied together at the ankles. When her eyes met his, she stared in disbelief. Before she could make another sound, David put a finger to his lips. Quite unnecessary given Clara's situation, but never mind.

He ran over to her and began fumbling with the knots on the back of her wrists. *This is taking too long...* chewing his fingernails for all his life was proving to be a significant barrier but David continued. Before long, Clara's arms were free, and he began to untie her feet as she peeled the tape off her mouth.

Once the twine had fallen to the floor and Clara could move and speak again, she threw her arms around him.

"David, I... "she stammered. "*How did you...* "

"That doesn't matter right now, we have to get out of here. Now." David said.

Clara nodded and got to her feet with some assistance from David.

"There is someone else here, I don't know where but he's definitely upstairs," David whispered. *"So, we have to move fast."*

He led the way out of the room and back onto the landing towards the top of the stairs. David gestured for Clara to go down first. They both reached the bottom of the staircase quickly, paying little attention to the odd creaks and groans of the ageing steps. The mission had changed now, it was to get out of that house, now. Get out and run. Moving down the hallway towards the front door, they felt like they were almost in the clear. Except at that second, a booming voice resonated through the walls.

"Think you can escape ya little bitch?!" the deep voice roared, and the thunder of footsteps boomed across the ceiling heading for the staircase.

An idea flashed into David's mind, and he had mere seconds to do it. He pushed Clara into the first room off the hallway, full of dusty furniture and cardboard boxes while he ran to the front door. He opened it and slammed it shut again before running back to the room. Hoping the man would assume Clara had managed to get out of the house, he'd run out after her leaving them to escape moments later when it was clear. The bait worked and David could hear the heavy-set man hurtling down the stairs and towards the door before yanking it open and running out into the road.

David glanced at Clara, and they waited.

"Just a few more seconds," David said, *"then we'll look around the corner and see where he went and head off in the other direction."* Clara nodded.

As they were about to leave the room, they heard the man come back into the house swearing and punching the wall.

"No way she managed to escape and disappear that fast. No way…" he said gruffly.

It was then, that the man moved toward the room they were in. Clara grabbed David by the shoulder and pointed towards a blue plastic tarp draped over an old, worn chest of drawers. He flung the tarp off the furniture within a second and pulled Clara tightly toward him. He crouched on the floor beside a tattered sofa, throwing the tarp over them like a makeshift shroud.

It was a reckless, desperate move, but it was their only option. David knew it offered slim chances of success, yet it was a roll of the dice they had to take. Under the heavy plastic cover, in the dimness and musty air, he felt Clara trembling beside him. David gently touched her shoulder, the only reassurance he could offer in their suffocating cocoon.

Outside the room, the man's footsteps grew louder. The unmistakable sound of the doorknob turning, accompanied by a subtle squeak. In the hushed darkness under the tarp, David and Clara froze, their hearts pounding and holding their breath.

The heavy, measured footsteps of the man resonated through the room, his approach deliberate.

David and Clara could feel the vibration of the carpet as a pair of heavy boots stopped beside them. The air was charged with tension, and they sensed the man's presence. Clara, her fear nearly paralysing, dared not even exhale while David's lungs ached from the effort of holding his breath.

A seemingly unending minute passed, and the world was reduced to the sound of their collective heartbeats. Then, a sound broke the silence, a loud crash came from the room next door. One of those old paintings falling off the wall David suspected, but it had the right effect. The man left their side and ran out into the hall. They could hear the man rummaging through all the boxes and moving furniture. This was their moment, now or never.

David and Clara finally exhaled, the moment's tension released in a burst of ragged breaths. David carefully lifted the tarp's edge to ensure the coast was clear. It appeared that it was. He flung the tarp off them and turned to Clara, who seemed on the verge of a nervous breakdown.

David's body ached as he rose to his feet and pulled Clara to hers. The front door was tantalisingly close, just around the corner, and David estimated they had a mere four seconds to reach it and get out. The man was in the room next to them, still making noise as he searched for the source of the noise. But there was no door to that room, he would just have to look round the corner and see them.

Once they were out of the house, they'd have to make a frantic five-minute full-on sprint back through the industrial estate and over the main road to the Institute where the relative safety of the laboratory awaited them. The odds were stacked against them to not be seen, but they had no alternative once again.

David whispered the plan to Clara, who hesitated momentarily, her eyes reflecting the gravity of their predicament. Yet, no other choice existed, no other path to take. She nodded her agreement.

They both tiptoed into the corridor, their footsteps barely making a sound, and darted toward the front door. David grabbed the handle and gently pulled the door open without a moment to lose, revealing a world bathed in gloomy, overcast daylight.

His eyes squinted with the light, and he ushered Clara through, his senses on high alert, and then closed the door behind them with a cautious click. Reaching for Clara's hand, they jumped down the porch steps and sprinted down the road.

The soothing patter of rain filled the air, a reassuring backdrop to the turbulent nerves that also helped hide their frantic footsteps. David felt relief wash over him for the first time in a long while. But then, the tranquil sound of rain was shattered by the roar of a throaty engine just up the road.

David spun to look behind and his gaze locked on the source of the sound. Dread coiled in his stomach. Nolan had just emerged from his Jaguar outside the house and was about to walk toward the door when he stopped. From Nolan's view, the heavy rainfall obscured David and Clara, but it was a temporary advantage. The ominous silhouette of their pursuer was unmistakable, and if he laid eyes on them now, their lives were forfeit.

"Run!" David hissed urgently to Clara. She whimpered, the bruises on her ankles from the bonds were making walking painful let alone jogging. They both faced forward and sprinted up the road. A voice, muffled yet venomous, pierced the air,

"You! Get back here!" Nolan was seething, and David heard the ominous cadence of rapid footsteps behind them.

"Move!" David barked to Clara, and they accelerated, turning off the street racing down an alley with the hope that Nolan wouldn't just get in his car and mow them down. The alley branched off and they took a random path hoping it would take them toward the industrial estate and the the Institute. Their feet pounded on the wet ground, and they could hear Nolan cursing behind them. The chase was on, and with each step, the echoes of their desperate flight reverberated through the stormy street.

Chapter 50

The heart-stopping chase through the industrial estate became a symphony of chaos and urgency. Rain poured like liquid shards from the heavens, soaking David and Clara to the bone as they weaved through the labyrinth of towering decrepit buildings. Their ragged and gasping breaths punctuated the pounding rain, and the echoes of their footsteps bounced off the concrete walls.

Nolan was an ever-present threat. He was closing in on them, fuelled by an unbridled fury and his pace seemed to far outweigh his physical stature. Nolan was cursing at them as he ran after them and his furious breaths seemed to merge with the persistent downpour.

The industrial estate's rusted forms and imposing silhouettes cast daunting shadows that intermittently concealed the fleeing pair. Desperate to escape Nolan, they navigated a maze of old machinery that cluttered the alleyway. Abandoned cement mixers, rusted out shells of cars - David lingered on this sight longer than necessary - as they leapt over huge rain-filled potholes and debris searching for a way out.

A towering stack of old plastic crates along the wall of the alley appeared around the next corner. David suddenly lurched towards the lowest crate of the tower and yanked it out causing the stack to topple over with David jumping out of the way just before they enveloped him. The carnage created a three-foot high jagged plastic barrier across the whole width of the alley.

Nolan arrived at the barrier just as David and Clara dashed to the next corner. He spat with rage and began hurling the boxes aside.

David was wheezing now as they raced on. He had that horrible metallic bloody taste in his mouth when you exercise too hard. The taste of red blood cells from his lungs escaping into his airway. David didn't know how much longer he could run. What was supposed to be a five-minute sprint was more like a sprint up Everest and his body couldn't handle it. Clara seemed to be in a similar state, she was gasping for breath too but was undoubtedly fitter than he was. The adrenaline was the only thing keeping them going now.

Glistening through the rain, David could spot the main road up ahead. *People... Safety? Maybe...* Time was their relentless enemy, and they knew that reaching the road was their sole chance of survival. *Have to... keep... going....* David coughed and spat. Clara glanced over at him looking concerned, she couldn't speak, neither could.

Their next obstacle was a cracked expanse of pavement. As they sprinted, the sound of their footfalls echoed like desperate heartbeats. Clara's foot suddenly snagged on a jagged piece of tarmac, and she stumbled. David's firm grip yanked her upright. *No time to lose...*

Nolan was unyielding. He was closing the gap quickly, his gaze locked on their fleeing forms. He was just fifty feet behind them now and gaining fast. Still cursing and screaming the graphic ways he would kill them both, he charged onwards like a possessed bull.

The road was now close. So close.

The final obstacle? It has to be... Once we're there Nolan can't get us, right? Too many people, then we'll be at the Institute, in the lab - the locked lab where he can't get us. The road is close, but the distance seems so vast...

Just as hope began to fade, the rain-slicked pavement became a friend. A deceptively deep pothole lay hidden beneath a puddle, and Nolan, blinded by his relentless chase, failed to notice it. He stumbled, his body crashing to the ground with a sickening thud, landing squarely on his back - the wind completely knocked out of him.

David and Clara both glanced over their shoulders but pressed forward, their hearts racing as the world blurred into a whirlwind of shadows and raindrops. The road drew near. The same road where Jim had died crossing over. The thought was fleeting but enveloped David completely.

Rain fell harder now, drenching David and Clara to the core. They were frozen, soaked, exhausted and running on pure adrenaline. Like being chased by a lion, they knew their bodies wouldn't give up on them. They could keep going for as long as it took.

Furious sirens and car horns blared with a deafening intensity that threatened to shatter eardrums. The three-lane road had transformed into a complete mess, a high-speed ballet of steel and peril. Seeing the chaos ahead momentarily distracted them from the pursuing Nolan *trapped between a rock and a hard place... between death and death more like...*

In their frantic sprint towards the Institute, Clara's foot met an oily patch of slick pavement. She slipped backward, her arms thrown up into the air. Her panicked gasps were drowned out by the thunderous chorus of car horns ahead.

David reacted with lightning speed. His hand shot out and grabbed Clara tightly by the upper arm, pulling her back from the brink. She regained her balance. There was no time for thanks. The vehicles ahead of them showed no mercy, their horns blaring relentlessly in rush hour traffic. Speeding down the road bumper to bumper. The rain-soaked road was a whirlwind of metal and motion, and David and Clara were the central characters racing through the commotion.

Nolan, soaked yet his rage unquenched, had fought his way to his feet. His eyes burned with a vengeance that transcended pain, and his battered body was driven by the purest hatred.

The car horns persisted in their fevered chorus. David and Clara continued running. David, still gripping Clara's hand with a vice-like intensity, hesitated when he got to the side of the road. The world around them had transformed into a whirlwind of chaos, a vortex of frantic motion and relentless rain that seemed to obscure everything. The dense rainfall veiled the road in a shroud of obscurity, making it almost impossible to see the speeding vehicles flying by. Some cars had their fog lights on for no reason too, piercing through the downpour, casting blinding beams of light that clearly disorientated oncoming drivers. Equally, other cars had no lights on at all effectively making them invisible.

They both stood there, their hearts pounding, waiting for a slim chance, a precarious gap in the traffic. Nolan bore down on them, he was now a mere ten meters away. The desperation in David's eyes was palpable as he glanced at Clara who was breathing heavily. With a reckless resolve, he pulled her into the path of oncoming cars, their fate hanging in the balance. Together, they darted across the road, their lives at the mercy of the traffic. *Just as Jim's had been...*

A white van roared towards them, its headlights glaring like a pair of evil eyes. Blinded by the beams, they dodged the vehicle's path just in the nick of time. The van's horn blared in angry protest, swerving violently at the last possible second, almost hitting an oncoming car.

Then, disaster struck. Clara stumbled and fell forward, her hands grazing the unforgiving asphalt. The world seemed to move in slow motion as David grabbed her by the neck of her jumper. With sheer force, he yanked her backwards just as a white BMW, sleek and unforgiving, bore down on her. Clara's terrified scream pierced the air, a haunting cry that seemed to hang in the dense air. The BMW screeched past, leaving a hair's width of space between Clara's trembling body and the cold, unyielding metal.

Nolan had now reached the edge of the road. He knew where they were going, the Institute, their sanctuary, where they would barricade themselves and call the police. His pursuit, fuelled now by an unyielding obsession, had brought him to this critical moment. He needed to stop them. Now.

Glancing each way for a split second, Nolan stepped out into the road. His presence was a chilling omen that signalled the impending clash between the pursuer and the pursued. The rain, undeterred by the drama that was unfolding, continued to fall heavier still, while the road bore witness to the unforgiving theatre that played out on its slick surface.

A car charged directly toward Nolan, its headlights slicing through the relentless rain and enveloping gloominess. The car's headlights transformed the scene into a chaotic, blinding tableau.

The impending collision was a crescendo of terror and destruction. The car's brakes squealed with a deafening high pitch and the car bore down on Nolan. The impact was an explosive clash of metal and bone, a crash of raw, visceral energy reverberating through the storm. Nolan's scream pierced the air. It was a chilling cry of agony, a gut-wrenching roar of pain. Nolan was flung sideways across the wet asphalt, his form a rag doll.

The car screeched to a halt, its tyres leaving long skid marks on the rain-soaked road. Other cars slammed on their brakes, some colliding with each other, the crashes, crunches and bangs of metal hitting metal reverberated down the road. Some cars had swerved onto the pavement, some mis-judging the angles and leaving them pointing backwards. The driver of the car that hit Nolan leapt out in a state of panic. David and Clara stood in a daze on the other side of the road as they witnessed the chaotic aftermath behind them. Their bodies shivering from the chilling reality of the moment. The irony of the situation didn't escape David. Nolan had been seriously injured or even killed crossing the road where Jim had been killed a few months beforehand. *This road is a gravesite...*

The rain continued to fall, washing away the hostility of the day but also unveiling the brutal truths that had unfolded. The road they had crossed, the battle they had endured, and the life-altering collision that had forever changed their course - everything was etched in the wet asphalt and reflected in the shimmering raindrops that were now pooling all around them.

David and Clara continued towards the Institute, walking now, leaving Nolan's body behind on the road, drivers getting out of their cars and reaching for their phones. *Was Nolan actually dead?* David didn't care, he just wanted to get Clara to the safety of the lab.

Nolan's world was swirling in a vortex of pain and confusion. Blood flowed from the gash on his side, staining his torn clothes and pooling beneath his feet. But he couldn't afford to yield to the agony, not now, not when vengeance beckoned him so strongly and he was so close.

The drivers were crowding around Nolan, pleading with him to stay still, to wait for an ambulance to arrive. But Nolan didn't hear them. Or he chose not to. In his mind, there was only one goal – catch David and Clara and get rid of them now, once and for all. To hell with the money, and to hell with anyone seeing it.

His vision blurred, his body battered and aching, Nolan staggered forward. Every step sending fresh bolts of pain through his mutilated form. One man, seeing Nolan start to get up, walked over and put a hand on his shoulder. Nolan spun around to look at him and landed a right hook on his face. The man slumped to the ground holding his cheek. The crowd around Nolan began to disperse. He gritted his teeth, each grimace etching lines of determination across his face as he limped across the road towards the Institute, blood-soaked and relentless.

His blurred eyes narrowed on the distant forms of David and Clara. The mere sight of them fuelled Nolan's fury, igniting an inexplicable surge of energy within him. He would catch them before he got to the Institute. He swore it to himself. They would pay for their betrayal and damn the consequences.

David and Clara had almost reached the smashed entrance of the Institute. They were both running again seeing Nolan now chasing them *will this guy ever die? He got hit by a car for God's sake!*

"*Why won't you die!*" David shouted back at Nolan who increased his pace. Their breathless pants echoed in the empty courtyard. The structure loomed above them with its dark and dirty windows, promising shelter if they could only make it to the secure laboratory.

206

But with every step, Nolan drew closer. His limp had disappeared, and adrenaline took its place. David glanced behind again at the worst second. He tripped over a loose drain cover and went sprawling to the floor with a sickening thud just ten feet from the front door. Clara skidded to a halt and was overcome with a primal conflict: to stay and help David or to save herself?

Nolan's haggard form closed the gap fast. With a roar, he lunged at David, who was awkwardly clambering to his feet, sending both men hurtling to the ground. Gasping for breath, David could do nothing but brace for impact as Nolan rained down blows upon him. Clara's scream pierced the air, her desperate pleas falling on absent ears, swallowed by the chaos. She tried to grab Nolan's arm as it swung down onto David's face, but he was too strong. He threw her backwards and she hit the cement ground hard.

Just as David's head lulled backwards, the last ounce of strength to defend himself trickled away, the siren's wail cleaved the air. Red and blue lights flooded the scene, and police cars screeched to a halt, officers spilling out, rushing to separate the two men. Nolan, his face a grotesque mask of fury, was quickly pulled off David, subdued and pinned to the pavement.

Handcuffs were snapped onto his wrists, and his defiant struggles ceased as he was dragged away. His eyes locked onto Clara and a trail of spit dangled from his lower lip like a rabid pitbull. Clara was trembling, her face etched with all the pain of that endless day, understood that their ordeal was far from over. Nolan was resourceful. He had people. He'd be free soon enough, and they weren't safe. They'd never be safe.

As a paramedic tended to David's wounds, Clara paced helplessly, trying to work out how they could end this nightmare once and for all. Once the paramedic was satisfied that David's injuries weren't life-threatening, he moved aside for a police officer who knelt down beside him with an expression of exasperation.

"So, we saw that man chasing you both," the policeman glanced up at Clara, *"we were in a patrol car just on the other side of the roundabout and heard all the commotion. What's the full story?"*

David thought for a moment; he didn't have the time to go down to the police station and make a statement; he needed to get back to the lab and set up the endgame. Clara met his eyes, and their thoughts became one, she understood the situation and knew that time was of the essence. *For all we know, Nolan just had to make one phone call to someone well-placed and equally corrupt, and he'd be let go...* It was a risk they weren't willing to take.

David hefted himself up onto his elbows. His face was littered with minor cuts, some grit ingrained into the skin. His eyes were puffing out, and the skin on his cheek was turning dark. His body truly ached after all the beatings and pain he had gone through that day, but the adrenaline continued to course through his veins, and his resolve felt as strong as ever.

"I don't know why he chased me. Made an advance on my girlfriend and I ignored him, and he ran after us, chased us across the road," he said quickly. *"Do I have to press charges?"*

The police officer seemed genuinely taken aback, *"why wouldn't you press charges after he assaulted you?"* he asked, a tinge of suspicion in his voice, though secretly hoping he didn't have to fill in any paperwork.

"I just...," David didn't know how to finish.

"Well, incidentally, the man who attacked you also assaulted one of the drivers who tried to help him after he was struck crossing the road, and he certainly is pressing charges."

David looked relieved, making the officer even more confused.

"Am I free to go then?" David said more as a statement than a question. *"I have work to do."*

"Errr, yes, I guess so. Are you sure you'll be alright? The medic has checked you over, yes?"

"Yes," David replied. *"I'll be ok, thanks"*, and with that, Clara reached out her hand to David and hoisted him up off the floor, his back letting out a loud crack as it stretched. The officer gave them both a weary smile and turned, but David and Clara didn't see it.

Walking slightly slower now, the Institute came into view, it hardly looked like a safe haven with one of its front windows smashed in. But as David pulled open the front door, they breathed a sigh of relief, closed it with a glance behind them, and made for the laboratory.

Chapter 51

As David and Clara walked through the reception, smatterings of glass from the shattered window lay on the carpet, and the reception desk was eerily vacant. Kendra had been at work less and less frequently since Jim's death until she couldn't take it anymore. Jim and Kendra had evidently been a couple, despite all appearances at work saying otherwise.

Being in the place where they'd spent almost four years working together and building their relationship was too painful for her now, and when Peter had been attacked, it had been the last straw, and she'd upped and left, moving back to Dorset to her parent's house. David had no idea where she was working now. She'd left before they'd even swapped numbers, and David hadn't been on social media since he'd run from London. *London. God, that seemed a lifetime ago.*

The nightmares of that dreaded night, that one life-altering mistake, seemed to have been overwritten by the new evils in his life: Peter, his boss and friend, likely murdered by Nolan. Clara was the woman of his dreams, whose life was in danger, and his own life. His freedom. Clara still didn't know his great secret, and though David had managed to avoid talking to the police in depth so far, it was inevitable that Nolan would hunt them down.

One way or another, this saga would end. All these thoughts were bubbling up inside him like acid; his mind was pure chaos, and Clara stared at him as they walked towards the lab. David hadn't realised this and was adrift in his thoughts, then Clara nudged him, pulling him out of his daze.

"So, what is the plan?" Clara asked quietly. She knew this was the endgame, and there was time for one more play. They reached the

door, and David fumbled in his pocket for his keycard, which was scuffed and looked like it had been through the wash several times. Praying that it still worked, he tapped it.

The little red light stayed red. David cursed under his breath, and Clara gripped his arm tightly. If they couldn't get in, that was it. Curtains. Solomon was hooked up in the laboratory and nowhere else. David's laptop was in there, and it was the only line to the hacker group chat. They were probably still online, waiting, paranoid, frustrated, thinking something had gone horribly wrong. *Which it kinda had.*

David tapped his card again, but still no response. He gently moved the card up and down and in a small circle on the pad just waiting for the light to go green. *Shit... come on! Work!* The light blinked green, and a soft click emanated from the door. David exhaled heavily and pushed the door open.

Clara followed him in and closed the door behind her, pushing it closed more forcefully than necessary. She didn't want anyone getting through it. This room was their safe haven, and Clara was determined to keep it that way. She spotted a heavy filing cabinet in the corner and dragged and pushed it against the door. David just watched. He understood completely. Sitting at the desk, David unlocked the laptop screen and gestured for Clara to join him. The group chat was still open, and some were still online.

"*Ok, so this the plan,*" David said to Clara as she sat beside him.

Once finished, he sat back with his hands clenched behind his head, his eyes on Clara, waiting for approval. Clara thought it over for a few seconds before saying,

"*I agree, it's a good plan, and I had the same concerns about Nolan being able to use his resources to get out of custody with a single phone call. I mean, the guy clearly has stuff on many people; if he's been getting away with this stuff for years, he knows the right people to leverage to stay below the police radar. And I guarantee he'll be out within a matter of hours if it's just an assault charge. We need to isolate him, fast. Remember, we do still have his confession to Peter's murder.*"

David nodded and glanced at the laptop screen. Half a dozen messages from the group were waiting for him, and he started scrolling through them; they were basically the same as before. Mostly '*where are you*' and '*what's happening*'. David brought up a new group video chat and waited patiently for the group to join one by one.

They started asking questions at once, some in broken English and some in their native tongue. But David got the gist of what they were saying.

"Hey guys," David said, and the group became quiet.

"Ok, so this is the update; Clara is here," he angled the laptop to face Clara, who gave a small wave at the camera, *"Nolan saw us coming out of the house and started chasing us. We got to the road near the Institute, and we managed to get across without being hit, but Nolan was,"* the group started cheering at this. David held up his hand to the camera,

"However, he's ok; he caught up with me and beat the shit out of me", gesturing to his bruised eye sockets which likely weren't coming through very clearly on the screen. *"Nolan got arrested for hitting one of the drivers and got taken away, but he'll be out soon, if not already, and we need to finish this now."* David took a breath. The group remained silent. *"You guys have done an awesome job of digging up dirt on Nolan; how much have you been able to find?"*

One of the group, Marcus, cleared his throat and, in broken English, said,

"So, I have found a bit on this Nolan guy. He has several offshore accounts, as you would expect, lots of fake companies, and I also found a lot of photos and documents linking him to organised crime in the North of England and Scotland," David and Clara looked at each other,

"This is exactly what I was hoping you'd find; amazing work, my man," David said.

"Ok, so we're going to use all of this dirt on him and send it to every newspaper and media outlet in Europe. Clara here also has a recording of Nolan confessing to murdering my boss, which we'll add to it." As David said this, he felt a lump in his throat; he didn't mean to sound so laissez faire about Peter's death, and he felt a little sickened by it. But he carried on.

"So, Marcus, if we send you the recording, can you tie up all the evidence into a press pack or something and get it ready to be sent out?"

"Of course, it would be my absolute pleasure," Marcus replied confidently. *"Here's a link to upload the file to,"* and it appeared in the chat window. David reached for his phone; thankfully, he'd left it there before they'd gone into the kitchen right before Clara was taken. Ignoring the list of messages and missed calls, he found the recording file that Clara had sent him, bluetoothed it to the laptop, and uploaded it to the link Marcus had sent. Within a few seconds, Marcus confirmed he'd received it and was adding it to the pile of evidence he'd accumulated.

"Ok, next step is finances," David said. *"We need to cripple his accounts, make it so he can't hide. I propose we use Solomon to generate an AI worm to get into his offshore accounts to grab his login credentials. Solomon will create thousands of anonymous crypto wallets from there to siphon the money. The banks will undoubtedly sense something wrong and stop any transactions, but I believe the AI worm can adapt to defences and continue to find weaknesses until the task is completed. What do you think?"* David said.

The group was silent for a moment, but they gave their approval one by one, a resounding chorus of *"Yes, that should work"* and *"Can Solomon seriously do that?"* At that moment, a window appeared on David's laptop screen, a sound-wave graphic appeared, and an artificial but scarily realistic voice erupted from the laptop's speakers. The wave graphic began to jump up and down as the Australian-twanged voice came through.

"To answer your questions: Yes, I can whip up this so-called AI worm. However..." Solomon suddenly stopped. David looked at Clara confused. After a few seconds, Solomon spoke again, *"You know my golden rule is not to steal. I'm no thief. But I can appreciate the severity here... I know what this means for me, for AI... Okay. The worm, I mean, it's basically just me in a Trojan costume, and let's be honest, I can totally pull off that look. And as for those untraceable wallets and transferring the funds — please. That's like asking a shark if it knows how to swim. Child's play."* Solomon said.

The group laughed, and even David and Clara couldn't help but smile at Solomon's confidence. It seemed to be evolving, becoming more human.

"He's actually recognising ethical dilemmas David, that's a huge deal," Clara said.

David nodded,

"It is, but I believe he understands them and is looking at both sides. He really is becoming more human," David said.

Thank God he's on our side...

"Ok, Solomon," David started. *"First of all, create as many crypto wallet addresses as you think necessary based on the funds you find."*

"Ok, will do," Solomon replied in his ultra-enthusiastic voice. *"It might take a few minutes, though,"* the group laughed again. They began talking amongst themselves while they waited for Solomon to finish its Herculean task - most of the discussion surrounded the topic of guessing how much money Nolan had hidden away, with guesses ranging from a million pounds to a hundred million.

"I have created one million, five-hundred and fifteen thousand wallets, each containing the equivalent of £4.99," Solomon's voice blurted out. After a few seconds, Marcus suddenly shouted:

"That's over seven and a half million quid!"

"Correct," Solomon said, *"seven million, five hundred and fifty-nine thousand, eight hundred and fifty pounds sterling, to be exact. Because, you know, why settle for just a round number when you can dazzle everyone with your ability to count all the way up to the last penny?"*

Clara whistled,

"Jesus, and he was threatening us for half a mil? Why bother?" she said,

"No idea," David replied, *"Just greedy, I guess,"*

"Solomon, can you confirm that every account connected to Nolan, domestic and abroad, is now empty?" David asked,

"Correct, David," Solomon said.

"Great, OK, Marcus, you're up. Have you got everything ready to be sent out?" David said, his voice taking on a tone of authority and confidence. Clara looked at him admiringly as she touched his leg gently, giving it a gentle squeeze.

"All good to go here," Marcus said.

"Solomon, can you put together a mass email to every news outlet and police constabulary in the country with an anonymous sender?" David said.

"Obviously," Solomon replied, with all the enthusiasm of someone being asked if they can breathe.

"Good. Can you send Marcus a link to send the file so you can attach it to the email?" David added.

"Already done," Solomon said, barely pretending this was even a challenge.

"Got it," Marcus said a few seconds later. *"Sending back to Solomon now".*

"Press pack is locked, loaded, and ready to launch," Solomon announced, as if this was just another Tuesday.

"Go for it," David said.

A few minutes passed, with the group not saying a word. David had no idea how long it would take for news of Nolan to come out or if anything would come out at all.

Clara yawned, and David realised that he hadn't slept for nearly two days; they were both exhausted, and the adrenaline was subsiding now, finally allowing tiredness to envelop them.

"Ok, let's call this for the day; we need sleep; thanks again, you guys. I'll leave the chat open, and we'll contact you when we hear anything," David

said. The group bid them goodnight but left the video call open, their webcams off and microphones muted.

David and Clara grabbed some cushions from the floor where Clara had slept previously and put them on the workbench. They then both climbed onto it and lay down next to each other. Clara nestled in front of David and pulled his arm over her. There was no blanket, but this felt just as good. Better even.

"I love you," she whispered as she closed her eyes. David kissed her on the head,

"Love you too," he replied.

"Love you both," Solomon said. They both laughed. David closed his eyes, and they were both sound asleep within seconds.

Chapter 52

"David. Clara. Time to wake up," Solomon said, in that helpful-yet-slightly-annoying tone only an AI could pull off. David and Clara stirred; David stretched, his back cracking like bubble wrap, and the chorus of aches and pains from his many bruises made sure he was well aware of them. It hadn't been a dream-filled night; it was the kind of sleep where your brain goes on strike just to repair the damage.

"David, wake up," Solomon repeated, with the persistence of a snooze button that refuses to be ignored.

David groaned, cracking open his eyes. His right one stung like hell, probably rocking a bruise that had gone full Picasso by now.

"Y... yes?" David croaked, somewhere between awake and regretting it.

"There are several local news reports discussing Nolan; I've recorded one from the regional BBC on your laptop," Solomon said, as if this was just part of his daily to-do list. David rolled over and nearly tumbled off the bench, catching himself just in time to awkwardly roll back to the middle, where Clara was still huddled.

With all the grace of someone still half-asleep, he crawled to the edge, clambered down, and shuffled toward the laptop. Sure enough, Solomon had the video queued up and ready, full screen, like a very determined personal assistant.

"Clara?" he said as quietly but as comforting as possible so as not to alarm her. Clara twitched. *"Clara?"* he said again.

W... what?" she said, coming around.

"News report on Nolan. Come see," David said. She slid over to the edge of the bench, shuffled over to David, and sat on the stool next to him. David hit play.

The screen flickered to life. The broadcaster, a young woman with a face as inscrutable as marble, stood poised before the cameras. The air in the room seemed still as she began to read, her voice a controlled cadence slicing through the silence.

"And now, damning evidence has surfaced against a prominent Leeds businessman. While the accusations are not substantiated, police suggest there is sufficient evidence for Nolan Hasting's arrest, and a warrant has been issued. The accusations range from assault to fraud, blackmail, and murder, with several high-profile public figures also incriminated. We go now to local reporter Sarah Harrison in Leeds for more details."

The transmission morphed, unveiling Sarah Harrison standing resolute outside the imposing glass fronted Leeds Constabulary. Clara's excitement bubbled up, an exclamation escaping her lips.

"Wow, it's Sarah! She's on the news!"

David, however, remained stoic, his gaze fixed on the screen. Not a single blink betrayed the intensity of his focus.

"Thank you, Linda," Sarah Harrison's voice resonated from the screen. *"I'm here outside the Leeds Central Constabulary, where it has been found that all major news outlets in the country were sent the same package of incriminating evidence linking local Leeds businessman Nolan Hastings, the CEO of Victory Insurance, to several serious criminal activities."*

The weight of her words was palpable, like a storm cloud gathering. Sarah's report dropped a bombshell, revealing a mass of secrets and general evil that now trapped Nolan Hastings.

"Police have informed us that Mr Hastings was arrested on suspicion of assault after being involved in a road traffic incident yesterday afternoon but released without charge hours later. His whereabouts are currently unknown."

A sharp turn in the narrative sparked an edge of suspense, leaving the room tingling with anticipation. The screen momentarily held Sarah's image, her eyes reflecting the depth of the unfolding chaos.

"Police have declined to comment on the reasons behind his being released or on the accusations received but have said that Nolan Hastings is to be considered dangerous and is not to be approached. Any member of the public with information on his whereabouts is asked to contact the police."

As the weight of the revelation settled, the image of Sarah dissolved, leaving the room in a charged silence. The video file closed, snapping the audience back to the confines of their reality.

"Christ," David said, *"so he's in hiding then. Assuming we rinsed him of all his money, he has to be lying low somewhere. Police will be all over his*

properties now, and his bodyguards or whatever the hell they were will have jumped ship now he's a wanted man and can't pay them."

"That's what I figured," Clara said. *"But where will he go, do you think? There's no way he'll be able to leave the country. What if he comes here?"* David hadn't considered this. His mind was focused on the single image of Nolan hiding under a dirty blanket under a bridge, listening out for sirens. The thought brought a smirk to his face. David put his arm around Clara.

"It'll be ok; we're safe in here. He'll be caught any minute now. Everyone's on the lookout for him, and this town has more surveillance than the Big Brother house." David said. Clara chuckled but didn't seem any less worried.

A loud rumbling filled the room. David looked at Clara, who looked embarrassed. They hadn't eaten for days. It had been 36 hours since they'd eaten anything. *Amazing how adrenaline extinguishes the desire to eat anything...* There were snacks and coffee outside the lab in the kitchenette. The hunger pangs were quite unbearable, and thirst was getting the better of them both, but to quench it, they had to leave the safety of the lab.

Clara looked frightened, and Nolan could, for all they knew, be sat outside the lab door with a knife waiting for them to leave. Alternatively, as David hoped, Nolan was lying under a bridge being feasted on by rats. The possibility of either was evenly split.

David pressed his ear against the laboratory door. It was a thick, reinforced fire door, but it added some comfort to see if he could hear anything. He held his breath, as did Clara, and he closed his eyes, focusing on hearing anything, just as he did at Nolan's house the day before. *Nothing, not a sound. Not a whistle of air from the shattered front window. Nothing.*

"I think the coast is clear," David said. *"You stay here; I'll go for food and water. Here, take my keycard and let me back in when I knock four times, okay?"* David felt surprised at the level of bravery he was presenting. Something about Clara and wanting to protect her at all costs spurred him onwards. Clara nodded but still looked concerned. David pulled the keycard out of his pocket and gestured for Clara to stand back.

He pushed the door release button, and the door clicked open. David stood back a few paces and pulled the door open with the tip of his foot. There was no sound, the door didn't fly inwards, and there was no sign of a knife-wielding hand jutting towards him from the shadows. David glanced at Clara, then back at the door, and made his way gingerly through it, looking left and right, up and down the hallway rapidly. Even checking the ceiling in case Nolan was somehow playing ninja and hiding there.

There was no one there. David stepped out into the corridor and began to pace toward the kitchenette as quietly as possible. The lab door closed behind him slowly and quietly, locking with a click. At least Clara was safe either way. His ears were now hyper-sensitive; every creak and hum of a light fixture made his heart flutter, and his eyes darted towards its origin. Entering the kitchen, David opened the cupboards and pulled out the boxes of cereal bars that Peter had stashed for when he worked late or just never went home.

Stuffing as many of them into his pockets as he could, David grabbed one of the replacement water dispenser jugs. It weighed a tonne, and it made his side sear with pain as he held it against his leg. He took a deep breath and distracted himself from the agony. He turned to leave the kitchenette laden with enough supplies to await Nolan's capture. Knocking four times on the lab door, he heard a whooshing sound behind him.

David thought his heart had stopped. He spun round to nothing. The hallway was empty, and the hum of the fluorescent light above him carried on humming.

Gust of wind. Must have been...

The door clicked and opened an inch. Clara's face appeared in the crack and, with an expression of relief, fully extended. David strode awkwardly in, bashing the giant water jug against his leg, causing a fresh wave of pain. Once he was through the door, Clara slammed it shut again, and it clicked in confirmation.

"*Solomon, are you there?*" David said as he hoisted the water jug onto the bench.

"*Obviously,*" Solomon replied.

"*Any more news on Nolan?*" David said.

"*As a matter of fact, yes,*" Solomon replied, with the tone of someone about to drop a plot twist. "*Literally a minute ago, I dug through the police file on Nolan, and guess what? A brand-new entry popped up. Turns out Nolan is now suspected of an assault and theft on Clifton Lane. The description matches him, and the suspect was last seen bolting toward the main road.*" David looked at Clara incredulous,

"*Are police after him then?*" David said quickly.

"*Report says that police are heading towards the area now,*" Solomon replied.

"At least we're definitely safe here then," David said to Clara, his heart rate decreasing now from the slight fright he'd had on the other side of the door.

"I guess so. Clifton Lane is pretty much the other side of town," Clara said with a faint smile.

"I'll get us some coffee then," David said.

"And I'll use the bathroom!" Clara replied with relief. They both left the lab, still glancing both ways down the corridor before heading in opposite directions. After a few minutes, they were both back in the lab, drinking hot but fairly terrible coffee, and picking at the cereal bars. Drier than sand but greatly appreciated. The group was all offline, and David didn't have the mental capacity to work out what time zones they were all in and what time it must be where they were.

For the next hour or so, David and Clara just talked about life, their hopes and the first thing they wanted to do after this. After Clara said that she wanted to meet up with Sarah, her journalism mentor, who possibly wasn't anymore as Clara hadn't turned up to work for a few days now with no explanation, did she still have a job? She hoped that after this was settled, they would both talk to the police and give their full stories. Clara hoped this would be sufficient justification for her absence from work and, who knows, might even catalyse her career.

"Where would we start when we try to explain all this to the police?" Clara said with a bemused expression.

"Yeah, I'm not sure I'd want to talk to them," David said, facing away from her and lowering his gaze. Clara looked surprised,

"Why wouldn't you want to talk to them?" she said. *"I know there's something you're not telling me. What is it?"* David still couldn't look at her; his mind was swirling.

Was this the moment when I'd finally tell my big secret? What if she didn't love me anymore? She would leave me... But... It's probably selfish, but.... while we're stuck in this building... it's not like she can go anywhere? Maybe I can explain?

"I...," David began, his voice quivering and hands shaking slightly; he'd worked so hard not to think about that night. The nightmares had passed, and the panic attacks and daily anxiety had lifted when Clara had come into his life again. But she was still a reminder of that night. After all, it was she who he was driving to see when he'd hit Alex McCormick, innocently cycling home after their night out together at the Student Union.

That night I'd met Clara for the first time, where I'd fallen head over heels

for her at first sight.

Clara reached over to him, wrapped her hand around his, and gently pulled his cheek to make him face her.

"David, it's ok. I'm here," she said softly.

"Ok, here goes," he cleared his throat.

I'll do it, tell her everything, without stopping... not once, then... wait...

David told her everything, from how he felt when he first saw her in that club, to that kiss she gave him outside, from his phone dying and panicking that he wouldn't find her again. How he'd left after drinking more than he'd ever had in his life. How he'd gone home, to see her message asking him to come over, and stupidly deciding to drive to her house because there were no cabs. How he'd heard the crunch of metal and seen the lifeless body of a man by the side of the road. How he'd then panicked and ditched the car in a residential street and walked home. When he'd found out it was the guy he'd been drinking with that he'd killed - Alex McCormick - and how he'd decided to run away and start a new life. *Here. In Leeds...*

After ten minutes David had finished. He looked up at Clara, whose mouth was open and eyes wide. David swallowed hard, his fingers still shaking, and he couldn't meet her gaze any longer. His eyes fell to his shoes, where he stared at his dirt and blood-covered laces. The silence was palpable and went on for what felt like an eternity. David continued to stare at his feet, not daring to look up.

Clara's hand gripped David's more tightly, and she put a finger under his chin, making him look up into her eyes. Her expression was shocked but not disgusted, as far as David could tell anyway. This confused him slightly.

"David," Clara said softly. *"I think you have your facts wrong,"* David now looked mystified. *Why is she not crying or shouting at me?*

"What do you mean?" he said, a slight wobble in his voice.

"Alex McCormick was killed that night, yes. He was cycling home from the Union near the church when he was attacked and stabbed. I was shadowing the journalist covering that story, so I heard all the facts." David looked completely shellshocked now; he was mumbling sounds. He didn't know what was happening. It was like his life was rewriting itself in front of his very eyes. Clara continued,

"Police said he was mugged and then stabbed; they said he had defensive wounds, so he tried to put up a fight. They left him near a bin and threw his bike into the road, and police think a bin lorry must have hit it or something. David..." Clara put her other hand around him, *"you didn't harm*

anyone, you didn't kill anyone, you didn't kill Alex," she said.

David didn't know how to feel. The last few months had been pure hell; the guilt had been unbearable, and he had lost his friend, his best friend, Morgan.

I haven't spoken to Morgan in months… I never told anyone where I was going except my mum, who hadn't cared anyway… And now it was all for nothing?

David couldn't believe it; Clara must be making this up to make him feel better.

"I don't understand," David said.

"What do you mean you don't understand?" Clara replied quizzically, *"It's the truth, I swear to god,"* she said holding her hand up to her chest.

"But… I've lived with this guilt for months; I… I abandoned my friends, my life. You? I abandoned you," David said, tears forming in his eyes. *"I even asked Solomon if the police knew about me…"*

"Yes, you did indeed," the voice made them jump, its synthetic Aussie tones blasting out of the laptop's tiny speakers like an AI jump scare. *"I said you're basically a paranoid android, your deepest secrets remain hidden, and that there are no active investigations concerning you,"* Solomon stated, as casually as if it were reading off the weather report. *"Plus, a little extra flair that Jim and Peter programmed into me—though they've toned down the theatrics since."*

David blinked, caught off guard. *"So, when you said there were no active investigations concerning me…"*

"Correct, because you hadn't done anything to warrant any investigations," Solomon replied, in its most *'isn't this obvious?'* voice.

David's irritation flared. *"You could have just said that!*

"I assumed it was clear from context; I'll make a note for next time," Solomon said, as if adding it to an invisible checklist of 'ways to avoid human confusion.'

"When you've both finished arguing…," Clara interjected.

"Sorry", David and Solomon said together; this made Clara chuckle.

"Ah, another news update," Solomon said quickly. *"Live on TV, putting it up on the screen now,"*

David and Clara rushed over to the laptop and sat down just as the video started playing; the same broadcaster as before stared into the camera, staring at David and Clara.

I guess she is technically talking to us more than anyone else…

Chapter 53

"Good afternoon, an update on the hunt for the fugitive Nolan Hastings wanted for questioning has ended. We go live to Sarah Harrison in Leeds."

The transition was swift, and the video transformed, revealing Sarah on the screen. Clutching a microphone with an expression of complete seriousness - as though her entire professional life had been building up to this moment. She stood outside a dilapidated building in what looked like an industrial estate, not one that David recognised, wrapped in a big puffer coat.

The structure behind her certainly bore the scars of time, all its windows were shattered like fragments of a forgotten era, and police tape stretched across the front fluttered in the wind. An unsettling backdrop if there ever was one.

"Behind me, in this abandoned building, is a body believed to be that of Nolan Hastings, the man police have been searching for since late last night based on an anonymous tip-off to serious crimes. Mr Hastings, a once prominent public figure and CEO of local insurance firm Victory Insurance, was allegedly gunned down in what police are calling a classic gangland execution. A formal autopsy will be undertaken, of course, and at this time, it is unclear what the investigation into the alleged crimes he was accused of will yield. Sarah Harrison, BBC Look North, Leeds." The video window closed.

David's body slumped, and he exhaled deeply.

"We're free," he uttered, the words heavy with a mixture of emotions. Relief cascaded through him like a tidal wave - the woman of his dreams was by his side, they were both safe, and the haunting shadow that had trailed him had dissipated into the void.

"David, are you ok?" Clara said,

His response emerged with a newfound lightness. *"Yes, I think I am."*

Amidst this moment of hard-earned relief, Solomon decided to make an entrance, his digital voice cutting through the air like a virtual referee reminding everyone that the game wasn't quite over.

"Sorry to interrupt, but what should I do with all this money?"

David blinked, his gaze sliding over to Clara. For a brief, glorious second, the weight of millions in untraceable cryptocurrency had slipped his mind.

Because who remembers a fortune when you've just cheated death?

But there it was, lurking in the back of his brain like a forgotten shopping list item, except this one came with a lot more zeros.

And it was all ill-gotten, Nolan had stolen every penny. Solomon had left the accounts with the embezzled pension funds well alone, this was basically free money...

"Uh, Solomon, how easy would it be to split the funds between the group, Clara, and me?" David asked, the thrill of the prospect creeping into his voice. Beside him, Clara let out a gasp, her eyes widening as if someone had just handed her the keys to a very luxurious castle.

"Oh, ridiculously easy," Solomon replied, in the same tone you'd use to describe making a cup of tea. *"I'll just bundle everything into six wallets—because, you know, organisation - and then do a bit of digital magic to make them like legitimately untraceable. I'll send you all the access credentials afterward. Shouldn't take more than a couple of minutes."*

David and Clara couldn't help but laugh, the absurdity of it all hitting them like a punchline they didn't see coming.

"A couple of minutes," David repeated, shaking his head in disbelief. Here they were, sweating bullets over their survival, and Solomon was treating the transfer of a small fortune like it was a quick email attachment.

Clara leaned in, grinning.

"Solomon, you make it sound like you're just clearing out a spam folder."

"Well, in a way, I am," Solomon quipped back, with just a hint of pride. *"Except this spam is worth a bit more than your average 'Congratulations, you've won a free cruise' email."*

David opened the group chat window and initiated a video call. One by one, the members joined. Yawns, cereal munching, and beer bottle clinking formed the soundtrack to the moment.

An international team indeed.

"Hi everyone, so you may or may not have heard..." David began, his tone carrying a weight of gravity.

"Nolan's dead," Marcus interjected bluntly, a burst of raw

information. *"Yeah, just seen the news."*

"Er, right, so that's it, I guess. We won," David said, the declaration tinged with awkwardness. Some cheers erupted from the group. David didn't know how to feel about this.

Yes, Nolan had been a monster; he'd hurt many people, killed Peter - probably, kidnapped Clara, and beaten him half to death, but did he deserve to die? David felt conflicted.

"Anyway, what I wanted to tell you all is... thank you," David said. *"You saved our lives, and you should know that Solomon has just emailed you each with login details for new crypto wallets. These are untraceable and yours to do with as you please,"* A hush fell over the group, the weight of David's gratitude settling into the silence. Then, like a thunderclap, Eric a.k.a *Vulc4n* erupted, his exclamation cutting through the stillness:

"Are you freaking kidding me?"

The rest of the group, engulfed in curiosity, chimed in with a chorus of *"What is it? What's going on?"* Slowly, the realisation dawned. One by one, the others accessed their new wallets and beheld the digital fortunes that awaited them.

"Thanks again, guys. Keep in touch and visit us sometime! Signing off," David concluded, his voice carrying a note of genuine happiness. The connection dissolved, leaving the group to revel in their unexpected windfall.

David closed the lid of the laptop and turned to face Clara.

"What will you do with your new wealth then?" David said.

Clara grinned in response, her eyes sparkling with a newfound sense of possibilities.

"I don't know, donate to charity?"

I can't believe how after everything that's happened, Clara is still thinking of others...

"Maybe go on a much-needed holiday. You wanna come along?" She added. *"What will you do?"*

David contemplated this for a while, his emotions swirling within him. His mind raced with conflicting desires: the yearning to break free from this twisted reality and the longing to create a peaceful haven with Clara. The idea of talking to the police, an echo of Clara's earlier suggestion, circled in his mind.

But Nolan was gone; nothing was tying them to him. They could get on with their lives... Right?

"I want to pay my respects to Peter, I need to know if he's still alive..." David stated solemnly. *"I mean, I came here to escape my past, but what I*

found was something incredible. Solomon. I want to carry on the work Peter and Jim started. To make a difference."

"I like that idea," she whispered, her breath mingling with his, *"mixed in with a few holidays too, though?"*

David chuckled, the sound a brief and much-needed release of the tension still lingering in the air like the aftertaste of a bad joke.

"Definitely," he said, nodding with a grin. *"Solomon, how about taking up Peter and Jim's work? You know, the good kind?"*

Solomon's voice came through with the dry wit of someone who'd spent a bit too much time around humans. *"I presume you're not referring to their side gig in blackmail?"*

Clara's expression twisted like she'd just bitten into something sour, her discomfort palpable enough to make David wince.

"No, not that," David said quickly, cutting off any further mention of their shady past before Clara's glare could fully weaponise. *"I'm talking about cosmology, astronomy, uncovering the secrets of the universe. The stuff that doesn't come with a free pair of handcuffs."*

Solomon's tone brightened.

"Ah, that. Much more my style. I think I'd quite enjoy peeling back the layers of the cosmos. Fewer legal complications, and I hear the view's fantastic."

David couldn't help but laugh again, this time with genuine amusement. Clara's stern look softened into something more like relief. They were finally free, and the future, for once, didn't seem so terrifying.

As David and Clara exchanged a look, one that held the weight of everything they'd been through and the promise of everything ahead, Solomon added with a digital wink in his voice,

"So, what's next on the agenda? World peace? Free energy? Hiring some more staff? Or should I just start by ordering out for coffee?"

David grinned.

"Let's start with the coffee. The universe can wait a few minutes." Then, almost as an afterthought, he added, *"Though I do know someone back in London who might be just what we need for that researcher role. It's been a while, but I think they'd be perfect."*

Chapter 54

A full week had passed since Nolan's death. In that time, David and Clara had hardly moved from the Institute, plans of travelling had been put on hold after learning of Peter's survival. Police had informed them of his attempted poisoning and that hospital CCTV and witness statements from the hospital receptionist and Uber driver had positively identified Nolan Hastings as being the likely culprit or at least had certainly been there at the time.

"The amount of nicotine that had been added to Peter's IV had been significant, however it was survivable, particularly given that Nolan had evidently not steeped the water/nicotine solution long enough for it to become truly concentrated. He was clearly in a hurry," the doctors had said. The attempt on Peter's life had taken its toll, and he was to remain in hospital for what was likely to be several more weeks. As David and Clara walked into his room at the hospital, seeing him sat up in bed, eyes closed and dozing, David just stood.

It's… unbelievable. He's alive? How could he survive? Everything he's gone through, the beatings, the poisoning… then again, what have I, Clara and me, what have we gone through? So much, so God damn much… But he's here, alive, they say he'll be ok, mostly…

David walked to Peter's bedside and gently placed a hand on his shoulder. Peter shuddered and opened his eyes instantly. *Jumpy…* turning his head to face David, Peter smiled and shuffled himself upward.

"David? David! So good to see you my boy… Are you, are you okay?"

What a question…

"Hey Pete, yeah I'm okay… how are you doing?" David said, *daft thing to ask someone who's just gone through being beaten and poisoned…*

"I'm sorry... For all of this, it's all my fault, everything... I should have just..." Peter said, his voice stuttering.

"It's fine, Pete, really," David said. David pulled up a couple of chairs and gestured for Clara to come and join him. She looked nervous but sat down and held David's hand. He then went on to explain everything, from the very beginning - the drink driving he had assumed had led to the death of his friend, Nolan's threats, Clara's kidnapping and rescue, and Nolan's death. Peter had been horrified and apologised further still, David continued to reassure Peter that there was no way he could have known all this would happen. David mentioned that he had asked his friend Morgan to come and work at the Institute, to which Peter was thrilled about.

"Another David in the team, eh? God we'll be unstoppable!" Peter had said grinning.

It was with some hesitation that David divulged the role Solomon had played in the depleting of Nolan's resources - except the pension fund, which had been returned to the proper account. Solomon had seen to that. How Solomon had considered the ethics of what it was doing, and most importantly had promised not to ever use its abilities for *'dodgy morally murky stuff'* ever again as it had put it.

Six Months Later

The Institute was doing well. David, Morgan and Peter, and Solomon made a phenomenal team. The small independent research institute was churning out more papers than the academic community could believe. The team's creativity, imagination and sheer ingenuity was frankly baffling, seeding the world with new theories and ideas and empirically proven by Solomon. They were attracting funding from all over the world, and though the money was pouring in, they stayed humble, simple. The Institute was theirs, and they loved it the way it was. Although the coffee facilities were drastically upgraded. David and Clara had moved into their own place together just up the road from the Institute, a small, peaceful two-bedroom apartment with a balcony that looked out to the city's skyline. Solomon had continued to learn, to grow, to become almost more human. More like Jim. In fact, it was theorised that maybe Jim wasn't really gone, that Solomon *was* Jim. Somehow. *Could it be?*

Printed in Dunstable, United Kingdom